BARKER & JULES®

LAVA DREAM


**First Edition. Published by BARKER & JULES®.**

**Paperback ISBN | 979-8-88691-173-2**
**Hardcover ISBN | 979-8-88691-174-9**
**eBook ISBN | 979-8-88691-172-5**

**Library of Congress Copyrights Control Number:** 1-11261463169



**Printed in the United States.**

**Book cover design by** Mariana Galindoe | **BARKER & JULES®**
**Book interior layout by** Norma Garay | **BARKER & JULES®**
**Illustrations by**

**BARKER & JULES® and their affiliates are an imprint of BARKER & JULES, LLC.**

**BARKER & JULES, LLC**
**3776 Howard Hughes Pkwy 549, Las Vegas, NV 89169**
**barkerandjules.com**

# “LAVA DREAM”

THE CHRONICLES OF PANAMERIA

*Book 1*

*Written by J.A. Ramonet*

BARKER & JULES

*I dedicate this book to the two most important women in my life.*

*To my mother, who gave me life and instilled a passion for literature in me. She accompanied me in my first readings, and she was also the first critic of my writings. Thank you, Mom.*

*To my wife, Arelia, the brightness of my days and the light of my nights, because, by your side, any fantasy world is possible.*

*I love you, my queen.*

# ACKNOWLEDGMENTS

*First, I want to thank my wife and children for their unconditional support during the many months of writing this novel. There were long nights shut-in, sacrificing family time, but they understood and accepted it, helping me make my dream come true.*

*I also thank my Beta readers: Adriana, Jorge, and José, for taking the time to read my writing and give me their comments. I really value your opinion.*

*Last but not least, to my Instagram community, the gameritos of @gamerbloodlife, to those writers who showed me that it IS possible and that it is just a matter of hard work and dedication. Thanks to JJ @dadosymazmorras, Yolanda @adidegalatia, Mano @manodemithrill, Cas @c.g.forne, Laura @laura_bewolf, David @d.o.martin, Raquel @rhueteiglesias, and many others who struggle day by day to deliver their beautiful works.*

*Without all of you, this story would not have been finished.*

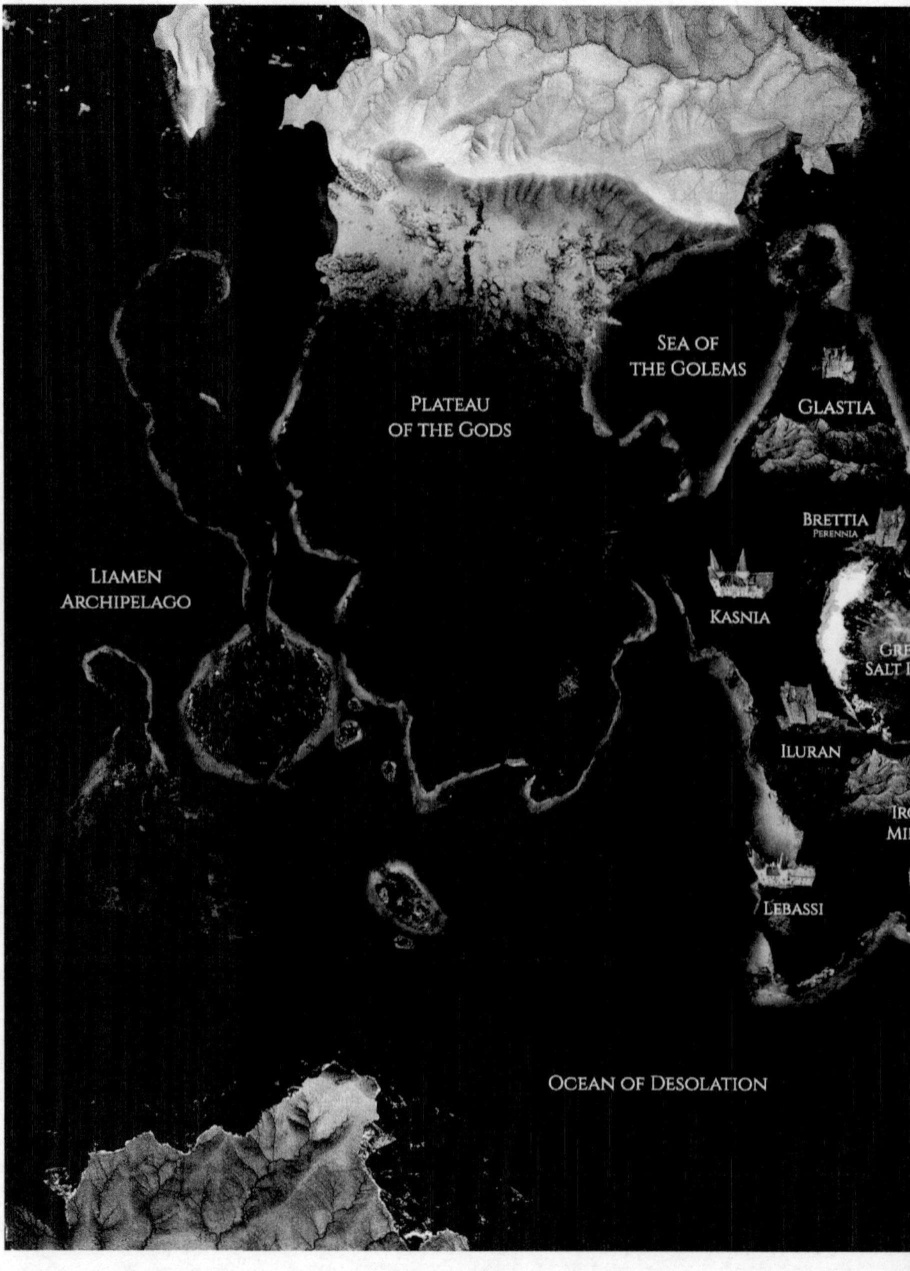
Sea of
the Golems
Plateau
of the Gods
Glastia
Brettia
Perennia
Kasnia
Liamen
Archipelago
Iluran
Lebassi
Ocean of Desolation

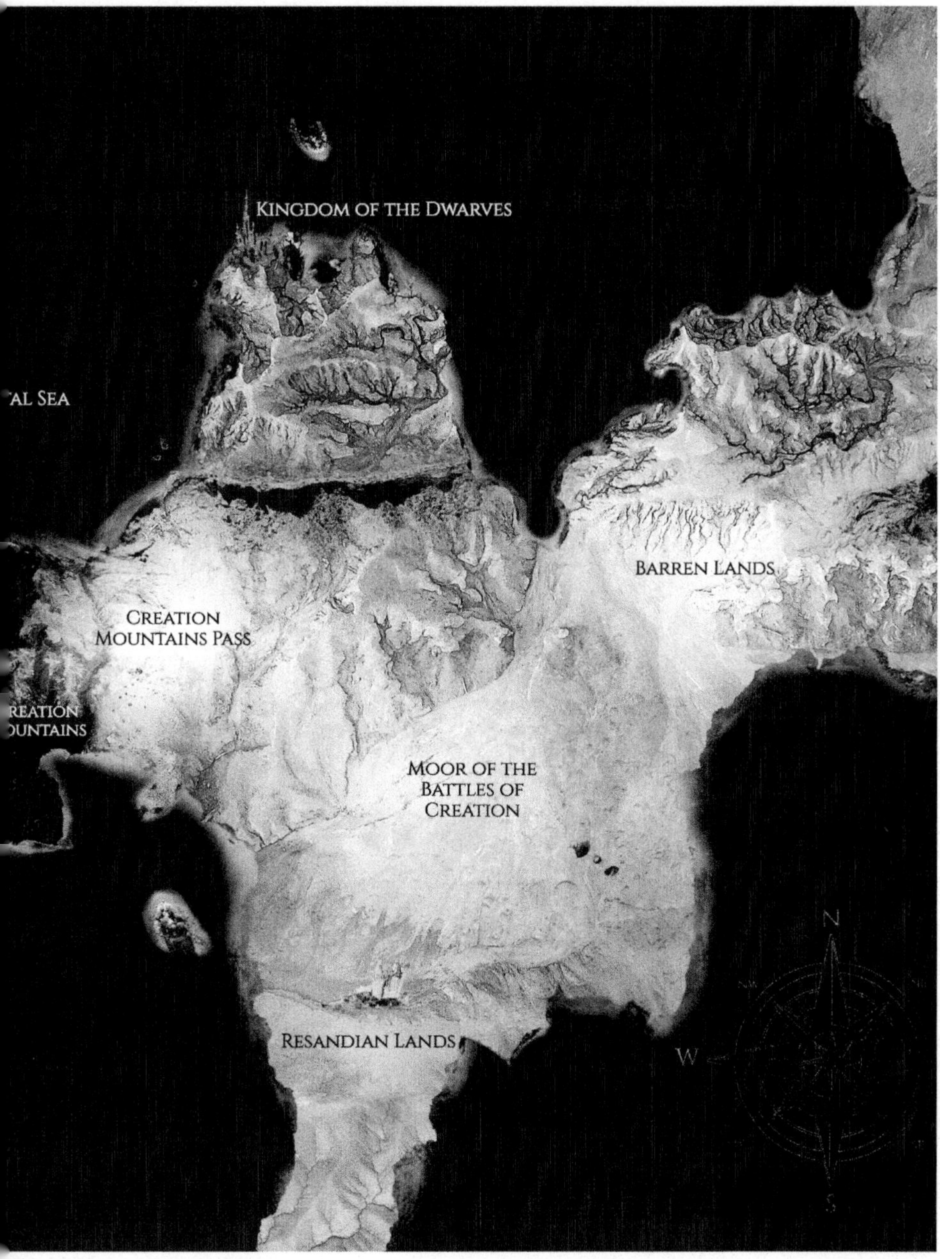
Kingdom of the Dwarves
Barren Lands
Creation Mountains Pass
Moor of the Battles of Creation
Resandian Lands
N
W
S

# CONTENT

# PROLOGUE

Nadia followed Oliver deep into the woods, away from the overbearing gaze of their master, Zerun. They had been studying together for over forty years under the tutelage of the head of the Council of Mages; their knowledge had grown during that time, as did their love. So many nights together, long training sessions, and many broken bones and wounds. The connection created between them was real and beautiful, capable of surviving a thousand storms.

The forest was dense, almost impenetrable. Their master lived in an old mansion in the middle of the Forest of Sighs, a beautiful, lush place in the territory of Kasnia, one of the six human kingdoms of Panameria.

They overcame the obstacles. They knew the way. They reached their secret place. Under the leafy shade of the tallest oak tree, they embraced and frolicked on the ground like the teenagers they had long since ceased to be. Being mages didn't make them immortal, but it did make them long-lived. Oliver looked into her eyes and kissed her tenderly, melting into her, synchronizing their souls.

Nadia watched him as he undressed her. He was tall and slender, with thick jet-colored hair that fell loosely down his back. Oliver's lips ran down her naked torso, making her skin tingle and her heart flutter. And, with the utmost gentleness, he kissed her stomach delicately. He looked into her eyes, then tilted his head, placing his right ear on her shapely abs. She knew he felt it too, heard it, that new life growing inside her. Their child, their baby, the fruit of their love.

And then, Oliver went a little lower. Nadia waited for the surge of pleasure, but her eyes met the imposing figure of her master. The blue robe gave off little flashes of lightning that matched the glint in Zerun's gray eyes. There was a grimace of reproach, no, of disappointment and anger on the old man's face.

"Mast..." she began.

"Shut up," shouted her master. "You have betrayed me, Nadia. Your lust has poisoned Oliver and caused him to stray from the path of knowledge. I took you into my home when your family rejected you for being a witch. I taught you; I took care of you. I broke the rules for you by taking on a second apprentice, and this is how you pay me. I am very disappointed."

Nadia didn't understand; her mentor had always been strict, but to blame her alone... She looked for Oliver, who was cowering away from her like a scared rabbit.

"This cannot stay like this. What I must do will hurt me more than it will hurt you. You are almost a daughter to me, but sometimes a father must take drastic measures to teach obedience to his children. But, sometimes, he must also understand when they cease to be his children."

Several roots came out of the ground in unison. Nadia tried to dodge them, but they held her tightly, leaving her at the mage's mercy.

"I can't let this happen," muttered her preceptor as he bent over her.

The apprentice felt her master's hand pierce her stomach as if it were a burning knife. His fingers delved inside her, found the little life growing there, squeezed, and tore it out. The scream of pain from her throat was lost in the immense forest. With tears in her eyes, she could see her child in the old mage's hand, only to see him disappear in a small violet flame a few seconds later.

Nadia gasped, struggling inwardly not to faint. She began to summon all her power to fight back. She gathered enough energy to erase the bastard from...

A cruel slap from Zerun made her lose all concentration.

"Stupid girl. I am Zerun, head of the Council of Mages of Panameria. How dare you rebel against me!"

Before losing consciousness, she heard her master's last words:

"I banish you to the barren lands beyond the Creation Mountains. May Salmur have mercy on your soul."

Nadia woke up disoriented, sore and covered in sand. Blood had formed a dry crust on her abdomen. She felt her belly. She felt nothing. There was no life left inside her.

Where was she? A crimson moon illuminated what seemed to be a desert! Banished! Rejected by her own master! Abandoned by her love!

The barren lands were the lost and unexplored lands of Panameria, where the worst horrors brewed, or so the myths said. Located to the east of the known world, they were nothing more than a forgotten and devastated wasteland. Now she could see it in the flesh. Wherever she looked, nothing; only rocks and sands. No trace of life. Like a grimace of fate, a deafening roar reached her ears. What creature could it be? Staying there to find out was madness. She tried to open a portal. She did not succeed. She was exhausted. She scanned the horizon: dunes and desolation. If the position of the stars didn't deceive her, she could make out a faint bluish glow to the south. Any direction is good when you don't know where you're going.

She began to walk while a seed of hatred grew inside her.

# I
# THE CHRONICLE OF DESIRE

# *1*

After seven years of waiting, he received his mage's call while practicing with his bow on the parade ground; Égnever's penetrating voice resounded in his head: *"Come to me."* At last, what he longed for, his greatest wish would come true, and his dreams of glory would be fulfilled. He drove one last arrow into the heart of the doll he was using as a target and headed for the castle.

The soldiers stood to attention at the sight of him. The maids bowed in reverence. He strode down the corridors, his steady strides echoing off the stone walls until he reached the entrance to the dungeons. He pushed open the old oak door. Winding, mildewed stairs plunged into the depths. He picked up one of the torches and started down.

The foundations of the Lebassi Castle were buried deep into a rocky cape in the south of Panameria. The beginning of the construction dated back to the reign of his great-great-grandfather, Thomas the Madman. In the end, it was his grandfather, Gregor the Peacemaker, who finished raising it. The Fortress of Foam (as some nicknamed it, because of the continuous breaking of waves of the

Ocean of Desolation that continuously beaded its foundations) was the neuralgic point from which Lebassi and the other three southern kingdoms, Kasnia, Tolm, and Iluran, were governed. He hated that way of referring to his fortress; it reminded him of children's games, not at all appropriate for a warrior.

He slowly descended the last few steps, not wanting him to notice his haste. He breathed in and out deeply, trying to get his breathing back to its usual rhythm. The smell of dampness and mildew tickled his nose.

Up to now, he had always gone downstairs seeking to speed up the process somehow. However, he knew he was getting nowhere with the insistence of his visits; he would be ready when he was, not before, just in his own time. And that moment came. Nervousness and happiness overwhelmed him. What would it be like? How would it feel?

The dungeons were a labyrinth of cells and dead ends. A continuous drip testified to the proximity of the sea. The mage's enclosure was at the bottom in the deepest part. He could see a bluish glow seeping under the door from where he was standing.

He approached. He took a deep breath, calming his anxiety. He did not knock. He firmly opened the small door; it was his castle, his kingdom. At least he owed himself that respect, even though he knew that his authority was lessened there. He was not afraid. He could not harm him; he owed him absolute obedience. But, for Salmur, there was too much power in that wiry body, gnawed by the passing of the years, to take it as a joke.

He crossed the threshold. He was so tall that he had to tilt his head to avoid hitting the doorframe. A spider's web caught in his dark brown hair. The man who came into view in the middle of the stone enclosure was tall and stooped. He cloaked his existence with an ebony-like tanned cloak that swept his footsteps. His hands were raised, forming intricate figures. His long white hair was knotted with a red ribbon at his nape and then dispersed over his back like a silver waterfall on basalt rock. His fingers were long and extremely thin as if the phalanges were barely covered by skin, a skin of a waxy-white tone under which black veins throbbed.

Triar, King of Lebassi, would be more at ease if his mage worked with a huge cauldron. Instead, in front of him floated a sphere of changing light. Over the years, it had grown larger, and this never ceased to disturb him. The old man's words were always scarce and terse: "The larger it gets, the closer your wish will be," was the first thing he had said to him seven years ago when a luminous spot appeared just a hand's breadth above the ground. The current size attested that it really had to be close.

He was about to speak to him when the mage turned to him. His hands stopped dancing, and the right one pointed at him with a long, sharp fingernail. He frowned, his eyebrows coming together, and his eyes armed with a look, his look, so steely that it pierced him until it reached his brain and made him sweat.

"You have come," Égnever proclaimed.

"I felt your call." He couldn't look him in the eyes. He lowered his head to meet the mage's bare feet; he never wore any shoes. "If you made me come, I guess it must be ready; you've had plenty of time."

"I need more."

More? He had been locked up there for over five years, and he still had not been able to hurry to finish his job. He didn't seem to remember that when he did, he would be able to leave, he would have broken his bonds, and he would be free.

"Then why did you call me? You know I cannot rush you, and you are the one who sets the time."

"I am close."

"I'm glad to hear it. Days?" The mage did not react. "Months?"

There was no response.

"A year?" Triar inquired again.

"There is no point in talking about it."

"No!" He immediately realized the mistake he was making, but he couldn't rectify it. "I am a mortal, a man whose days are numbered like any other. You may have all the time in the world, but I do not."

"You must confirm your desire," the mage requested.

"Of course I confirm it," asserted the king. "Why do you think I regularly come down to see your work? I long for my desire. I want to see it. I want to have it in front of me as you promised. Not only do I want it; I need it."

It was exasperating. A thousand detours for such a silly question. More than anyone else, he should be sick of standing there every day, waving his hands, repeating words or whatever he did, and not even seeing the sunlight.

“From today on, I will not be able to stop it.”

Triar looked at him decisively, with no more fear.

“Perfect, Égnever.”

“It’s dangerous,” the old man announced.

“Are you afraid?”

“No.”

“Go ahead and let me know when it’s ready. I won’t come back down until you tell me to.”

“Get ready.”

“Come on; you do not have to worry about me.”

“I do not,” replied Égnever, smiling, as he turned away to continue his concentration on the sphere.

The king understood that he would not be able to get much more information out of the old man. It didn’t matter. After so many years, the wait would be over. From his grave, his grandfather would be proud of him. He would prove to the kingdom, to the entire coalition, and even to Panameria that he lived up to the legend of the Peacemaker.

## *2*

Triar settled back in his armchair, still enjoying the taste of the supper's viands and rocking a glass of wine in his hand. Logs crackled on the hearth warming the room and complementing the lighting of candles and torches. Ancient battle banners were hanging on the walls, which he required the servants to keep scrupulously clean and preserved as if it were only yesterday that they had just been embroidered. He was proud of the coat of arms devised by his grandfather: a black dragon, wings outstretched, on a red background. Simple. Straightforward. He had never seen a dragon before. The last ones were said to live in the north, on the Plateau of the Gods.

Outside, a storm was raging, and the wind was intensifying with terrible fury against the castle walls. They had been suffering from such nights for weeks. The sky had enough energy to spare, and so did he.

Once of slender figure, his wife sat slouched on a bench, embroidering flowers or something feminine on a handkerchief. Her blonde hair fell ungracefully over her face. Only a couple of generations ago, the monarch's wife would have been found mending her husband's war uniform or making new flags to be worn on the battlefield. He was fed up with her, how the years turned her fat, and the inactivity she professed. Luckily, she still knew how to stay quiet, if nothing else. He had been procuring warmth at night with the virtue of one of the maidens for many years. The touch of his queen's flesh was repugnant to him. As a king, he had to keep his marriage to set a good example. This sacrifice made him weary, and he cursed having married her every day.

The chubby-cheeked brat, Gregor, lived close to his mother's skirts. He was never able to instill in him the warrior spirit he possessed. At times he could understand it; life today was capable of making anyone lethargic, but, on the other hand, he detested the boy for his lack of strength. Right now, he was playing with wooden carts. In his childhood, he only spent time with swords. Seeing him there, playing on the skin of the largest brown bear that had ever inhabited his land and that he, Triar, shot down with a single, accurate arrow, made his contempt grow. His son could not stand hunting; he was very weak, and, once, he had cried when he wanted to force him to take part in a hunt in the woods. What angered him the most was that he gave his son the same name to honor his grandfather's memory. Damn! His grandfather would roll over in his grave if he saw such a pusillanimous great-grandson. That's why he hadn't called him by his name for years.

"My husband, we are having a stormy night again," Queen Angela murmured.

Triar snorted. He saw a plea for an answer in his wife's face, if not affectionate, at least kind. He drained his glass in one gulp, and a couple of drops trickled down his gray-free brown beard. He wiped them away with his forearm in a mechanical gesture.

"Woman! Pour me more wine."

Angela rose wearily to take the wine from the large dining room table. She grabbed the earthenware pitcher and approached him. She shuffled her feet and kept her head down. Triar stretched out his arm without taking his eyes from the hearth fire. She poured it for him. A thunder boomed, and she, frightened, spilled some of the liquid on her husband's hand.

"Stupid!" His hand shot towards her face, whipping her violently. Her upper lip was cut and swelled instantly. "You are a stupid woman; you can't do anything right."

The child began to cry and rushed to hug his mother.

"You, shut up! I am just asking for a quiet night, and I have to put up with you." He got up heavily and headed for the stairs, turning his back to them. "Woman, go and tell Katrina to come up to my rooms."

## *3*

Katrina trembled. The queen had ordered her to go up to the tower where King Triar now had his chambers. She was a simple maid who sometimes helped in the dining room. She never thought the king knew of her existence; she had barely crossed paths with him half a dozen times. This could not be happening to her. She shook her head; it could not be, but it was. She sighed.

The steps became interminable. The higher she climbed, the farther away she got from the bustle of the lower floors. She stopped at a landing. She peered through a small window. The view was breathtaking. She could hear the distant crashing of the sea waves on the coast as if her ear was next to a conch shell. She searched within herself for courage. She resumed his ascent.

An oak door closed the king's room. She let out one last sigh before knocking quietly on the wood. The shutter opened softly, revealing a sparsely furnished room, dimly lit by the glow of a fire.

"Your Majesty," she announced herself in a low voice.

Triar's imposing figure pushed the door wide open. He must have been two or three palms taller than she was. She felt even more helpless. She bowed her head submissively as she pressed her feet against the floor so he wouldn't notice her legs trembling.

"Your Majesty. You sent for me."

"Come in. Come closer so I can get a better look at you." Triar crossed his arms and leaned his back against the wall.

She was terrified. She knew exactly what it meant that he had made her go upstairs. Several of her companions had had such a privilege. He was the king for a reason. She could not refuse. She advanced; it was a royal command. She suffered a strange pain inside her, and her breathing was ragged. Surely when she came closer, he would yank off her dress and throw her on the bed with ease; despite so many years, he retained the vigor of his youth. He even was attractive when seen on the parade ground with his naked torso and making a fool of soldiers twenty years younger than him. Attractive! How could she think such a thing? He was nothing more than a tyrant who enjoyed bending her to his will.

"Don't be afraid, Katrina. I would be incapable of hurting you. I have not the slightest intention of forcing you to do anything."

He smiled at her to show his sincerity.

"I know what you want from me, Your Majesty."

"Are you sure you know? You only know what others have given me. It doesn't occur to you that I might have other plans for you."

"No!" replied Katrina sharply.

"Well, at least you're honest. All the others have gotten something in return; none have left empty-handed. What do you want? Let's see. Maybe I could buy you with gold; that usually works well. Although jewels are not to be despised either, right? Of course, nothing forces me to do so. I am the king, which gives me absolute right over everything, everyone, and, of course, every woman. Come on, girl, don't be shy and ask."

"I just want to leave, please."

Tears ran down her cheeks, and she bowed her head even more. Triar reached out and stroked her long black hair.

"Calm down. Tell me, how many men have you been with?"

"With none, Your Majesty."

Then he took her in his arms. Katrina laid her head on his shoulder. It was so nice to feel his warmth next to her. She crossed her hands over the regent's back only for a few seconds. But she understood at once what might happen and rejected him violently, so much so that she braced herself for a scourge that never came.

"I'm sorry you thought I would take advantage of that moment of weakness. I am not like that," the king apologized.

That he wasn't like that? She couldn't be talking to the same man who slapped his wife more than he spoke to her, the one who beat his own son just because he was not like him. It had to be a ruse to lure her into his claws. She took a couple of steps back and sipped her tears. Her green eyes were still red and inside her remained the fear that he would abuse her.

"May I leave?"

"You are free to do so whenever you feel like it."

"But..."

"Yes, I know. A few minutes ago, I wasn't talking like that."

Katrina turned around and walked towards the exit. She felt that she was leaving a lion behind her, ready to pounce and devour her completely.

"Katrina."

She knew it; he would not let her go that easily. She turned to him with her face pale with fear and her heart about to burst in her chest.

"Yes?"

"Good night, sleep well." The smile seemed sincere.

"Ah!" she mumbled in obfuscation. "Good night, Your Majesty."

## 4

As she approached her room, the first thing she noticed was that her parents were awake, not the slightest doubt as to why: they were waiting for her. She clenched her fists when she stood in front of them.

"So, you're the king's new whore," her mother shrieked. "Tomorrow, the whole castle will know, and the next day the rest of the kingdom will too. Whore!"

"Be quiet, woman. It is an honor for our daughter and us that the king has set his eyes on her," replied her father.

"His eyes! I wish it had been only that."

"You don't know what you're saying. He must have rewarded her well; he's a just man. Let's see, what did he give you?"

"Father, he did not..."

"What do you mean? Didn't he give you anything in return?" her father shouted as if he didn't give a damn about waking up the others.

"No," she felt her throat close, letting out only a voice trickle, "I didn't want to sleep with him."

"You have done well, my daughter..."

"I told you to shut up. Don't make me hit you." Katrina could see more than anger in her father's eyes. "How could you do that? The king can't be denied anything. You know very well that he can throw us out of here whenever he feels like it. I assure you that life outside is not easy. You haven't thought about that; you haven't thought about anything, maybe only about keeping your virtue intact, right? Right? Answer!"

"No, I..."

The backhand of her father's calloused hand struck her hard on the cheek, throwing her to the ground. Her watery eyes perceived her mother trying to approach and being brutally repelled.

"I will tell you what you will do tomorrow, not tonight since I am afraid you could wake him up. You will go to his quarters and give him your body and whatever else he wants without any complaints. If he asks you anything, which I doubt because men don't care about words at such moments, you will tell him that you were scared and nervous because it is your first time, isn't it? Otherwise, I..." he threatened her, raising his hand again.

"Yes, it is."

"Good. Besides, as he is the king, you were afraid, I mean, you didn't want to disappoint him because of your lack of experience. That will soften him up. Then don't forget to tell him that he was fabulous and as ardent as the best stallion in the stable, that you enjoyed plenty being with him, and that he can have you as often as he wants. You won't ask for anything; hopefully, he will offer it to you. You may have wasted a great opportunity. If he gives you a choice, take the simplest with humility so that he doesn't think you want to take advantage of him. Do you understand me?"

"Yes, father."

She tried her best to wipe away her tears. Her father was leaving when he turned to her. Katrina dared to imagine that he would help her up. That didn't happen.

"Ah, don't be so naive to think you're special to him. You weren't the first, and I assure you won't be the last. Get it through your head."

Katrina waited a few minutes for her parents to leave before going to her room. It was a small room with a straw pallet and a small table where the light of a candle trembled tremulously, above which hung a broken oval mirror.

Her reflection showed her a sorrowful face. Her father was right. She had behaved like a fool. Life in the castle was good; they lacked nothing. It was quite possible that the king would send them away tomorrow. Stupid! What if she went up again? Maybe she could make amends tonight. No, no, she did not want to do that. She did not want to, but she had to.

She grabbed the door handle to open the door. Would she, or wouldn't she? She hesitated. According to her father, the timing was not right. She closed the door. She would go tomorrow. She would give herself to him. She would be his.

She took off her fatigues. Tucked behind the door was her worn nightgown. The reflections of the chandelier allowed her to admire her young body. Next summer, she would be nineteen. Her shapes were not exuberant. She held her own breasts gently. It was what she had; it should be enough for the king.

She dressed the camisole and curled up to sleep. *"I am not like that."* Triar's phrase took over her mind, and she fell asleep thinking about him.

At dawn, a storm was unleashed. As lightning and thunder crashed over the Kingdom of Lebassi, as the sky threatened to fall, and as the sea waves tried to destroy the castle's steep foundations, Katrina dreamed of the king.

# 5

To ride together! Angela couldn't remember the last time her husband had asked her for such a thing. When Triar was courting her, he traveled fortnightly to her aunt and uncle's farm south of Tolm. She was an orphan; her parents had died in a fire when she was little, and her father's brother and his wife had raised her; she became the daughter they never had. He would always invite her to ride through the fields and woods back then. She, only eighteen years old, was enraptured by the boy's regal bearing and exquisite manners. When she met the young man, he had just turned twenty-five. And the king celebrated his birthday with a great feast in the city of Lebassi. He was a tall, handsome young man with a short beard in shades of brown matching his hair. A simple invitation raised the memories of those distant times.

She tried to stuff herself into her riding outfit: a light green skirt and a white bodice. The seams complained. She expelled air and held her breath as she knotted the last few loops. *Phew*, she finally managed to close the garment. She breathed.

She froze when she saw Triar in the stable. He was standing in front of his favorite horse, Hunter, wearing black leather breeches and a sky-gray jerkin. In his forties, her husband's body had gained muscle and retained the agility of his youth. Her husband's face was strong, with a square chin, a slightly elongated nose, and deep wrinkles on his forehead. For a few seconds, she evoked moments of happiness by his side. The equine neighed playfully as his rider stroked his sea-foam-colored mane.

"Come on, woman, hurry up," Triar urged her.

The king's call brought her out of her reverie.

It had been so long. She approached the brown steed that was ready for her. She interlaced her fingers without daring to mount it.

"Will you help me up?" begged Angela.

She knew she could provoke him in this way. It had been a long time since he had sought her company simply because he wanted her. Perhaps there was still some hope. She still loved him.

The king approached and stood behind her. He held her by the hips until she put one foot in the stirrup. Then, he gently urged her forward by placing his hand in the middle of her buttocks. Her blood warmed slightly, and a blush lit up her cheeks.

"Triar!" exclaimed the queen in surprise.

"What's wrong? Did I do something wrong?"

"No!" exclaimed Angela, blushing.

Triar nimbly jumped on Hunter and started whipping him into a run.

"Come on, follow me!" he shouted as he trotted out of the stables.

It could not possibly be happening. That shout. The same shout she heard the first day they rode together, the first day he kissed her. The same shout he repeated the rest of the days they rode. She couldn't understand; yesterday, he had hit her again without going any further. It did not matter; he was her husband, and she would always be his wife.

The queen smiled, tightened her grip on the reins, and dug her boots into the steed's flanks in pursuit of her spouse. If there were a chance to get him back, she would catch it on the fly. She owed it to herself; she owed it to her son, Gregor. The boy was a beautiful-hearted young man who took refuge in her arms without his father's love. She owed him. There had to be some way to erase the last few years and regain the lost romance, the lost romance, and the lost family, and build a home again

## *6*

"Why did you have to change? You know I loved you. You could not stay true to the image you gave me when we were young. You always said you were enthusiastic about my ideas; we had drawn up many plans. But no, years went by, and you drifted away from me," Triar explained.

They walked along the beach below the castle. The horses were left grazing high up after more than an hour of riding.

"I never did that."

Triar faced her and put both hands on her shoulders. "You felt less and less like going out riding or coming for a swim. You stopped doing so many things."

"I am the queen; I cannot behave like a young girl. I had to assume my role."

"The queen is the king's wife, and, to him, she owes absolute obedience, just as the subjects owe it to us. Who would say something to you? Not me, and the opinion of others lacks importance." He let her go and kept walking.

"Despite that, I still loved you. I would have done anything you wanted to please you. You never said anything to me. You took refuge in the parade ground, hunting, and so many other activities that you left no room for me."

"I was waiting for you. I wished you would come to my side, that you would notice my need for you and come closer. You didn't; you thought that trying to talk during meals was enough."

"But I didn't know..."

"I know; you don't have to tell me. I got tired of waiting, Angela."

Triar picked up a stone and threw it far out into the sea. He continued walking. After a few seconds, he realized that Angela was not following him. He turned around, looking for her. Sitting on the sand, the queen was crying while she kept playing with her wedding ring. The same wedding ring that he put in her hands the day they married belonged to his grandmother. That day, she had also cried; her aunt had tried to calm her down without success until, smiling, he approached his fiancée, held out his hand, and said: "Come on, follow me".

He walked over to his wife and crouched down beside her. Her countenance lit up with a smile when he took her hands.

"What are you telling me that for now?" Angela mumbled between sobs.

"I may have hurt you with my attitude. I guess no woman likes to see that her husband prefers others to her." He stopped and looked out to sea. "I would like you to forgive me for all I have put you through."

His wife's green eyes lit up.

"Triar!" The queen embraced him without hesitation.

"Does that mean you do?"

He felt her lips on his and experienced a sense of horror. He did not remember how impulsive his wife could be.

"Calm down, Angela." He hardly managed to say it; she kept kissing him. He lifted her in his arms. "Come on, I feel like repeating our wedding night."

"Are you sure you can carry me all the way to the horses? I've put on a little weight."

*I know you have, you disgusting witch,* Triar thought.

"No! I'm going to take you to our bedroom like this."

"Oh, but how gallant!"

He began to climb the steep path slowly. He didn't even remember when the idea formed inside his head. He had his doubts; he recognized it. He weighed it, analyzed it, and assessed the risks. In the end, he was convinced that it was the right decision. From now on, his life would experience a great change. His life would go well again. He cursed that he had not thought of it before; he would not have wasted so much time. It was curious to him that the pieces fit together perfectly.

He paused midway to catch his breath. They were high enough. The impact from there would be strong enough to kill her.

"Don't tell me you've had enough. Let me walk. You'll need your vigor for later."

"The only thing I need is to regain some strength to do it."

Saying this, Triar lifted her over his head. He felt her writhe.

"What are you doing? Put me down!"

His muscles groaned as he hurled her towards the rocks at the bottom. His wife fell, flailing arms and legs and screaming until the stones on the beach broke her fall.

He watched her without missing any detail. He thought the body would bounce off the rocks, but it didn't; it just settled brutally, like a pebble in mud.

When he went down to look for her, he stopped to arm himself with a boulder, just in case. Before reaching the sand, he rolled his body on the ground; as if, when she slipped, he had tried to hold her but unfortunately did not succeed. He reached her side. It was unnecessary to finish her off.

She laid on his back with her eyes open. A pool of blood was clotted under her head, and her arms showed small tears. Otherwise, it was as if she were asleep.

He dropped the rock and bent down to pick up his wife's corpse. Like a game of fate, she now felt less heavy to him. He caught his breath before starting up the slope. There was still a long way to go.

# 7

The kitchen chats were always of the most varied nature. Today, new love affairs and the ailments of the elderly had no place. No one in the whole castle brought up any topic other than the queen's death.

The few who saw the king arrive recounted the terrible scene. The monarch, covered in dust, with several scratches and the inert body of his wife in his arms. When they wanted to give him a glass of wine to revive him, his hands could not hold it. He sought the shelter of his armchair after leaving his wife in expert hands. Then, he went upstairs to suffer the loss in solitude.

Next to Katrina, her fellow tradeswomen commented on the tragic accident.

"All I know is that I can get something out of this," said Melissa, the stable manager's daughter. She was only a couple of years older than Katrina, and, unlike her, she had a voluptuous figure, dark skin, and curly hair cut short at her neck. Besides, everyone knew that she had been the monarch's favorite for about two months.

"Look, pretty girl, if anyone is going to get anything out of this, it is going to be me. I'm not going to let any clever little girl come along and take it away from me. If I find out you've tried anything, I swear I'll scratch your eyes out. And that goes for everyone, including you, Katrina; don't think you're fooling anyone with your prudishness. As if we didn't know what you did yesterday. It's a worn-out trick to make them beg, so they find the fruit tastier later on." She was around her thirties, but her beauty was still smooth. She also exhibited a generous cleavage, which she never hid, and wide hips, whose swaying bewitched the eyes of more than one man in the castle. "You heard me!"

"I wouldn't do that, Martha," Katrina replied.

"You have been warned!" concluded Martha.

One of her friends gave her a poorly disguised nudge as if trying to get her to leave the conversation.

Martha walked away from them. Katrina watched her in silence. *"I am not like that."* Triar's phrase flew into her head again. What if he wasn't looking for a warm body to unload his masculinity but for a partner who understood him? What if she, a poor naïve girl, was so stupid that she did not realize she was still fantasizing? Something told her that he really was not like that, that he was looking for someone who really understood him, and she felt connected to him. She felt connected to him. Could it be possible?

She unconsciously shook his head, saying no to her own thoughts and maybe, just maybe, to her heart.

# 8

Triar swung his legs over the abyss, attentive to the distant crashing of the waves, which was barely a murmur. He loved the peace that reigned in the whole place. There, sitting on the granite blocks, he felt at ease again. All the bad memories were behind him. It was time to build a new future, a new life, remake his history, and think big.

Tomorrow he would speak to Omar, one of his captains, to take his son away from there. A week's ride away stood the Falcon Tower, just at the foothills of the Iron Mountains. That place had been abandoned for years; it would be perfect for imprisoning the brat, for taking him and training him to be a great warrior. He would give him absolute power over the puny child. He would not even reproach him if he suffered physical harm. Perhaps then he could make amends for the wasted years. Extreme measures were needed for extreme cases.

The mage assured him that it would not be long, although he did not say anything about the exact date. He was still in a hurry, but the wait would be more pleasant now.

The night threatened to freeze. Surely the fields would be covered with frost at dawn. In a few weeks, the first snow might come. He joked with the thought that his men would have a much harder time digging his wife's grave in the frozen ground; doing it now would not cause them to sweat too much.

From behind him came the sound of the door opening. Who dared disturb him? He jumped to his feet. He went in to face it.

"Your Majesty."

The voice bit his ears lasciviously, like a snake crawling on the sand.

Martha was wearing a cotton nightgown that a few winters ago might have been white. Her hair waved loosely. He perceived a faint fragrance of orange blossom. Her lips glowed a fiery red as if from hell itself. The king remembered: that not only her lips were an invitation to sin, but her whole body was also a true temple of pleasure. He thought it was a good way to alleviate the mourning that filled his spirit.

The woman advanced a few steps toward him. Her hands undid the knot that closed the garment over her chest and pulled it until it fell at her feet. The night breeze blew against her skin, making her clench her teeth to keep from chattering.

"Your Majesty, I am cold."

"You read my mind," Triar exclaimed hoarsely. "Come here."

He took her in his arms and sought her hungry mouth. Martha kissed him back, and they surrendered to passion in front of the fireplace.

## *9*

Hundreds of candles illuminated the hall. Incense burned on four pedestals. Katrina moved in silence. She could not help a shudder when she saw the body lying on the table: she was wearing a white dress with a veil, and her hands, crossed over her chest, cradled a red rose. The funeral masters had managed to make the queen's face look flawless, with no trace of the accident.

She hurried her pace to approach the stairs as quickly as possible; she wanted to leave death behind. These events made a strong impression on her. When she was five years old, her uncle, her father's brother, when repairing a roof, fell from a considerable height onto the cobblestone of the entrance. She was crossing the road at the time and saw the fall and heard the screams of agony. Her uncle resisted for half an hour. As she approached to help him, he grabbed her hand and did not let go for several minutes, which seemed like hours to her. She did not like death. The farther she was from it, the more difficult it would be for it to reach her.

As she climbed the steps, she thought about why she was going up to see him. It wasn't her father's words that motivated her. No, it was not that. It was her decision. She had control over her actions. She was going up because... because... she just wanted to see the king; she had to see him. She was still afraid of him. She went over the conversation from the night before. *"I am not like that."* Actually, he had not forced her; he had not forced her into anything. When he saw her fear, he let her go. He was kind to her. And not the kindness of a king to a maid, but a man to a woman.

She ran up the stairs on tiptoe. She did not want him to hear her. She wanted to get in without the king noticing. It could be in her head, but she remembered the casual tone of yesterday's conversation. Maybe that was good for her; maybe her father was wrong. What did her father know!

The door was only a few more steps away. She steadied herself to catch her breath. It was no use not being able to talk to him when she saw him. She breathed very calmly as she summoned the courage to present herself with her eyes up.

When she was younger, her heart was kindled by the son of the palace carpenter; Thomas was his name. They would sit in the courtyard in the evenings and chat. She even allowed him to kiss her one evening. They had been in this routine for several months when she discovered that he had spent many evenings with one of her friends. Katrina always turned him down whenever he insisted on sleeping with her, saving herself for marriage. She never thought he could look for what he couldn't find by her side someplace else. On that occasion, the pain that shot through her was visceral, tearing her soul, reminding her of the falseness of men, the lies, the deceit, reminding her that she should not trust. That pain was not even close to the pain she felt when, upon entering the monarch's bed-chamber, she saw him wrapped in furs cavorting with Martha. It was not only as if her heart had been ripped from her chest but also thrown against a wall of rusty iron spikes.

"No!" she wailed helplessly in what she thought had been a whisper.

Triar became aware of his presence at that moment and tried to sit up. A hand grabbed him by the shoulder.

"Katrina, I..."

She watched as the hand squeezed harder on his shoulder, pulling him towards the bed.

"Leave her. Make me yours," demanded Martha.

Katrina ran out of there, repeating to herself that she was no one to dream about, that there was nothing special about her, and that men were all the same. Tears flowed from her eyes, blurring her vision. Stupid, stupid! The king only wanted one thing; he did not care which woman gave it to him. She was not going to succumb to his lust; she would not accept him in any way.

When she reached the end of the stairs, she ran to her small room as fast as possible. That night, she did nothing but cry.

## *10*

Dawn was breaking when the haughty figure of Égnever crossed the main courtyard, heading for the castle's entrance gate. There was nothing left for him to do in that place. His work was done, and, with that, his sentence, his condemnation, to be precise, was over. Seven years! For a mage, that amount of time was like a wisp of straw in a barn; he was over three hundred years. It was not the length of the chastisement; it was the punishment itself that tortured him day after day. Being chained to fulfill the wish of that grotesque king was an ordeal. Today it ended.

He stretched out his hands and looked at the dark metal bracelets on his wrists. Damn cryol metal! Legends said that this metal forged the gods' weapons, Salmur and Rumlas, and those of their minions. In his case, the mineral was not used as a weapon. The metal had completely covered his arms for seven years, imprisoning his powers; as time went by, it was unraveling, allowing him to have more access to and control magic. His former master, Shao, the same one he had tried to assassinate to take his place as head of the Council, had been in charge of placing them on him. The pain he felt was as if worms were burrowing deep into his skin, devouring him without doing so, tormenting him day and night. The martyrdom was still there, binding him to the Council and limiting him. He hoped that, in a few months, they would finally be gone, freeing him completely.

The soldiers on guard automatically drew their swords and cut him off.

"I am King Triar's mage. You'd better stay out of my way!" said the old man.

The guards did not lay down their weapons and did not make way for him. Suddenly, one of them raised his eyes to instantly sheathe his steel. His companion imitated him.

The mage turned around, looking for the cause of the change in the men's attitude. The king was watching the scene from his keep. Égnever looked at Triar carefully, remembering the day he had appeared at the castle.

The first autumn leaves were beginning to fall when he offered the king his powers to fulfill any wish he had. The cretin didn't waste a day thinking about it, as if he had been holding the same rod all his life and waiting for the first tug before pulling in his fish. He wanted the old glories of his kingdom to return. His fields were to be strewn with corpses, and blood was to flow. The shadows would have to give birth to a new enemy, a strong entity before which he, ruler of Lebassi, could draw his sword and fight a matchless duel. He did not specify anything else, but Égnever understood him very well. From that day on, he worked in the dungeons, cursing his doom, accessing the magic of Panameria to create that dream, make it real, and give the sovereign what he so longed for. He accomplished his task.

In what could have been a farewell gesture, Triar bowed his head slightly.

The guards stood back and lifted the iron gate.

Égnever walked away on an upward trajectory, thinking he was leaving Triar just as the fun began.

## *11*

"We will be there soon."

Mounted on his horse, Gregor followed Captain Omar to an uncertain destination. His father only told him that the old soldier would train him. That had been almost a week ago. The soldier had turned out to be quite jovial all the way, explaining details of the forest to him. He was almost as tall as his father, with a long, bristly black beard that contrasted with his shiny bald head. A thin scar ran down his face from his right temple, bordering his eye, to his aquiline nose. He had a slight limp on his left leg, the result of a revolt five years ago in one of the villages, as he told him on the second day of their journey.

In the evenings, his new guardian forced him to set up camp. He had to prepare the tent, tend to the horses, replenish the water rations, fetch wood for the fire, light it, and even cook whatever his companion hunted in the forest. He had blisters on his hands, and his back ached from riding so much. No one attended to his wounds or his suffering. His mother was gone.

He remembered his mother's funeral. She looked beautiful in her white dress. Her father, the king, led the procession that escorted the body to the family cemetery. Behind him, two snowy horses pulled the wagon where the queen's coffin rested.

The cemetery was a small stretch of land to the south of the castle. No more than a meter high, a stone fence surrounded the grounds. There was an archway with a dragon with outstretched wings engraved at the top at the entrance.

In the retinue, he distinguished Captain Omar and other high-ranking military officers. Behind his father was Daniel, his closest friend. Some servants, the most elderly, joined the procession.

Two laborers lowered the coffin with ropes. His father, before the grave, gave an insipid eulogy in which he spoke more about him than about his mother. Shovelfuls of dirt fell on the grave. The two men finished in less than a minute.

Then, as everyone was leaving, he approached. He carried in his hand a single white rose. He squeezed it so hard that the thorns cut his skin. Drops of blood fell on the grave. He knelt. Lovingly, he placed the flower, praying for his mother's soul. Tears streamed down his face. He didn't understand. Why did she die? He started digging, trying to find an answer. He scratched his fingers. He pounded his fists, again and again, on the freshly dug soil. It was pointless.

That was when he noticed the white marble tombstone which, written in elegant calligraphy, read:

"Here lies Angela,

wife of King Triar."

Was that all she was? Wife of the king. She was not good. She was not loved. She was not a mother.

Thinking about it again rekindled the pain he harbored in his heart. He repressed the tears and stared at the road.

He saw it! At the edge of a pond stood a circular tower of three or four levels, he could not say for sure; beside it, a small house with a rickety door and shutters about to fall off the windows. The roof, slate, seemed to be in no better condition. An orchard, or what may have been an orchard, loomed to the right of the house. Behind the buildings, the massif of the Iron Mountains could be glimpsed, the place where the metal in the kingdom was extracted from.

This would be his new home: the Falcon Tower.

"I told you we were about to arrive, or I didn't tell you," boasted Omar.

"Yes, you told me."

They dismounted. Omar pushed open the front door of the dwelling, which opened with a loud creak. The inside was in no better condition than the outside. Furniture was smashed. Mice scurried in the corners. Fat spiders draped the ceiling with their webs. Scant furniture, most of it broken.

"Nothing that can't be fixed with a little grease, wood, and nails. We have a lot of work to do before we start your training, Gregor, a lot of work."

The young prince snorted. This was his father's punishment for being weak. Crying was useless. He did not wait for any orders. He took an old broom in his hands and started sweeping.

## *12*

Katrina sighed before entering the great hall. She knew he was waiting for her. He was very forceful when, about two weeks ago, he had demanded that she attend to him upon the mage's departure. She was to serve his meals, take his clean clothes to him, everything. He was always correct, trying to be affectionate. She repelled him coldly.

The maidens and not-so 'maidens' who tried to keep the king company in his bed-chamber were expelled. He slept alone. Some said out of respect for his dead wife. She knew that was not so.

He paid attention only to her and the soldiers with whom he fought on the parade ground. He dedicated every day to training and preparing her men. He repeated to his soldiers repeatedly that they had to be prepared, that the old glories would be reborn.

Katrina approached, carrying a platter full of roasted deer. She tried hard not to look him in the eye. She placed it in front of him and withdrew her arms quickly, not wanting to be grabbed by his hands. She filled his wine glass and prepared to leave.

"Stay."

The order left no room for discussion. She stood a few feet away from the table.

"I am not going to eat you; come closer. No, you'd better take a chair and sit down. You must be tired too. I'm worn out. I spent the whole day training with my men."

She moved to the other end of the table. She had to keep her distance.

"Don't do that. You act like you're afraid of me," the king complained.

"I am."

"I see. Why are you afraid of me?"

"You, no, sir..."

"So you're afraid of someone you address without respect," Triar interrupted.

"I didn't mean to. I'm sorry, Your Majesty."

She thought he might hit her for saying something like that. She bowed her head so as not to look at him.

"What are you thinking about?" asked the sovereign.

"Nothing at all, Your Majesty," Katrina lied, looking at him, trying to make him believe her.

"Come on, I'm old, not stupid," added the regent, smiling.

She couldn't trust that smile.

"Let me guess: you think I may hurt you, that I will treat you like all the others."

"Yes."

"Well, at least you're back to addressing me the way you feel you should." He skewered a good piece of meat and greedily brought it to his mouth. He lifted another piece and pointed toward her: "Do you want to eat?"

"No, thank you."

"Well, I cannot force you to do anything." And he swallowed it without chewing.

"May I leave?"

"No, absolutely not. I want you to spend the night with me."

Katrina's eyes widened in surprise. She blushed completely and began to tremble.

"If that is what you want," she said.

"Then it's settled. Just let me finish, and we'll go upstairs."

She waited with resignation as he devoured each slice of deer one by one. He accompanied the meat with several glasses of wine. As he drained the last one, he slammed it down hard on the table.

Katrina jolted in her chair.

"I'm ready!" announced Triar.

The king rose from the table, stood behind her, and stroked her arms.

"Come on, let's go."

Katrina felt like the world was coming down on her. Before she could get to her feet, he lifted her with ease. One of his hands was just below her chest, and she didn't dare breathe so he wouldn't brush against it.

"Stop being so stiff; you look like a corpse," grumbled the king.

Katrina's mind immediately flew back to the night she walked across that enclosure to see Triar passing by Queen Angela's body. Just as then, she now got goose bumps.

## *13*

Nervous, Katrina waited as Triar lit the fireplace. Not that he didn't trust her to warm him with her body, he told her, but that a chilly breeze was blowing outside. It took very little time to light the logs. The light bathed the room and formed shadows that looked menacing to her.

"Come warm yourself by the fire," the king invited her.

She sat down next to the sovereign. She expected that, at any moment, he would put his arm around her and then kiss her; it could not happen any other way. Instead, he stood quietly contemplating the flames.

Several minutes passed before he addressed her again.

"If I asked you to undress, you would, wouldn't you?"

"You are the king, and I would have to do it."

"If I asked you to jump into the void, would you do it too?"

She did not know what to answer; that was different.

"I thought so." He thought for a moment before continuing, "What's the difference? Both times I would have you do something against your will."

"But it is not the same. My father..."

"Yes, I can imagine what your father says. I'm sure it's because of him that you're willing to give yourself to me. And he's also the reason you went upstairs last time."

"No, not that time," she admitted.

"You mean you wanted to make love to me because you felt like it?"

"Yes, I mean, no. I just wanted to talk about what happened the night before, nothing else."

"I didn't understand it either. I'm used to women coming to me and being willing to do anything but always waiting for their reward."

"Like Martha."

"Like Martha and many others. In so many years, you have been the only one who... I don't know how to say it."

“That was scared?” Katrina ventured.

“No, please, there have been several of those. You’re not the first virgin I’ve met. But you, despite all you could get, were not willing to sell yourself. I can’t understand the difference between you and the others.”

Triar picked up another log and threw it into the hearth. There it collided with the others, raising burning blades.

“Come on, tell me something,” Triar requested.

“I don’t know. I just do what I feel. I can’t delve into the reasons of others. Some people want to go very far in life; money is very useful.”

“You talk as if you don’t want the same thing.”

“No.” Although, at the same time, she realized that she didn’t say it with much conviction.

“You are lying. We are all the same.”

“Maybe, but there are many ways to live life; maybe that’s the difference.”

“Nonsense. I am a king, and you are a maid; there is more than one difference between us, but it is not the same between two kings or two maids. For example, my grandfather and I were identical,” Triar concluded.

“Why are you talking about your grandfather and not your father? He was also a king.”

“Because… because... I don’t like to talk about my father.”

"Why?"

"I don't know; I don't want to talk about it," Triar insisted.

The king stood up with a sullen expression and went out to gaze at the sea.

Katrina waited, sitting in front of the hearth. The dance of the fire was hypnotic. Some of her fear was fading.

The sovereign returned, then sat down next to her. He did not look at her; his eyes were fixed on the fire.

"I'm going to bore you." But, before she could say anything, he continued, "We got along very well in the beginning. He had me when he and my mother were young, not like I did with my son. He taught me how to ride horses and many other things. I loved him as much as a son can love a father, but then everything changed. When I was about ten years old, my grandfather began to tell me stories of the previous wars. I loved those stories. The fights, the sieges, it sounded so heroic. On stormy nights, I would sit in front of him in the great hall; while he drank mulled wine, my grandfather told me about his battles for hours. My grandfather was a great warrior who unified the southern kingdoms. The later it was, the sadder his voice became, and I could see in his misty eyes that his mind was lost in those distant years during which he fought with determination and bravery. My grandfather had ideals. He had a purpose.

"My father always told him to forget the past, that those were sad times when misery populated every village and death laid behind every tree. But he never shut up. He was a very stubborn old man. Well, in the end, he had to; we all have to go some time. Although my father had always told me that men didn't cry, I cried over my grandfather's grave. I miss him very much."

Katrina rested her head on the king's shoulder as she listened. His arm wrapped around her, instantly sheltering her close to his muscular body. The feeling was pleasant. Fear left her completely. She was comfortable listening.

"From that day on, life in the palace changed, as if my grandfather's death had buried the last bastion of past glories. It was all a charade to keep him happy, to avoid conflict; after all, he was the king. I don't know, I don't know why it changed, but it did."

Triar interrupted his story. Katrina heard him sigh, perhaps seeking strength. When he spoke again, his voice sounded sad, broken, as if the ghosts of the past were returning:

"I felt that my father disowned the rest of the family, all our ancestors who had once shed their blood to bring peace and security to the town. I hated him ever since, even more, when one night I heard him tell my mother that, luckily, they had gotten rid of the old man.

"That same early morning, I escaped to the cemetery to swear on the sacrosanct land of our family that I would never forget the past. I silently wished a new war would break out just to see those who disowned the roots die. But years passed, and nothing of the sort happened. Life went on as usual and..."

Triar interrupted her story. He turned his head to look at her. Her eyes were closed, her mouth half-open. She was breathing softly. He watched her.

"I bared my soul for the first time, and she wouldn't even listen to me," Triar mumbled through his teeth.

He carried her gently to the bed and tucked her in with the best furs. He sat down beside her to contemplate her. He gently stroked her temple, outlining her black hair. He ran his fingers down her cheek. He ran his fingers down her graceful neck. He stopped his hand on her upper chest. A few seconds. She was breathing hard. Gently, his fingers moved down.

He shook his head sharply and removed his hand from Katrina's chest. He clenched his fist tightly and returned to the fireplace, where he began to stoke the fire. He placed more logs to warm the room.

## *14*

Far, far away from the lands of Lebassi, in the Creation Mountains, a thick blanket of clouds began to swirl over one of the peaks. The moon, which until then had been shining brightly, became misty with mourning, plunging the region into total darkness. Lightning flashed across the sky, crashing against the base of the mountain.

The ground groaned. The mountain peak opened, expelling black puffs that thinned the air. Panameria suffered.

A few minutes later, the ash was accompanied by a faint reddish glow illuminating the peak and its surroundings. Then sparks flew as if a giant blacksmith had his forge inside the mountain. There was a continuous wailing sound.

Then silence took over the area as if nothing was happening. No sound, neither from the mountain nor from any animal. Nothing. The stillness remained for several minutes.

Suddenly, the earth opened its bowels to the sky. Huge debris emerged, tracing arcs of fire in the foul air. A gigantic rumbling was heard as if the tectonic plates were gears in a gigantic mechanism. A torrent of lava raged through, like blood from a deep neck wound. The ridge of the mountain was shattered. The molten rock dragged down the accumulated ash forming a crimson front adorned by black measles.

Clouds of sulfurous gas hissed as they escaped from the wave of liquid material.

Amid that trail of destruction, a hand rose; it stretched out as far as it could as if it had just awakened from a nap. The rest of the body followed it, as white and perfect as ivory. Lava trickled over the woman's skin as if it were warm water. She rose to her feet and, with magma up to her knees, began to walk slowly to get out of there. At first, her steps were shaky. Gradually, they gained strength and confidence.

Behind her, Panameria's sigh could be heard, just like a mother's after giving birth.

## *15*

Katrina opened her eyes and found Triar's figure in front of her. He had taken off his shirt and was smiling mischievously at her. She noticed herself; she was completely naked and bound hand and foot to the bed's four corners.

She looked at the king again and found him menacingly changed. His eyes seemed to glow with flames, and his fingers grew long and sharp. The wolfish smile persisted as if telling her that he had been waiting for this moment for a long time, and he would not let her escape; he would make her his.

Katrina screamed loudly and tried to break free from her bonds when he put a knee on the bed. He could be sure she would not be easy prey.

She let out the shriek so loud that she felt her arms break free.

"Nooo!"

Sitting in the middle of the monarch's bed, she could not believe it had been a dream. The last thing she remembered was sitting in front of the fireplace with Triar while he told his grandfather's war stories.

She spotted the regent poorly settled in an armchair, barely covered by a blanket. He was snoring loudly. She threw one of the furs over him and then went to take care of the hearth.

The morning was near, and the first voices of the day came through the window. Most of the stable boys should be ready to milk the cows.

She sat down in front of the ruler of Lebassi to wait. Minutes passed. The beautiful cacophony of the castle's labors rose to the tower.

When Triar woke up, she was looking at him.

"Good morning, Triar."

She dared to call him by name. No majesty, no sir, just Triar. She felt the night had changed them, perhaps even brought them together.

“Good morning,” replied the king.

She watched him, captivated. She had an accomplice smile on her face. Her eyes sparkled as they never did before. She walked up to him and took the monarch’s hand in hers.

“Thank you. I didn’t think you would respect me. While we were sitting, I was afraid to fall asleep because I thought you would take advantage then to abuse me. You didn’t. Thank you,” Katrina repeated.

“I am not like that,” Triar emphasized.

Her smile became much broader, more radiant; her heart swelled with a warmth unknown to her.

“Do you want to have breakfast with me?”

“But I’m just a maid!”

“You’re right. The king could get very angry.”

They both laughed.

Katrina stood up and invited him to do the same, pulling on the king’s hands. The man was much taller than she was. She stood on tiptoe, daring to press her lips to his. In response, Triar’s hands embraced her waist in a loving gesture.

“Come on, follow me. I’m hungry, and I’m sure you are too,” said the monarch as he held out his hand.

She accepted it, accompanying him as they walked down the stairs to the great hall.

## *16*

He walked. One step after another. For the past few weeks, Égnever advanced northward. His arms were heavy. The cursed cryol still curbed his powers and slowed his march. Each night, like a vile mortal, he had to rest. Until his shackles finished undoing, his powers would remain sapped. One step at a time.

A few hundred yards away, a squadron of horses was approaching at a gallop. Only a dozen, although he guessed that this was only a small fraction of the contingent that must be waiting behind. He sensed a faint trace of magic in the men approaching; nothing to fear.

Five of them surrounded him. Their armor was completely black and made of leather, tough and practical to a large extent.

"Let me through," commanded the mage. His eyes gave off an icy look, but none of them backed an inch. "I am a mage," warned Égnever.

Their reaction was different then. They drew their swords and charged at him.

Without even moving from where he was standing, Égnever prepared his defense. He flicked his hand with a sharp flick of his wrist, and all five riders went to the ground.

"I said let me through!" yelled the old man.

Without waiting any longer, he resumed his pilgrimage. He did not understand how they could think of attacking him, simple soldiers against a mage. It was clear that their leader's only ambition was to kill for killing. Triar would be pleased.

The defeated men returned to their mounts and escorted the lone traveler along with the rest.

Without slackening his pace, Égnever watched them suspiciously. What were they looking for from him? To attack him? To stop him? Why were they escorting him?

After three hours of walking, Égnever could see a monumental camp. He could well go around it, just walk past it. This convoy had the mission of accompanying him to their leader. Something inside him told him that they were waiting for him. What could he lose by talking?

The guards at the entrance ignored him. Half of the horsemen went in another direction. Égnever advanced, followed by the same five horsemen he had knocked down earlier. The vast majority of the soldiers encamped there took not the slightest notice of him; others, the fewest, paused their activities. The mage wondered if they knew who he was. The makeshift barracks would hold no more than a thousand men. It was a good number for such a short time.

He arrived at the center of the cantonment. The stench of magic was more than noticeable; it emanated from a majestic tent that ridiculed the poor tarpaulins worn by the rest of the troop. Six soldiers, who Égnever sensed were the army's captains, wearing similar leather armors and swords in their belts, emerged from the tent and positioned themselves in front of him in a crescent formation.

The figure that emerged next was not as tall as the captains. Equipped with copper-toned armor that shimmered below the sun's rays, the female warrior looked imposing. Her long hair matched the armor, falling down her back in light curls. The skin of her face was an immaculate white, like the first snowfall of winter, dotted with a beautiful shade of green nestled in her eyes.

"Égnever, beloved father!"

At that moment, the noises from the camp ceased. A thousand pairs of eyes were watching what was happening.

"You've grown up so fast," said Égnever.

"No, I was born an adult. I see you underestimated your powers."

"Maybe."

The woman drew the sword from its sheath and raised it towards the mage.

"Are you challenging me?" questioned Égnever in amusement.

"I was born for destruction. You interfere in my designs."

"You are crazy. You have no designs."

The mage extended his hand, repeating the same gesture that had served him to subjugate the riders just a few hours ago. He was bitterly surprised to see that his opponent did not even stagger.

"My turn!" announced the woman.

The sharp steel descended swiftly upon the old man leaving a glittering arc in its wake.

Égnever had to focus a lot of energy to repel the blow. The weapon slammed into his hand, shattering in two. He smiled.

"You will need another sword."

"Nonsense, you gave me a little bit of yourself."

With a quick gesture, the lady swung the sword to the side. A crimson glow ran over the metal, easily reintegrating the broken blade.

"You see? I'm ready again."

The mage's smile transfigured into a grimace of disbelief. He focused the energy he drew from the earth, creating a sphere in his right hand. He threw it with precision towards the female's face. It would blow her head off.

With a nimble feint, his enemy dodged the magic projectile and launched a fierce attack on him. He tried to raise his hands to defend himself. His arms were so heavy that he was unable to do so. It was as if chains were holding him down. He pulled hard. Nothing.

An instant before the thrust reached his head, he understood. The cryol bracelets not only limited his abilities, but they also served as a link to Shao, the one who put them on him. It was him. He felt his hand in all this. He was bending him, leaving him helpless before his creation. Seven years was not the penalty the Council had craved, of course. They had tricked him into believing he would be free later. Mages didn't kill each other, funny! They turned his own creation against him.

He sank into utter darkness.

## *17*

"You eat more every day."

It was as if history was repeating itself. Before long, she would be piling on fat and reneging on promises made only a few months before. What else could be expected from such despicable beings as women? They had only one mission in this world. Why did he have to marry her? How could he have been so stupid as to fall into the nets of another? He was old enough to know them perfectly; they were all looking to get married and have their husband carry them for the rest of their life.

"Triar," he managed to hear the honeyed tone with which she pronounced his name, "it is just that I have to eat for two."

"And what the hell is that supposed to mean? It's just an excuse to make you look like a cow. You are all the…"

The last word died in his mouth. She looked at him expectantly.

"Two? You mean..."

Katrina nodded and smiled at him.

"I'm going to be a father." He got up from the table and walked to his wife. "I'm going to be a father." Triar took her in his arms and held her tightly. She began to cry tears of joy seeing him so happy. "How long have you known?"

"Just a few weeks," his wife confessed.

"Weeks! This is great news to keep hidden. If it's a boy, he will be the best of warriors; if it's a girl, she will be as good and beautiful as her mother," Triar said.

He wished it were a boy. He wished to make amends for his previous parenthood. He would love him dearly and would not allow anyone or anything to take him away from him. He would teach him to hunt and ride horses, they would be the best of friends, and he would be king at his death. By Salmur, the prince was to be born!

"So, it doesn't bother you anymore that I eat so much?"

He noticed in her voice a kind of pleading. Surely, she remembered the obese figure of the former queen and the despotic way he treated her.

"Forgive me for saying it like that. In your condition, you have to eat as much as you need. I want our child to be born strong."

He immediately kissed her, trying, in that way, to further seal their bond and show her that he truly loved her.

"Your Majesty!"

The voice came from the entrance of the hall. Who dared to disturb him at that moment? Triar turned in displeasure to find the figure of Daniel, one of his captains, whom he had entrusted, weeks ago, with getting information about the troops advancing through his kingdoms.

"Come closer, my friend," the king demanded.

It seemed that the soldier could barely stand. Limping, he approached the table.

The king quickly approached the soldier and invited him to sit down, dragging a chair.

"Katrina, quick, bring wine for Daniel."

"They were following me, Your Majesty, but I managed to lose them," explained Daniel.

"Well done."

Triar noticed that his left leg was soaked in blood. He bent down to check the wound as his wife poured the wine. It was an arrow, or what was left of it. Daniel must have broken it. The tip was still inside.

"Wake up Aurelius, the healer. Have the maidens prepare a room to accommodate him. He will stay in the castle," Triar ordered.

He and Daniel grew up together; he was like a brother to him, a training buddy, a wine-night companion, simply a friend. He was only a couple of years younger than him, and he had three beautiful daughters and a wonderful wife. They lived on the outskirts of the town, on a small farm where they raised sheep and lambs, which Lily, his wife, sold in the town square or to the castle itself. He would not lose his friend tonight when he was celebrating that a new life was on the way.

Minutes took forever. While Daniel sipped the wine, he squeezed the wound.

"Aurelio is not here; he went out to take care of a sick person," said his wife.

"Damn it! Bring me Iron Moonshine," said the king as he pulled his knife from his belt. "My friend, you are going to need something stronger than wine for me to get the arrow out of you."

He held the bottle his wife held out to him, took a long drink, and then passed it to Daniel. The dwarven master blenders distilled Iron Moonshine. The most praised of its healing properties was that it could put a man to sleep all night; other uses were also known: a worm killer, a rust remover, and a remedy for forgetting sorrows.

Dagger in hand, he waited for the captain to down a quarter of the bottle and saw a thick fog appear in his eyes. Triar made a clean cut with a skilled hand, barely half a finger's length. He pulled firmly and gently. The arrow resisted. He tried again. Daniel groaned in pain.

"Drink more, Danny," suggested the sovereign.

He cut again. The blood prevented him from seeing. He probed with his little finger to understand what he was dealing with.

"Bastards! What scoundrel uses three-bladed arrows?"

"Triar, please take care of Lily and the girls," Daniel implored.

"You will take care of them, for Salmur, for my kingdom; you will do it."

A group of servants milled about at the entrance to the hall. Katrina, by her husband's side, dared not utter a word.

"It's going to hurt, but I have to get it out," warned the monarch.

He held his breath. One, two, three. He pulled hard. Daniel screamed until he lost consciousness. The arrow's tip was indeed three-bladed, and each blade was serrated to inflict greater damage and pain.

"Give me a burning log from the hearth," said Triar to his wife.

Too much blood. That was not good.

He held the log Katrina brought him and poured a generous dose of schnapps on his friend's leg. He brought the fire close to the wound, which instantly ignited. He waited a few seconds and covered the cut with his own hands, extinguishing the small flames.

A strong smell of burning flesh permeated the entire room. Several maids fled, suppressing their retching.

"Take him away. Let him rest. I want someone with him at all times. If there is any change in his condition, let me know immediately."

Several of the servants carried the captain in their arms with great care.

Triar sat down dejectedly, looking for some peace. His wife's hands sought shelter in his.

"What happened?" muttered the king. More than a question, it sounded like a claim to himself.

Two soldiers rushed into the large hall.

"Your Majesty, intruders!" announced the tallest of them.

As if stung by a scorpion, Triar jumped out of his chair and faced the guards.

"Intruders? Where"?

"Your Majes..."

"Tell me where!" said the king with rage.

"At the main gate," replied the man, bowing his head in submission.

"Give me your sword," ordered the ruler.

Without waiting, Triar snatched the steel from the young man's belt and began to run.

"How many are there?"

"Twenty horsemen, my Lord..."

"Archers to the embrasures!" shouted the king as he descended the stairs leading from the hall to the main entrance.

Like a stampede, the two loyal men began to run towards the castle's militia barracks.

It was inconceivable that hosts would threaten the castle. He was the king by right, the sovereign of Lebassi. What audacity!

He opened the double doors and witnessed the bustle in the front courtyard, a wide, open esplanade from which the many towers of the wall could be accessed. Within seconds, the turrets were illuminated with torches. Archers were stationed in the embrasures, ready for the royal command.

Triar trotted towards the gate; a small platoon joined the sovereign with swords in hand. While the threat worried him, pride coursed through his body at the swift response of his militia. The training paid off. They were prepared for what was to come.

Fearlessly, he unbolted the main locks of the gate. He saw them. Twenty horsemen clad entirely in black, light armors made of what appeared to be leather. His trained eyes distinguished eight archers in the group. One of these fuckers was responsible for his friend's wound.

The warriors waited at the other end of the stone bridge that connected the castle to the rest of the continent. The majestic fortress stood on a rocky outcrop that gave it a strategic advantage against invading forces.

Triar's boots heavily thudded as they traveled along the arched walkway. He stopped in front of the henchmen, backed by his men.

"Give us the spy!" demanded the stranger.

"HA, HA, HA!"

The king's laughter echoed through the walls of the royal citadel. At the same time, he raised his left hand with all five fingers extended.

The whistling of arrows followed his movement. Ten horsemen fell to the ground.

"There are no spies here. I only see corpses riding horses; well, some corpses don't ride horses anymore."

"We followed the spy here. Hand him over!"

Triar closed his fist, leaving his index finger raised. Several bows released their projectiles until only the one who seemed to be the strangers' leader was left standing.

"You are in no position to demand anything. On the other hand, I, Triar, King of Lebassi, and the coalition of the four kingdoms, will demand your death."

"With the cowardice of your archers?"

"No, you will die by my own hand," said the ruler as he lowered his left hand and walked towards the enemy with his blade ready for combat.

The jet-clad fighter dismounted with dexterity, drew the sword, and walked toward the king.

"You are a damned scoundrel. You come to my kingdom demanding a friend's head, whom you call a spy. This is my kingdom! There are no spies because these lands belong to me by right. I am the king! I will not allow anyone to threaten this kingdom nor its inhabitants; I will not allow anyone to threaten me, my wife, or my unborn child. You and your hosts are just misbegotten usurpers. This ends today."

This enemy was a joke. Stupid mage!

He launched a thrust at the assailant's chest. His blow was repelled. He insisted on a second attack. His enemy's arm moved with alacrity. The swords clashed countless times.

In a last attempt of the king, their swords crossed in front of each other. He could see the soldier's empty eyes through the leather helmet as if a white membrane covered them. He closed his left fist and struck hard at the face of his enemy, who had to retreat to keep his balance.

Triar took advantage of the misstep to throw a slash that cut through leather, skin, and flesh from top to bottom. He spun around and, taking advantage of the momentum, slit the attacker's throat, whose head rolled over the stone bridge.

"We won!" Triar proclaimed haughtily.

He turned towards the castle, raising both hands in triumph. Blood dripped from his sword, and his troops cheered him on. A gleam of confidence settled in his eyes until he heard a loud laugh behind him.

The miscreant's head moved his jaw as if he still had life in him, and a burst of sinister laughter came out of his mouth.

"I will wait until your pain is deeper!" predicted the head in a deformed and malignant voice.

Angrily, the king kicked his face, propelling helmet and flesh over the balustrade. The laughter did not cease until the castle's foundations abruptly halted the fall.

## *18*

From inside her tent, the desire-turned-woman was pleased. She loved playing with her puppets. Although she maintained control over each of her militiamen, nothing compared to completely overriding the will of one in particular and using them as a flesh-and-blood puppet.

The maneuver turned out better than anticipated. She did not need to chase any spy; she only intended to plant the seed of doubt in the king. The stupid long-tongued man blurted out information that delighted her. A son was on the way. Her design was to bring destruction and pain to Panameria. To kill Triar's unborn child would be painful, but to let him enjoy the creature in his arms and then take it away from him would be even more unbearable for the new father.

A pause in her way toward Lebassi would allow her to achieve two goals. First, it would allow time for the pregnancy to proceed naturally. Second, it would allow her to prepare herself; the king turned out to be a better adversary than expected. She defeated others without difficulty by handling her human puppets, but not Triar. His army was well trained. She had to subdue him, not only with mastery of combat but also with an overwhelming number of soldiers. She would extend her tentacles to nearby towns. She would increase her military might with fresh blood. She would prepare them and enjoy every moment until she plunged her steel into the chest of the ruler of Lebassi.

She got up from the improvised armchair, made of wood and cowhide. Her two main captains, inside the tent, imitated the warrior's gesture.

"Cedric, Karl, we have a lot of work to do."

# *19*

From the corridor, he could hear uninterrupted moaning. The maids kept coming in and out carrying containers of hot water. Why did they need so much? When Angela had her son, everything was rather quick. The former queen was more corpulent; that was what Gertrude, the midwife, had said.

On the other hand, Katrina had narrow hips, which complicated the delivery. A few minutes ago, the old woman told him that it was possible to lose both the mother and the baby. He reacted like any good husband; if that happened, he would have the old lady's head cut off, as simple as that.

A faint smell of smoke seeped into the corridor. He approached the window. In the distance, a column of black soot was rising. How did his dreams become so twisted? When did it happen? Maybe when he thought he put an end to his wish by slitting the throat of that poor wretch controlled by someone. How stupid!

His wife was suffering; she was in danger of dying. Three platoons, about five hundred of his soldiers, were fighting against the sinister troops withering Lebassi and the other kingdoms with their filth. They were raiding, burning, kidnapping men, young men, and women to create a colossal army, or so the rumors said.

He noticed a firm hand squeezing his shoulder.

"Your Majesty."

"Daniel, how's your leg?"

"Ready to ride alongside you, drive these bastards out of the kingdom, and then get drunk out of our minds."

"Thank you, my friend."

At that moment, the door to the royal bedroom opened, making way for the matron with a marked expression of exhaustion carved on her face.

"Your Majesty, it is a boy. The queen is also alive."

Triar didn't need anything else. He hugged his friend, who congratulated him effusively, and then ran into the bedroom. Katrina was lying on the bed. The maids hurriedly removed the red-stained basins and sheets. The queen was barely keeping her eyes open.

"Triar, meet your son," Katrina whispered.

Next to his wife, the smallest baby he had ever seen was kicking.

*But he will grow, he will grow, and he will become the greatest warrior and king this world has ever seen,* he thought proudly.

Katrina tried to smile as he lifted him.

"I love you."

These were the only words he found suitable to dedicate to his wife; he placed a kiss on her forehead and cradled the child in his arms. He would protect him. This little creature was his responsibility and represented the future when he was gone. Here, he repeated to himself that, in his arms, he would be safe.

A small tear ran down his cheek as he thought that sometimes it's not a good idea for longings to come true.

## *20*

The sun was high; after finishing his shift at the western mine, Gregor walked back to the Falcon Tower. Today was the end of another week's work. On his belt, he had a small bag with the week's wages; a mere fifteen small bronze coins, which people colloquially called 'dogs'. For someone who grew up in the abundance of Lebassi Castle, that wage was a pittance. It was a fortune for someone who had been away from that opulence for months. Points of view completely changed his perception of reality. Money not only served him to eat, but it also fed his pride and esteem. He worked. He earned it.

After tidying his dwelling about eight months ago, the first thing Omar did was to get him a job in the mine. It had to make him stronger, he said. An eleven-year-old boy had to be in better shape, he repeated. Following that plan, in the mornings, he worked as a miner; in the afternoons, he trained in combat with and without weapons.

Today, he was stronger; not only did he know how to hold a sword and strike with it, but today was his twelfth birthday. He didn't expect any celebration, no festivity. He didn't even remind his guardian, trainer, and friend. Maybe tomorrow they could treat themselves to some small luxury, a lunch, or a nice dinner, at the village inn.

He heard a rustling sound. He stopped. He brought his hand to his belt, where he kept his dagger. The roads around the mines were not safe, Omar had warned him from the first day: many highwaymen and bandits. One always had to be prepared.

The sound did not repeat. He heard nothing.

Surprisingly, the bushes on the left side of the road rustled. He stood on guard. A scared rabbit ran, zigzagging through the undergrowth.

"So frightening!" Gregor exclaimed. "It was just a damn rabbit."

Three individuals appeared from behind the bushes.

"You should watch your tongue, young man. What would your mother say?" the tallest of them, wearing a light green doublet and brown pants and boots, reprimanded him. His two companions laughed. "I think we can forget about your rudeness if you pay the road toll."

"Toll? What toll? There has never been a toll to pay for using the road."

"There's always a first time. The bag, give it to us!" ordered the delinquent.

Gregor stepped back. With one hand, he wielded the knife; with the other, he held the bag with his pay.

"Be careful with that. Lest you cut yourself."

The three miscreants searched for their own clothing. The blades of three daggers flashed in unison.

"Don't make us cut you. Just give us the bag."

The prince looked left and right.

His attackers reacted by spreading out as if trying to cut off his escape routes.

The shortest of them, who smelled like a pyre of pigs and had greenish teeth, made the first move. He dodged it with ease. He was even able to make a move that left a slash on the miscreant's wrist, forcing him to drop his weapon in pain.

Gregor felt happy because he had disarmed one of them. The lessons did not turn out to be as useless as he thought during the first few days.

His joy was short-lived. Another of the men, his back as broad as a closet and his face pockmarked, threw himself upon him, knocking him to the ground. In the clash, their blades flew apart. The robber was trying to hit him with his fists on his torso. He held his arms out to protect himself from the attacks. When the punches lost their rhythm, he kicked his assailant's crotch. The wretch howled in pain and rolled to the side, holding his parts.

Gregor wasted no time and stood up, facing the third man. He was not fast enough. An accurate blow to the stomach left him breathless. He doubled over and fell to his knees. The ring he wore around his neck, hidden inside his clothes, came into view.

"Well, well. What do we have here?"

With a strong tug, the chain was torn off. The tall man looked at the ring.

"A winged dragon! The emblem of the kingdom. Who are you?"

An arrow pierced the individual's face. Gregor looked for the source of the attack. Omar was about thirty yards away, holding his bow. Two more projectiles put an end to the lives of the other two thugs.

The captain approached him angrily.

"I told you to keep that ring in the tower. It's not safe to carry it around. No one should know who you are."

"I'm sorry."

"It doesn't matter. Good fight."

"Thank you, Captain."

"Let's go. Today is someone's twelfth birthday, and we should celebrate. How about your first beer?"

Gregor's heart rejoiced when he heard his friend's words, even more so when he put his arm around his shoulders.

## *21*

At last, his cursed desire was in front of him. He had news about the terrible defeat of his men. The pieces were not going according to the original plan. The enemy should have been wounded and weakened; his strategy of undermining them by sending a group of soldiers did not work. The army stationed there outnumbered them, possibly two invaders for every Lebassi soldier.

Hunter was uneasy. There was a strange feeling in the air. It reminded him of the times he went down to see Égnever's work. Magic!

"Easy, easy."

Next to him, mounted on a sorrel, was Daniel. The night before, his friend had begged him to allow him to accompany him. He tried to stop him from coming, for his wife, for his daughters. He did not accept. Together until the end.

He distinguished their leader. He wore copper-colored armor. His mount was a black steed. He was surrounded by a group of no more than thirty horsemen. To his right, there was a soldier of high rank, he imagined, tall, more than a head taller than their leader.

"Your Majesty, there are too many," acknowledged Daniel.

"I know," Triar admitted.

Tension was palpable. The troops were holding their position, waiting for the order to attack.

Combat would be suicide for his men. They would delay their arrival at the castle, where a small garrison would offer resistance. In the end, they would fall.

"I will settle this," announced the king.

He advanced his horse towards the enemy troops, hoping to invite them to parley. Triar's action met with the right response. The rival leader advanced toward him.

A fleeting thought flashed through his mind. His wife and child. Katrina was just beginning to recover from the strain and blood loss during labor. This was his fault. If seven years ago he had known this would happen... There was no use regretting it. His desire was raw, just as he dreamed it would be. A threat, a challenge.

"You are Triar. I have come to kill you and take your kingdom," the stranger proclaimed.

The voice sounded distorted through the helmet. It was cold, hard, terse, like a dagger forged in ice.

"This is my kingdom! You and your henchmen must leave. If you do so now, I will consider sparing your infamous lives."

The laughter that sprouted from the being reminded him of the laughter that erupted from the dead head of the henchman he executed on the bridge at the entrance.

"The little toy men you sent against me, we gutted them and fed them to the wolves."

"You had the advantage of numbers."

"Now too."

Of course, it was true; he knew it. How long could he drag out this pantomime? Why was he buying time? He was looking for a way out that would not end in the massacre of his soldiers.

"We are both gentlemen. What Égnever initiated focuses on us. We could face each other in a duel to the death, you and me. If I win, your men will retreat; if you do, you will take my kingdom."

"All right."

It didn't take him a minute to respond, not one. If he was so willing, he was surely hiding something. Triar cursed the mage for this creation. Now, the glory didn't mean so much in the face of life. For a few seconds, he was about to agree with his father. He gathered courage; he would not only fight for himself, but he also had to think of his family.

"You have the advantage. You are a creation of Égnever. It reeks of magic here. I'm sure you have some of his powers."

One against the other, without magic, he had a great chance. He was taller, burly, and skilled. His opponent looked much smaller; he had barely been alive for months. He had been training for years.

"I accept. After all, it is to you that I owe my existence. I will use only my body and my sword."

In unison, they descended from their horses. They walked a few steps closer. The swords gleamed out of their sheaths.

Throwing himself forward, Triar unleashed his weapon with force. Despite being more muscular than his opponent, his attack was easily repelled. Immediately, the enemy blade threatened to tear his stomach. He deftly moved his hand and saved the situation this time.

They stepped back. The king watched his adversary. He was looking for a gap in his impeccable defense. He found it. His rival slightly lowered his guard; then, he took advantage of the moment to confront him with a direct blow to the head. It was a trap; although he managed to hit him in the helmet, he felt how the steel bit his left arm...

"You will die, and I will take your kingdom."

The warrior stepped back and removed his shattered helmet.

Triar did not even pay attention to the bleeding cut on his adversary's cheek. His gaze focused on the long, curly, flesh-toned hair that fell down her back. The feminine features could offer no doubt.

"A woman!"

"Selena, future Queen of Lebassi and the rest of Panameria," proclaimed the warrior.

What a bloody mockery this was! He was not going to lose his kingdom to a woman. He wasn't going to lose his family. No, he was not going to lose.

His steel flew swiftly, seeking the graceful neck of the female, taking advantage of the fact that it was now uncovered. With a feline gesture, the woman dodged it by less than an inch, taking the opportunity to duck and counterattack.

The king felt as if a lightning bolt had pierced his abdomen. The pain was excruciating. The blade somehow cut through the steel and part of his insides. For a few seconds, he remained precariously balanced. His knees faltered, and he fell to his knees. He stuck the sword into the grass, clinging to the steel to avoid ending prostrated on the ground.

"Men promise and promise, but it is always over so fast."

"It can't be. Women don't..."

Selena kicked him in the face, throwing him backward.

"Destroy everything, leave none alive! But don't even think of touching Triar's son; do whatever you want with the mother. I'll take care of the child," she shouted to her captains.

The King of Lebassi could hear the first clashes of weapons and the cries of agony of his soldiers.

Selena crouched down beside him, pulled off his helmet, and ran her hand through his hair.

"Don't worry about your son. I will take care of him. He will be my slave for the rest of his life. Every queen needs eunuchs in her service."

Triar couldn't hold back his tears. His poor Katrina! He didn't even want to think about the future of his baby, who would never become a man.

While he was lying on the ground, the sun blinded him until, little by little, his sight became blurred. He tried to sit up in vain. He saw his sword nearby and stretched out his arm in search of it. It was as if it was moving farther and farther away. He wanted to wake up from the nightmare that his dream had become. He did not succeed.

# II
# THE CHRONICLE OF THE AWAKENING

# *1*

And the Fortress of Foam fell. It took Selena only two days to overcome the fierce defenses and take over the majestic stronghold.

Constructed of gray granite, the building stood proudly on a base of stone and rock. For over two hundred years, three monarchs worked on its construction, creating a structure of towers and rooms that loomed beautifully against the ocean.

The new queen proudly crossed the arched bridge. Inside the main courtyard corpses and prisoners, soldiers and servants alike.

"I am Selena, your new queen. Follow me or die!"

The prisoners bowed their heads. She delved into their minds. Anger, pain, rebellion. She had dealt with it all before; it was no surprise. They would get used to it.

Limping, an old man approached her. From his appearance, he could be as old as the castle itself, with three strands of combed hair, almost stuck together, trying to cover a bald head populated with reddish spots.

Next to her, Cedric drew his sword.

"Queen Selena, welcome to your castle!"

That was the welcome she deserved. At last, she was the queen.

"What is your name?"

"Marco, Your Majesty."

"Show me the castle."

"As you command, Your Majesty."

Selena dismounted and walked towards the main staircase, accompanied by Marco and Cedric. The castle was huge; it would take time to get to know it. She needed to find a room that was worthy of her. Something else troubled her: her powers were limited, insufficient. She could still feel her mind going into the minds of her men like tendrils, but the more they were, the more she was losing the privilege of overriding their wills. They were her toys; they were too many toys. She needed more magic; she needed to learn. The only mage she knew had died by her sword; yes, she had defeated him with ease. That victory haunted her; too easy, too simple.

"Cedric, take care of the old queen!" said Selena.

## 2

From her chamber, she saw the woman enter the main courtyard. She was death incarnated. Katrina had been mourning her husband's death for two days. Her guards had assured her that she would be safe there, that the castle would not fall. They were wrong. Somehow, the enemies took control. The kingdom was lost, and she had to flee.

She tucked Magnus, her son, into a black wool blanket. In turn, she covered herself with a cloak of the same color.

"I'm ready!" she announced to her escorts.

"Follow us, Your Majesty."

She trusted those men. They were the only ones left of her personal guard. The other five died trying to repel the invading forces.

Katrina took one last look around the room. Her life was shattered. After nine months of living in a paradise, everything was turning into hell. She couldn't delay any longer. It would take them a few minutes to go down to the dungeons. There, a narrow passageway would lead her down an escape route to the exit at the beach.

They were about to leave when the doors of the room opened. A huge shadow loomed in front of them. It held a sword.

"Behind us, Your Majesty.

Katrina recoiled in fear. Her heart was racing. Her body shuddered at the thought of the possible fate that awaited her.

Synchronized, their protectors unsheathed. They separated to make the enemy's defense more difficult.

Jonah struck the first blow. He was about twenty-five years old, and Katrina had known him since she was a child. He was the son of one of her mother's best friends, and he had enlisted in the army as soon as he turned fifteen. The stranger rebuffed his coup.

That's when Martin attacked. He was short and wide, like a barrel of beer. He unloaded the broadsword with strength, and the stranger recoiled from the impact.

The retort did not take long. Taking advantage of the length of his arm, the adversary unleashed a horizontal slash looking for the bellies of both soldiers.

Jonah turned to her.

"Run, Your Majesty."

The warning made the young man lower his guard. Cedric lunged at him, grabbing his armed hand and plunging his steel into the middle of his chest.

Martin screamed and rammed with his blade.

As if he were a rag, Selena's captain used the deceased's body as a shield. Martin's attack cut his friend's back.

Katrina was paralyzed. She could not believe her eyes. She began to cry. Her bawling woke the child, who accompanied her with a thunderous cry.

Martin turned to look at the queen.

Cedric threw the lifeless body toward the last of the escorts. The Lebassi warrior dropped his sword to hold his friend and instantly felt a flashing pain in his abdomen.

The queen screamed as she saw the soldier impale her two guards. The scream made her react, and she ran for the exit. It was up to her. She could do it. She owed it to Triar and her son; she would get him safely away from these murderers. She just had to get to the stairs. She was fast. He wouldn't catch her. She crossed the threshold. Now to the left.

A firm hand grabbed her by the hair. No, no, no. The bastard caught her. She rummaged through her clothes until she found a silver dagger. She turned to her captor and thrust the weapon hard into the man's chest.

Cedric stepped back and released her. Blood gushed from his chest. He threw a punch at Katrina's face, and she fell backward to the ground.

He was wounded. The bloody dagger bore witness to it. Her nose was bursting with pain. She watched him walk towards her. He was a mass of leather and muscle with blue eyes glowing wickedly.

"Please, no, please," Katrina begged.

She saw no trace of emotion on the henchman's face. She prayed to Salmur to take her and her son into his bosom.

"Please," she repeated softly. Tears ran profusely down her cheeks. Magnus couldn't stop crying.

The soldier raised his sword and thrust the blade into the queen's throat.

## *3*

Shao's robe was green with gold trim. His youth and hair were forgotten. His fingernails could only be shorter if they did not exist. He kept his head high and watched the rest of the members of the

Council from his chair at the head of the table as the leader of the mages. He inherited that position upon the death of Zerun, his master.

He had not gathered them together for seven years. The last time was to judge his disciple, Égnever, and sentence him for his fault to the Council: seven years of slavery, enduring the cryol chains and bound to King Triar to obey his will. The situation with Égnever ended with Selena's sword, with a little help from them. It was up to them to discuss what they would do with their former apprentice's creation.

The room was cozy. The flames gnawed greedily at the oak wood, thus preventing the cold of the eternal snow outside from permeating. Their glasses were overflowing, a small pleasure that no one refused.

Shao took a sip and spent a few moments pondering his words.

"Brothers, we must talk about someone we are directly responsible for: Selena."

## *4*

Cedric escorted one of the prisoners to Selena. He wanted to introduce her to the new wet nurse for Triar's son. It had only been a week since the girl had given birth to her own son. The child fell ill a few days later and died the night before. In his opinion, her breasts were overflowing with enough milk to feed the queen's new protégé. She was little more than a child, with light brown hair that fell without sensuality framing her face. Nevertheless, he recognized that she had very well-defined curves.

The door to Selena's room was closed. He knocked to signal their arrival, and it opened instantly. Selena was outside the tower, watching the sunrise, so he assumed she used magic to open it.

He stood to attention before her with the girl next to him.

"Your Majesty, I found this woman among the prisoners and wished to know if she is to your liking. She is young and strong. She can nurse and take care of Magnus."

"I see. Tell me, child, where is your son?"

"Dead, Your Majesty. He got sick and died yesterday. I buried him with my own hands," the girl confessed, sobbing.

Selena approached her and, placing a hand on her chin, made her raise her head.

"Don't be scared. What's your name?"

"Pamela, Your Highness."

"Do you know what we want you for?"

"Yes, Your Majesty. You wish me to take care of the former king's son. I assure you that I will treat him as if he were my own; you will have no complaints."

"Of course I won't have any. I'm sure you know how important this is to me."

"The child will want for nothing; I will take care of him as if he were my own."

"I am pleased to hear you talk like this. My generosity can be very great."

"Your Majesty, I do not need anything. To serve you is a privilege."

"Cedric, this child is under my protection from this day on. Let no one dare touch her. Pamela, you are free to roam the castle as you please. You will always have an escort to protect you and the child. If you need anything, anything at all, ask me. If you fancy a man, he will be yours; just ask."

"You are very kind, Your Majesty."

"Cedric, take her to meet her new son. Make sure my orders are carried out."

"You can be sure of it, Your Majesty," said Cedric.

## 5

Pamela washed her hands in the kitchen sink. She felt Cedric's gaze over her shoulder. She rubbed them again and again. She spread them out in front of her and looked at them. There was no trace of the earth from her son's grave. Fate was giving her a new chance to be a mother. She had to trust herself. Many babies died at birth; it was not her fault. Nonetheless, she would always carry the pain of losing him; she would never forget that.

"Are you done? The little one is hungry. And it's not in the best interest of either of us for him to have a bad time."

She turned to Cedric without saying a word. She hated men because they only brought her suffering.

"Yes."

"Then follow me."

He guided her, and Pamela simply followed in his footsteps.

Her former house had no floor other than rammed earth. It was a modest home with more warmth from his parents than from embers. She couldn't imagine what life could be like in a place like a castle. She thought about how cold its walls might be during winter.

When the soldiers entered the village, her father assured them that nothing would happen to them. He ordered them to stay inside and not to leave until he returned. She disobeyed. First, she peered out the window for a few minutes, just a few, but long enough to see her brother fall under the hooves of a brown horse with white speckles. She remembered it as if there had been no sounds, only the ringing of alarm bells. Then she left home, left her mother and sisters, and told them she would look for her father. She did not find him, and she never saw them again. She ran back and forth, dodging armed men everywhere. Without knowing how, her body crashed against the flanks of a steed. She was lucky not to break her head against the equine's legs when it reared. The rider controlled the animal and, after dismounting, rushed at her. Only his piercing blue eyes and the smell of his leather armor mixed with sweat and blood were etched in her mind. Then days became a coming and going of men; female prisoners were taken in separate carts. Usually, none remained there for more than a month. Pregnant women were allowed to live; they said that their leader wanted new men, that she had long-term plans, and that no one would ever stop them. Many others committed suicide when they saw what was happening to their loved ones and did not want to contribute with their children to the madness. She was alive only because she did not dare kill herself and had a lucky birth.

When they got to the room, she was crying.

"You will live here from now on. And don't be afraid. We will treat you well. You heard the queen."

Pamela tried to wipe away her tears. Her nose was completely congested, and her mouth was very dry. She had no choice but to accept the proposal to survive. To take care of someone else's child as if it were her own. What mother would accept that?

Cedric put a hand on her shoulder, and she felt as if she was being touched to the very bone. Past that first impression, she could feel the warmth of male fingers and cursed herself for thinking this man could be good.

"Don't touch me; don't you dare lay a hand on me again." And she turned her whole body sharply away from him.

"I'm sorry, I was just trying to be nice."

"Leave me alone. I have to take care of the child."

'Her new son', the queen had said. She deludedly dared to think that she could easily transfer her affection from one being to another. What was this illusion of generosity and kindness? Everyone in the camp knew she was a bloodthirsty, vengeful witch.

"As the queen said, you are free to roam the castle as you please. If you wish to wander around, an escort of guards will protect you and your son."

Pamela slammed the door in his face.

## *6*

She was surprised to smell the scent of roses and even more surprised to see a freshly cut bouquet adorning a vase on the dressing table. She wondered whose gesture it was. She looked at the furniture; she had never used anything like it. The bed seemed huge to someone who had always shared one with her sister. The sheets were white, they weren't new, but they had been made to look so. Two sky-blue dresses were placed on them. The floor was immaculate, carpets and rugs everywhere. The fireplace also looked clean and, despite the season, had a good pile of dry firewood beside it. The windows were wide open to emphasize the good weather, and she could hear the birds chirping. A light breeze played with the lace of the tablecloth on the bedside table.

Above all else, her attention was drawn to the cradle. It was made of black wood and carved with exquisite taste. Pamela made out snakes coiling around the legs and dragons standing sentinel on the bars. Winged horses tried to take flight from the crossbars on the roof while unicorns guarded the headboards. And a lot of other figures mingled among so many details.

Strange as it seemed to her, the boy looked happy, no doubt oblivious to all that was going on around him.

She took him in her arms. He must have been the same age as her son. In the kitchen, she heard they had tried to give him cow milk to feed him; although he drank it, he mostly rejected it. She sat with him on the edge of the bed. She could feel his little hands reaching for her breast. She scooted back until she was leaning against the headboard. His insistence was compelling as if he had caught the scent of a mother and knew what that carried. She felt a pang of pain; only a few days ago, she had cradled her son, her real son, in the same way. She could see the baby's distressed expression; he would start crying if she delayed much longer.

A few days ago, she had been a mother for the first time. When she had felt her son's lips on her chest, she could not suppress tears of joy, forgetting everything that had happened to her in that damned wagon.

She pulled the dress away from her breasts and brought the boy's head close to them; he did the rest. Pamela felt those tickles again and the lips sticking eagerly to her flesh, sucking, feeding.

At first, she thought she would not even dare to hold him, let alone give him a part of her to keep him alive. However, he was such an innocent and helpless creature himself that she could not resist. She knew deep down that Selena was right, so deep down that it would take her quite some time to admit it.

The child was not satiated with the milk of one breast. As he started with the other one, Pamela stroked his head. She saw those little brown eyes light up, and a smile appeared on her face.

She could not hold back a few tears. Then, when he had finished, she cried harder, praying to those cruel gods who wounded her so deeply but, at the same time, gave her another chance to start over.

## *7*

When Gregor entered the cabin, he found Omar gathering his belongings.

"What's going on?"

"Shut up and take your things."

"But what's going on?"

With a solemn gesture, Omar looked for a chair and invited him to sit with him.

"Your father is dead," he said.

"What? What happened?"

The captain shook his head.

"An enemy army has taken the castle. The king died challenging the invading leader. Lebassi now belongs to a woman named Selena."

A woman? The new ruler of Lebassi?

"What about my brother?"

"I don't know."

"My father's wife?"

"The news is confusing. A couple of soldiers who managed to escape reported to me. They went to the village. We will meet them in two hours to head north."

"Where will we go?"

"Far away," the man clarified. "The Iron Mines are strategic for the kingdom. Soon we will not be safe here."

"What happened to the other kingdoms of the coalition? Didn't they do anything?"

"I don't know. Stop bothering me with questions."

"I'm sorry."

"No, don't be sorry. Your father is dead; you are the king by right. Start behaving like one."

"How? Beating women and sleeping with maids?"

"Your father was more than that."

"Not for me," Gregor replied bitterly.

For him, he was never a good king; he was never a good father. Triar hated them, his mother and him. He made that very clear many times. He made it clear with his whippings, with his words of contempt. He made it clear with a tombstone that his mother was nothing more than a 'wife'. Nothing more than that.

He was not glad that he had died, but he did feel liberated. He knew he would never live up to the king's expectations. He didn't care either. He was free.

He removed the pendant from his neck. He removed the ring from the steel chain. He placed it on his right ring finger. The two small emeralds embedded in the dragon's eyes sparkled.

"I told you to hide..."

The words died in Omar's mouth.

Gregor fixed his gaze on the captain's eyes. They had been together for ten months. Ten months of hard training. Ten months of loading and pushing wagons in the mine had strengthened his muscles. Ten months of strict military discipline, rising at dawn, eating a frugal breakfast, and listening to the teachings of his master, had rebuilt his being, formed his character, and awakened a flame within him. These ten months served for him to find his voice of command today.

"Shut up, Captain. I will gather our possessions. Go get the horses and weapons ready."

"Yes, Your Majesty," Omar replied proudly.

## *8*

High above, the moon shone majestically over a clear sky full of stars. Standing on the small, snow-covered plain, Shao stretched out his arms. The icy air began to form miniature whirlwinds around his hands. Ice arcs were built connecting his body to the land, to Panameria.

He felt at peace, in complete connection with his surroundings. He chose that spot in the mountains for his dwelling because of its isolation.

A whitish glow burst from his fingertips and spread out into the ground through the ice arcs. It sank its tentacles into the cold ground, moving slowly through the earth's bowels.

The mountains were far from the Lebassi Castle, so it would take him quite some time to find his target. He was patient and in no hurry.

As he passed by, he perceived or saw the places' life. Animals fled in fear. Men and women who were sleeping squirmed and turned in their beds; those still awake shuddered as if the claw of death was caressing their backs.

He passed under the waters of rivers and affluents. He traveled through crop fields that burst with abundance.

Slight tiredness began to torment him. It was not much longer, just a little more.

There it was. At last, the castle. He saw the gray granite, the black slate roofs, and the torches shining brightly all around.

One last effort. He climbed the walls.

The horses in the stables whinnied and banged on the doors, trying to escape. A baby began to cry. Yes, Triar's son.

He reached the highest tower, following the smell of magic and the iridescent glow of power. There it was. Selena was sleeping.

The tendrils crawled over the cobblestone and climbed up the bed until they surrounded the woman. Minutes passed as he dedicated to cutting, one by one, the magical ties that bound her to Panameria.

## *9*

Selena woke up abruptly. She jumped like a feline out of bed. Two seconds were enough for her to be standing on the balcony wall. She sensed a very subtle presence in her dreams, very subtle and familiar, close to her.

She breathed in, trying to find more traces. There was nothing left. Whatever it was, it was gone, gone or hidden. Anything was possible.

## *10*

It felt eternal, maybe several hours. It took a lot of effort to make the necessary adjustments to break the ties between Selena and Panameria.

Shao walked calmly to his hut, observing the fogged windows and the snow accumulating on the roof. Once inside, he fastened the locks on the windows. A heavy storm was coming. He leaned back on his divan and savored the taste of the mulled wine. His hands were grateful for the warmth of the cup.

Selena would be cut off from her own essence from that night on. Her powers, weakened, would be difficult for her to execute. She would suffer from being deprived of what was once natural to her.

Shao felt the drowsiness of the wine. He sighed with delight and drained the last drops. He set his glass down and crossed his arms over his chest. It would be a restful sleep. He closed his eyes. He yawned without blushing.

She would be vulnerable. It would be easy to control her. He would give her the necessary support to turn her not into his ally but another instrument for his plans.

He heard the crackling of the embers. Outside, the wind whistled through the rocks and trees. A wolf howl; in seconds, there were several. His friends always came to keep him company on the coldest nights.

What if she turned against them? What if she sensed that it was a manipulation? No, it was impossible that Selena could attempt to act against the mages. If they continued to act from the shadows, they would stay away. Besides, he had enough tricks to repel any attempt of aggression.

His wolves arrived. He imagined the feel of their tongues as he fed them. Not tonight; he was tired. Just a few minutes of sleep was all he asked for. Then he would let them in and let them satiate their appetite.

He wanted to believe that Selena would never be a threat to his power. He remembered Égnever, who thought the same; poor thing, he didn't take him into account. Terrible mistake to underestimate the Council.

Shao began to snore.

# 11

And then there was light. Not slowly like the dawn, but all at once, suddenly, just like a fly dies under the weight of a hand.

Cedric's mind was filled with cozy sensations. His nose sniffed the freshly turned humus. His hands, full of dirt and calluses, felt the dry, sturdy wood of a plow. He walked, pushing and shouting at his two cows; his feet kicked up little clouds of dust, which began to tickle his toes. He knew that they would be shattered by the end of the day. The sun hurt his eyes. His forehead was crossed with beads of sweat. His shirt rested on a stone at the end of the field, his field, and his back burned, although he was used to it.

Camila would force him to wash up before going in for lunch. Even so, that would not stop him from giving his daughter a big hug first. She was about to turn fifteen, but he still saw her as that little creature who ran around with only a diaper for clothes. Her hair was tousled, and her rosy cheeks were always stained with something. The day she was born had been the second happiest day of his life. Surely, she would soon fall in love and leave home; it always happened that way, and, even if it hurt him, he was willing to accept it.

"Pull!"

It was going to be a good year for the harvest. The soil smelled alive, and hardly any fertilizer was needed. The plow blade was sinking easily into the soil; he didn't have to exert himself.

The cows stopped and raised their heads. He could hear the sound of their thick lips dilating. They were restless and refused to go on. He approached them and stroked their heads. Every once in a while, something like this happened. He thought the wind might bring them the scent of some wolf nearby.

But, this time, he saw the reason for their concern in the distance. A lone horseman was riding very fast in their direction. He could see the red flashes of sunlight; he guessed that he was wearing armor.

His house was only half an hour's walk from the village, but it was distant from the usual routes taken by travelers. It had been months since any stranger had appeared there. Maybe some knight from the neighboring kingdom came to meet with King Kirna. There were rumors of betrothal. It would be good to have fresh news.

He shouted for his wife to come closer.

## *12*

He bowed his head before the upright figure that descended from the horse.

"Welcome, sir. My house is humble, but you may rest at ease among us."

The newcomer made no sign that he had heard him, yet he went into the hut.

Cedric thought all nobles were the same.

"Would you like something to drink? It will still be a few minutes before lunch is ready."

The knight settled into the chair at the head of the table. He removed his sword and leaned it against the wall behind him.

"Where is your daughter?"

The voice was so cold that he thought winter had come early for a moment. In turn, the question chilled him. Before he arrived, he advised her to stay in his room. He knew the instincts that a beautiful young woman could arouse in men. They always thought they could do whatever they wanted. A heavy door opened in the back of his mind for a few seconds, allowing him to see something he had not remembered for years; he closed it violently, telling himself that he would never allow such a thing to happen again.

"What do you want her for?"

"Bring her. I don't have to explain myself to you."

He watched him carefully. Despite the armor, he was sure that he was much burlier. Besides, none of the men in the village could bend his arm when they measured their strength in the tavern. The other man may have had a sword, but he was right.

"Go away. You are not welcome."

"What's wrong? Are you still in pain about your sister?"

Cedric gritted his teeth. He wondered how he could know that.

His wife began backing towards the entrance to their daughter's room.

"Come on, bring her in. If you don't do it the easy way, you'll do it the hard way."

He clenched his fist vigorously as if he wanted to extract water from a rock. No matter how hard his helmet was, the blow would knock him to the ground. That way, he would know that he was not to be trifled with. But the impact never came. The knight raised his arm and absorbed the shock of the palm of his hand. Instantly he felt the tip of his boot in his stomach with such impetus that it made him double over and fall to his knees on the ground. A thick fog began to close in before his eyes. He bit his tongue to keep from fainting.

The pain and the taste of blood brought him back. The stranger stood up and walked toward his wife. He grabbed her by the hair, by that silky, golden hair like the sun that he had caressed so many times. In his other hand, he held the sword.

She saw him bring the blade closer to her neck. His wife's skin now had the texture of chicken skin. He could see how the steel dug into the flesh and...

"Noooooooo!"

He opened his eyes and found himself staring at the ceiling beams. He turned to his wife. She was still asleep under the blankets. She was curled up like a puppy looking for warmth. He could only catch a glimpse of her mane.

He was glad to know that it was a nightmare and that she was still by his side.

For the first time, he noticed his bedroom. The floor was not of rammed earth, and the walls were built of stone. Neither the bed nor the furniture was what he remembered.

He sighed, thinking he might still be inside the same nightmare.

"Nooooo!"

He put his hands on his head as he felt a flood of new memories. He saw himself in front of armies, following a woman to destruction. Again, he sighed, but this time in pain. He did wake up from a bad dream. Now he understood how horrible it was, especially knowing that it was not the result of his unconscious but belonged to his past.

He pulled the blankets away from the woman's body sleeping next to him and confirmed that she was not his wife. She had a certain resemblance to her; she was just a common substitute.

He served the current queen, Selena, the same one who slit his wife's throat in front of his own eyes and then murdered his daughter without him being able to do anything to prevent it. Nothing, because, even then, he could already feel that hypnotic influence with which she forced him to follow her, just as she then managed to add more strength to start and continue his mission.

All the images of the campaigns came to him at once, and he was sickened by the crimes he committed and ordered to be committed.

He went to the window and looked out. He was in the castle of King Triar. He killed the former queen. In the distance, he could still make out the traces of the bonfires. They burned people dead and alive, just as plague-infested rats would be burned.

Fate was cruel. He was not there as a mere lackey who could hide in the shadows of a stable from the queen's sight so he could suffer and try to pay his penalty. No, he was the right hand of that assassin. He had been by her side since she started her plan, the Plan, so to speak. It would not be easy to get rid of her wrath by trying to escape his present in such a cowardly way. She would kill him before he could even raise his sword to defend himself. But perhaps that was the only way out. He could challenge her and bid farewell to life by trying to eradicate such a monster. However, that would only be an illusion, a suicide, another cowardice.

He went back inside, poured water into the bowl, and rinsed his face. His eyes met their reflection in the mirror, and his hand clutched his chin, sliding his fingers over his cheeks repeatedly. He didn't recognize himself without a beard.

With a mechanical gesture, he took the clasp-knife. He contemplated it with familiarity for a few seconds, then tossed it into a corner. He would not shave; he had never liked to shave. It may be a mistake to try to go against her wishes; after all, she had suggested he take his beard off. It was about time he had some independence again.

## *13*

Selena grunted from one of the armchairs when Cedric appeared in the great hall.

"It's about time you came down. I've been waiting for you for ages."

"Good morning, Your Majesty."

"Yes, yes." He looked different, but she had too much on her mind to look at him in detail. "I'm bored."

But it was more than boredom. Since the morning awakening, she had the impression that something was wrong in the castle. Something was there, present with her; something changed. Magic!

It had to be that. She couldn't even claim that there were more mages than Égnever, but she was sure of it, just as she was sure that rain falls and men die when their hearts are ripped out.

"What can I do?"

"I want a mage to entertain me."

"A mage?"

"Yes, Cedric, a mage, a wizard, a sorcerer. Are you having a hard time understanding my words?" And right then, she saw it. "What, your companion didn't give you time to shave?"

"I have decided to grow my beard again; I hope you don't mind."

Selena smiled, just as a wolf would smile after licking the bones of a sheep.

"All right, I may welcome the change. Back to business, I want you to send a patrol to find a mage. I don't care if he's good or bad, just a real one. Warn your men that they will long live their death if they waste my time with an impostor."

"I'm sorry to say it, but none of them is an adversary for a mage. If he refuses, we will get nothing."

"You woke up very alert today. I thought of that. You'll give him a letter from me. That'll do." And she tossed him a rolled-up parchment.

"But, my Lady..."

"Égnever's daughter needs no more. He will not refuse."

"It will be done as you order."

"Don't waste any more time. Go and communicate my orders."

The queen leaned back with pleasure in the armchair. She closed her eyes in delight.

*Again.* How naïve of him. And how well he would have fooled her had he only thought a little more. The presence was not coming to her but to him. He broke the ties without cutting the strings so she wouldn't notice. His lack of wit betrayed him. She had to give him credit for wanting to impose his wishes. The best thing about it was that she would have fallen for it like a naïve girl.

It didn't matter. The cockerel had no business in this barnyard. And, if he remembered everything that had happened, it would be fun to watch him pretend to suffer in silence. Anyway, it wouldn't hurt to keep an eye on him. Then there would be time; then there would be everything she wanted.

"Marco!" Selena shouted.

The poor wretch who welcomed her to the castle appeared as fast as his arthritic knees would allow.

"My Lady. What do you want?"

She had to get as much out of him as she could while he was still alive. Surely he didn't have much left.

"I want to see the library. I want to see the magic books."

"Your Majesty, I am sorry to tell you that there are no magic books in the castle. I can take you to the library, but you will not find what you are looking for."

"We will search the castle from top to bottom if necessary. There must be one."

"I don't wish to intrude, Your Majesty, but there are no magic books as far as I know. Mages are trained by word of mouth. Each one learns from their master, who learned from their own."

"Are you refusing to follow my orders?"

"No, of course not, my Lady. I try not to waste your valuable time in enterprises of difficult success," the old man excused himself.

"Stop trying to ingratiate yourself with stupid resources, you dog, if you don't want to come to my call crawling with just your arms."

"Please forgive an old man who appreciates his life, Your Majesty. I was born to serve; I have done nothing else in my life. If I have disturbed you, I beg you to excuse me."

"Shut up and guide me."

## *14*

*"My generosity can be very great."* Pamela spent the night with that phrase running through her head. Her son's crying woke her from her first *son's* death nightmare more than once.

Now, in the daytime, she felt her skin tingle again. She told herself she would not cry; she could not cry. She had to face destiny as a new opportunity.

He approached the child's crib and watched him sleep. Under his eyelids, there were no traces of dark circles under his eyes, and his cheeks were rosy. And all thanks to her. The queen would be pleased. But what did that matter to her?

"Sleep, my child..."

She roughly pulled her hand away from the childish hair, realizing what she had just done. It could not be true, not so fast. It had only been a few days. Selena said it; it was a new beginning. Her heart would eventually accept that she had lost nothing.

He stepped back towards the fresh air from the window. She could see a group of ten riders galloping away from the castle. She imagined herself escaping from there and taking the baby with her. She could look for a faraway place where no one would bother her, some secluded spot lost in the forest or the mountains. "*... an escort of guards will protect you and your son.*" Not a chance of being able to get away, not from there, not from her.

She heard the child stirring. He probably wanted his breakfast. She would nurse him, and then they would go for a walk, maybe on the beach. She had never seen the sea before now.

# 15

"Are you sure there are no more books?"

"Sure, my Lady. Until very recently, this kingdom did not cease to fight, and there was not much time to dedicate to collecting copies," replied Marco, balancing on the ladder he was standing on.

"And are there secret rooms?"

"Just a leak path. But, there, you will only find rats and spiders; it has not been used for decades."

Sitting on one of the benches, Selena turned the pages of a heavy brown leather-bound volume. There was nothing but books on war and strategy. They were of little use to Triar. She threw it angrily into a corner.

"Hand me the black-covered one at the top."

"This one, my Lady?"

"Yes," Selena hissed.

The old man staggered on one of the steps. In a vain attempt to hang on, he dropped the book and reached out his hand for a handhold.

Selena watched him fall as if he were a feather. He curved his back, trying not to let his head be the first thing to touch the ground. His arms imitated the first flutters of a young sparrow, who knows it has to move its wings but does not know how. She also saw the book fall, hardback, and strangely glossy. She could glimpse some images between its pages that caught her attention.

As if it were an eagle's claw, her hand caught the copy, leaving marks of her fingernails on it.

"Your Majesty!" begged the old man.

"Poor coward. Come on, open your eyes."

She held him a tenth of a second before impact with her left hand. She held him as if he were only a cloak.

"Marco, do you think you can stand up?"

"Yes, Your Majesty, thank you."

"Well, but if you ever think of me that way again..."

The old man swallowed and backed away in fright.

"It won't happen again, Your Majesty."

"Now go and get me some wine."

"Yes, my Lady."

"Later, we will check that slip door and Égnever's chambers."

Selena went back to her seat. She leaned against the wall, feeling the cold of the stone. She opened the ebony-colored book. She concentrated, searching for some magical force in the copy. Nothing. Just another one on the pile. 'My travels through Panameria', read the title; written by Romina from Brettia.

She opened it and slowly turned the pages. It was handwritten in blue ink. It bored her to read. The illustrations attracted her attention much more. Bright colors reflected in her pupils. The authoress portrayed unusual places and various animals. They were drawings.

However well done they were, they were just that. Nothing of any use to her.

She stopped the movement of her fingers. There. Something. She turned back a page.

"It's beautiful," murmured the queen.

As if she were a little girl, she thought: *I want one.* At any cost, she would have one just like it. What nonsense; she would have the best one! She could feel the life in those green irises and guessed the power of the muscles under that black skin.

She brushed her fingertips against the illustration, imagining it to be real and not just a compendium of shades created by some mortal.

"Cedric!" Selena shouted.

## *16*

The warrior's yell pierced the castle's thick walls until it reached the parade ground.

Despite feeling free of her influence, Cedric felt the call not only in his ears but also deep in his brain like thunder on a summer afternoon.

"I'm coming, Your Majesty."

He sheathed his sword before unleashing a blow on a wooden doll, a doll where, until a few seconds ago, he imagined the face of the queen. He dismissed those thoughts. He felt vulnerable again.

That infamous harpy still held power. He could not, and should not, allow himself such licenses in his mind.

He hurried his steps to meet Selena. He did not run; that would have been expected of any other servant, not him.

He was unfamiliar with that part of the castle. He hesitated. The call was very clear. The door was ajar; before pushing it, he could see the warrior immersed in reading a book and surrounded by dozens of others.

"Your Maj..."

"Come closer, Cedric. Sit next to me."

It had to be very bad. She had never been so cordial to him.

"Did you send your men?"

"Yes, my Lady, they have already left."

"Good. I have a question to ask you."

She held out the book.

"Tell me, what is the name of this beast?"

Cedric focused on the image. It was familiar to him. He delved into his memories. His brain, free, or almost free, of the magical influence, allowed him to recall a morning in his town. He was walking beside his father, a big man with huge hands that left marks on his face and body more than once. A great bustle was rising in the main street. People crowded around a wagon advertised as the greatest compendium of wonders. A friendly little man perched on top of the vehicle was shouting at the top of his lungs for people to follow him to the outskirts of the town, accompanying his words with a waving cane.

He saw himself walking, trying to follow his father through the crowd, and dodging the brown puddles that bloomed on the road.

Then he saw only backs that prevented him from contemplating the wonders. It was like this until his father lifted him and sat him on his shoulder.

"Take a good look, Cedric. You may never see this again in your life."

A few yards in front of him were cages covered with blankets. The little man was shouting from his left, announcing what was to be seen in a few minutes.

A man suddenly appeared on top of one of the cages, pretending to be a strong man. Cedric was sure that a blow from his father would have crushed him. The strongman jumped to the ground and pulled back the blanket with a strong jerk.

"It is a panther, Your Majesty, a black panther."

Selena's eyes sparkled.

## *17*

There were three people with her. One guarded the entrance to the trail, and the others stood a few feet away.

As he walked down to the beach, he went over what he had to say. He still wasn't sure she was the one, but there was no one else. He felt that Selena couldn't, or rather wouldn't, access the wet nurse's mind and that she would let her work by keeping the reins loose.

He gave a stiff salute to the road guardian and walked toward the others.

"You may leave. I will take care of her."

"Sir, we have orders."

He thought so. While they were directly under Selena's command, they should still have some respect for their superiors.

"I know. I just want to talk to her in private; you know, male and female stuff. You know what I mean?" and he winked mischievously.

He saw them smile and walk away toward their partner.

He headed towards Pamela. She was barefoot, and, with the child in her arms, she was dodging the waves.

"Pamela."

"What do you want? I have nothing to talk to you about. I just want you to let me do my job."

"I wish to apologize for everything that has happened."

"Apologize? Why? Because you and your men enslaved me. Because your queen wants me because I can produce milk. Apologies are useless."

Cedric turned his gaze back to the soldiers and then focused on her again.

"You are right. Apologies are useless."

“Leave, go away,” Pamela begged.

“Please, I only ask you to listen to me.”

The farmer put his hand on his sword.

“Don’t hurt me; I’ll listen.”

“I won’t hurt you.” he finished removing the straps that held the blade and threw steel and leather on the sand. “Come, sit down.”

Cedric took off his shirt and spread it on the floor just as he did with his wife and little daughter many times.

“I don’t want you to be frightened or think I’m forcing you to do anything. If you still don’t believe me when I have finished telling you what I have to say, you can take that sword and slice me with it.

The girl’s face became skeptical.

“I’m serious. In fact, I’ll save you the trouble. After all, without you,” and he regretted having said it that way, “I have no reason to stay alive.”

“I’m listening.”

## *18*

“Greetings, young Béldar.”

“Master, you honor me with your presence.”

“Come on, come on, Béldar, don’t be so formal with me. You’re one of us. You mustn’t go on behaving like that frightened disciple who came under my tutelage years ago.”

Béldar shook his master's hands. He loved the old man dearly. He cradled him when the world had rejected him. He gave him security and initiated him into the world of magic. More than his mentor, he had become a second father.

"What brings you here?"

"Ah, my son, the Council makes obscure decisions that neither you nor I can understand and in which we must not dare to intervene. I see that you enjoy the viands of the forest."

"Do you feel like it? I have satiated my gluttony, and there is still enough left."

"Well, it never hurts."

He took a bag of wine out of his backpack and held it out to his student. They drank.

The young man watched him take the rabbit's remains between his round fingers. He remembered the banquets they used to feast on back in his hut. They were not long ago, and he thought he would never forget them.

He failed in everything he undertook before he found him. He was unable to enter the ranks of King Gregor's army when he was recruiting soldiers for the consolidation of the four kingdoms. Too weak, they objected. His four brothers were accepted and fought for their family's honor and their kingdom. From that day on, he was looked down upon at home.

He loved a girl; Sofia was her name. How many times had he murmured that name in his sleep, how many times had he kissed those lips in his dreams! Then came the cruelty of the morning, the disgusting real life. Even though those weren't her exact words, she didn't want him. It didn't matter if she disguised her rejection with reasons, like not being ready or not wanting anything serious at that moment. How could he be interested in anything that wasn't serious? He cursed that afternoon when he had her in front of him. Sitting by the village fountain, she snatched his heart, threw it to the ground, and stomped on it, wallowing in his misery. No, there is nothing exquisite about pain. Months passed, bloody months of seeing her and knowing she would never be his.

He had no choice; the fire of life did not dwell in him. He packed his few belongings and wandered into the darkness. No one batted an eyelid. Then his master, Darius, found him. He welcomed him into his home as if he were his son, gave him the fatherly affection he had never received, and instructed him in the ways of magic so that he could be his successor.

"Master," he addressed him as he watched him throw the last clean bones. "Your visit intrigues me. Have plans changed?"

"No, I am only here to give you this."

He held out what looked like a rolled-up papyrus. He could recognize Shao's seal closing it. Not just the paper. Something was hidden inside. It was hard to the touch and a little bigger than a pebble.

"Tell Selena's men that, in addition to the *Oxbius*, here is a gift from Shao, the head of the Council. That is how you must say it."

"What is it?"

"I'm curious too. The *Oxbius* should be enough; he knows what he is doing."

"Nothing else?"

"Nothing. Now I must leave."

"I hope to see you soon."

"Goodbye, lad."

"Goodbye, master."

He watched him leave with slow, sure steps.

What else would Shao send Selena? She was going to have an *Oxbius*. They were scarce. Just holding it was an honor.

He took it out of his robes to examine it again. It was spherical, no bigger than a baby's head. It was perfectly polished with a smooth surface, like a forgotten pond. Free of glitter and completely black, like a tar pit. On what would be the sides, two sets of five small holes where fingers fit. At the top, one last solitary hole where a quail's egg could fit.

*Oxbius* were said to be made of stellar material. Béldar did not believe that; if so, they would surely glow. They functioned as channels of connection with Panameria to facilitate the control of magic. Some masters used them to accelerate the learning of their disciples. He was not so lucky. Other rumors suggested that *Oxbius* could not only connect the mage to magic but also enhance it. Simple tales of apprentices looking for shortcuts to their learning.

It was time to wait for the soldiers to arrive.

# 19

Pamela watched him curiously as he told his story. Curious and a little afraid. She knew well what to expect from men. But then, when she saw him holding back tears as he spoke of his wife and daughter, pounding angrily and helplessly on the sand, sitting there like a helpless little animal, she understood that he wasn't lying. He may have been bad before, even if that sounded like nothing to him, but now he had again the pure soul of a farmer who never wanted more than happiness for his own and himself.

"Are you done?"

"Yes."

The wet nurse watched Cedric for a few seconds. His whole story was madness. A being created out of nothing, with a hunger and thirst for destruction.

"What do you think we should do?" questioned Pamela

"I don't know. I, more than anyone else, know the extent of her power. I'm sure that we wouldn't get very far if we were to escape, but the truth is that I don't see any other alternative."

"We could stay. She has promised to be good to me, and you can carry on as you are."

"Good? She doesn't know the meaning of that word. You'll stay alive until your son can fend for himself, don't get your hopes up; she doesn't want you for anything else. Do you think she'll allow you to raise him? You're nothing more than his sustenance, and you'll be expendable in less than a year. And me, do you really think

I can go on as I have been? You consider me so shallow as to not care for what happens to others. Look at you. You're just a child. I don't know what the hell I'm doing telling you all this. You, of all people, can't help me."

She got up from the sand and turned her back to him. She was nothing to anyone; to the queen, breasts overflowing with milk to feed Triar's cursed son; to him, a worthless child.

From behind her, his arms came around her. They were firm, muscular. The bare skin of his torso stirred heat in her loins.

"Don't cry. I don't want to think I hurt you. I shouldn't have spoken to you that way."

"Lie to me, Cedric; tell me that everything will be all right, and we will be able to escape."

The embrace grew a little tighter.

"I promise nothing will happen to you; I will make sure of it."

"Do you swear?"

She felt that she could come to love this man.

"I swear," Cedric lied.

Pamela turned, seeking his lips to kiss him. He leaned towards her. They kissed.

## 20

At the top of the tower, Selena gazed with delight at the scene on the beach. The captain and the wet nurse allied against her. How deluded! People were so predictable.

The previous night's event prevented him from controlling Cedric's mind. The same was not true of that silly girl's mind. It was a blank canvas where she could create anything.

Who said life wasn't fun?

## 21

A hundred yards away from the forest, a small group of riders was advancing along the road towards Tolm. There were ten of them. They wore light black leather armors and were all armed.

He formed a sphere of light between his hands and made it rise. The brutes might pass him by if they were not given a signal. It worked.

The soldiers left the road and approached the edge of the grove.

"Were you looking for a mage?" asked Béldar.

Two of the horsemen approached him. Neither drew their swords.

"Are you one?" asked the one who seemed to be in charge of the search.

"Yes, shall I show you?"

A sardonic smile surfaced on the mage's face.

The two messengers looked at each other for a few seconds.

"All right," said the same man who had spoken before.

"Perfect. Which of your men will be the lucky one?"

He snapped his fingers. Small flashes of lightning erupted from his hands. Both men stepped back. Perhaps they sensed that their steel could do nothing.

"Leave it. We trust your words."

He pulled a card from his bag with his left hand and held it out to them. They kept their right hands on the hilt of their swords.

"Take it; our queen sent it."

"Your queen is Selena. Am I wrong?"

"Yes, that's her."

"Well, let's see."

With slow gestures, he spread out the paper and read it. He didn't know what for; nothing would change his orders. Well, he did know; he loved to see the fear in men's eyes.

"I am sorry. I cannot appear before Selena. Give her my warmest regards."

"But you can't refuse."

"Why not?"

His eyes glowed like red-hot metal.

"Uh, she is the daughter of Égnever, a great mage. She is very powerful," explained the rider.

"Even if she were the sun's daughter, that wouldn't change my decision at all."

"But she..."

"Hm, so she would kill you if you came back empty-handed. Tell me. Who would you prefer to be killed by: her or me?"

They reached for their swords. The fear on their faces left no room for doubt.

"You."

"I see that what I heard about her was not a lie. Don't worry. I was just playing with you. You will take this artifact to Selena; she will know what to do." Béldar handed them the *Oxbius* wrapped in a black cloth. "Ah, give her this gift as well. It is from Shao, the head of the Council. See that everything arrives in order if you value your lives. I am leaving."

He turned his back to them and covered his head with his hood. He walked away serenely, lightly shuffling his bare feet. He had not walked twenty steps when he heard a whisper behind him.

"Son of a bitch. You, get the crossbow ready and shoot."

The dart flew greedily towards him. With his back turned, he was a perfect target.

At the last second, Béldar faced his attackers. With imperceptible movements, he caught the arrow between his thumb and forefinger.

"What you said was true. You'd rather be killed by me," said the mage.

## 22

Selena waited. Cedric was not usually late; of course, his captain was not usually free to choose. Now that he was a free entity, perhaps it would be pleasant to deal with him from now on. She should keep that in mind.

A large amount of food was laid out on the long dining table. The deer platters were smoking, giving off an incredible aroma. A pair of roast suckling pigs swam amidst an apple sauce that she imagined was delicious. It was strange to discover her sudden interest in such mundane pleasures as food. Her stomach thanked her for it. She remembered the repulsive pottage served during her campaign. She supposed that her men would have abandoned her if she had not influenced them. They could not complain about the bad cooking. It was fortunate to spare the lives of the castle cooks. Her mind played with the possibility of sending out patrols in pursuit of new recipes.

"What am I thinking? It's crazy. I'm sure I'll even start embroidering soon. I don't know where I can be getting this nonsense from."

She unleashed her sword on a piglet, splitting it in half.

The knock startled Pamela, who, accompanied by Cedric, was entering the room at that moment.

"I am sorry to have kept you waiting, Your Majesty. I ensured that the guard fulfilled their duties well with the wet nurse."

"You did well, Cedric. Always so diligent in your assignments. Now let's eat. You too, girl, join us."

"Thank you, Your Majesty."

"Is your child sleeping?"

"Yes, Your Highness."

"Well, put him on that divan; you have a few furs there. Then you can eat in peace."

"Thank you, Your Majesty."

Selena was at the head of the table. Cedric approached her with the jar of wine and served her. He could see in Selena's lap the book she had found in the library; she seemed to treat it as the most precious of her treasures.

The queen proceeded with the deer. She dipped bread in the sauce and tasted it. She dipped her lips in wine and let out an exclamation of delight.

"Eat, eat. Hurry up, or soon I won't leave anything for you," Selena warned while holding a piglet's leg. She took a big bite. "Delicious!"

## *23*

He could only distinguish one of the ten soldiers sent out. He was approaching very slowly. Cedric noticed that the queen was getting impatient. Selena did not like to wait. She sent two horsemen to look for him.

"Your Majesty, something must have happened."

"Yes, Cedric, but that doesn't matter; what matters is if they got what I wanted."

The captain felt the licks of small flames of fury in his heart; she only cared about herself; the others were nothing more than unwilling tokens to dispose of at her whim.

The horsemen caught up with the messenger. One of them took the steed's reins and whipped it to make it go faster.

"Well, here it comes."

The two men helped their companion to dismount. He approached her, shuffling his feet and firmly holding a blanket with which he covered his shoulders and head.

"My Lady," his voice trembled. Cedric could make out several missing teeth. "I have carried out your orders. Here is what you asked for."

A hand with only three fingers left held out a bundle wrapped in black cloth.

"I asked for a mage. I don't know what that is."

The queen unwrapped the package. The *Oxbius* caught her gaze, drawing her in for several seconds.

"You must present yourself to me as you should. Take that tattered blanket off your head," Selena reacted.

The soldier obeyed. The hand holding the blanket tugged on it, letting it fall to the ground.

Selena and Cedric recoiled in shock. The man's face was a sea of yellowish oozing pustules. One eye was completely closed, and the other was barely open.

"Was it the mage?"

The man shook his head affirmatively.

"You must have messed with him. Who came up with the idea, and where are the others?"

"Dead, my Queen."

The rider's legs gave out, and he fell to his knees with a loud screech of pain. His companions rushed to hold him down.

"You have not answered my question."

"It was I," the soldier mumbled.

The man began to cry.

Cedric sensed the pain he might be suffering. He had to end his life. It was not humane to prolong his agony. He brought his hand to his sword with the firm intention of slitting his throat.

"Stop," Selena ordered. Her gaze was on fire, and she gave off fury.

The captain restrained his hand and withdrew it from the hilt.

Selena approached the wounded man. She held him by what was left of the leather armor and lifted him.

"Anything else you want to tell me?"

"The mage told me to give you the artifact, that he would not come, that you would know what to do with it. He also sends you a gift..." The words were choked off in a cough accompanied by thick blood froths. "... a gift from Shao, the head of the Council."

"Where is my gift?"

"It is on my belt, my Lady, but I can't take it. I'm sorry."

More tears.

"So useless! Cedric, take my gift."

Burning with rage and compassion, Cedric rummaged through the man's clothes. He found the rolled-up parchment and showed it to him.

"Is this it?"

"Yes, sir."

"Take it, Your Majesty."

Selena grabbed the paper and tucked it into her belt.

"Your Majesty, may I dispose of the wounded man?" suggested Cedric.

"No, not at all. I'm not done with him." Turning to the messenger, she added: "Let's see, so you came up with the great idea of attacking a mage. When have I ever told you to think? I take care of that; me, Selena, Queen of Lebassi."

Cedric was consumed by fury. One chance. He just needed one chance.

"You wanted to force him to accompany you, didn't you?"

"No."

"What? What did you say?" Selena shouted.

"No, Your Majesty."

"Then why?"

"He treated us like children. I wanted to end his life."

Selena kicked him in the chest with such force that the two soldiers holding him released him. The soldier fell a few yards away, howling in pain.

"Damn it. You've soiled me. You deserve what he's done to you. You two, take him away and feed him to the pigs."

The two men bent down to pick up their comrade.

Cedric was accompanying Selena back to the castle when she turned to the guards.

"No, poor animals. Take him to the forest and leave him there. Who am I to interfere in the revenge of another?"

## *24*

The room was heated. He saw the white snow huddling against the panes of the small window. He laid on a bed covered to his chin by a thick blanket; a well-preserved old man leaned over him.

"Who are you?" asked Triar.

"That is not important. You will stay here for a while until you recover, then we will see what to do with you."

"But..."

"Sleep. You do not have to worry about anything else."

The bald man dressed in a green robe described an arc with his hand in front of him. The pain he felt in his gut eased, and drowsiness began to take hold of him. As sleep took over his consciousness, he remembered the combat against Selena, her sword piercing him, and the dishonor of defeat.

He thought of Katrina, of their son Magnus. He dreamed of revenge.

## *25*

The queen was sitting on the floor of her room. Her back was leaning against the wall, and her right leg was resting over the left one. Her gift was open in front of her, and she was reading. Her eyes roamed over the words, and the smile she had ready was cut short by an expression of impatience.

She heard a knock on her door. She focused her mind on opening it from there.

Nothing! Nothing? But yes, there was something; she felt a strong pang through her brain, a pang that immediately disappeared.

"Damn it, what's going on?"

She got up feeling heavy. Her mouth tasted horrible, and her stomach was turning.

She opened the door to find the monumental figure of Cedric.

"Come in."

She saw a look of doubt on her captain's face as he stared at her. She stepped back and went to sit in one of the armchairs.

"Bring me the water."

He approached her with the pitcher and a glass. After he poured it, she drank several glasses. She felt droplets of sweat on her forehead. What was happening?

"Your Majesty, are you all right?"

"Yes, of course, I was just thirsty."

"Dinner is ready, Your Majesty."

"Well, tell the wet nurse to come with us. I want the child to get used to my presence."

"As you command, my Lady."

"I'm sick of it; give it a rest. Treat me like you have always done. I'm Selena to you; stop with all those titles."

"Fine then."

## *26*

The Iron Mountains were a mighty mountain range that served as a natural boundary between Lebassi and Tolm. From the Fortress of Foam, the route northward skirted them, but they could not risk passing near the old castle nor the nearby towns.

John and Paul, faithful soldiers, were finishing setting up camp. The logs were crackling on the campfire, and two fat rabbits were slowly roasting over the flames.

"Show me the path you suggest, Omar," Gregor commanded gently.

The captain spread the map on the ground.

"We are here, Your Majesty," Omar said as he pointed to a spot on the paper with his fingernail. "If we leave at dawn, we will finish crossing the mountains tomorrow at noon. I expect no setbacks. Four or five days later, we can reach Iluran."

"Tolm is closer."

"Yes, it is, but Tolm suffered attacks from Selena's army. Rumor has it that King Kirna is no longer loyal. He made a pact with that assassin to save himself."

"Cowardly pig. Iluran then. What is known about King Sabilo the Right-Handed? Can I trust him?"

"Yes, you can trust him. The story goes that Faustino, father of the current king, fought alongside your grandfather, the Peacemaker. He was his best captain. When he was only ten years old, Sabilo accompanied his father in several battles. Unfortunately, a Brettian soldier cut off his left arm in one of the last battles. That is where his nickname comes from."

"A warrior."

"An old warrior, very old. He has no heirs; he never married. There are rumors."

"There is loyalty. I don't care about anything else," said the heir of Lebassi.

Gregor watched as the captain nodded. He stirred the coals with a stick. The rabbits were almost ready. The fat sizzled as it fell on the fire, and its smell intoxicated him.

"Let's eat," the boy invited.

## *27*

"Something is wrong with Selena."

Pamela blinked quizzically.

"What do you mean?"

Cedric stood a few steps away from her and turned his head to make sure no one was listening, trying to forget that Selena's eyes and ears were all-encompassing.

"There's a strange twinkle in her eye, and, tonight, before dinner, I could have sworn she was dizzy."

"What's so strange about that? For one thing, she is a woman like any other."

"Yes, but... Nothing like this has ever happened to her, and I've been by her side for a long time. What's more, I'm not sure she's really a woman like any other. I know she has certain powers and can control others very easily."

Cedric closed his eyes and tried to turn them inward, trying to rescue images and sounds from his still murky memories.

"She always says she is the daughter of Égnever, a mage. But before killing him..."

He relived the scene in his mind: the old man was escorted by several of his men, he was to Selena's right, and she was covered in her armor from head to toe.

"They talked, well, talked… words were exchanged. He commented something about her appearance... yes, he told her that she had grown up too fast as if he had not been present during her childhood, as if something had made him leave and abandon her. Maybe that's why she hated him and finished him off. The strangest thing was that she responded that..." One last effort; he had it right there, like having a fish on the end of a line and not knowing if it would hold. "… that she was already born big."

The child began to bawl in his crib. He was hungry.

"Wait."

Pamela carefully pulled him out from between the sheets. She sat down on the bed and uncovered her breasts for him to satiate his appetite.

"What you are saying leads nowhere. It doesn't make any sense to me."

"I know, but..." An idea began to take shape in his mind; he gathered his strength to clarify it.

"But?" she asked, trying to get him to continue.

"Give me a second."

Just a little more. He concentrated on the pursuit of the idea. But it ran away.

"Nothing. Damn it! Maybe later it will come to me again."

"We could try to escape."

He snorted and shook his head negatively.

"That's impossible, she..."

"You said yourself that something is wrong with her. Perhaps we could outwit her surveillance. And the sentries won't block your way."

"You forget your guard. They owe me respect; they owe her absolute obedience."

"They are only three people."

Her words caused a red burst before his eyes. That girl was talking about shedding more blood as if his hands hadn't shed enough, and he couldn't forget that all the soldiers were nothing more than puppets handled by Selena.

"I have no right to kill them; they are not masters of their actions."

"You don't have to; knock them out. Truth be told, they're a lot less manly than you are."

He could see a look of desire on Pamela's face. What happened on the beach was a mistake. He should never have responded to her kisses. It was too dangerous. The wet nurse was only a few years older than her daughter.

"I don't know. We'll talk tomorrow; it's late. You and the child must rest. Good night."

"Good night."

## *28*

Selena was lying on the bed. She was sick of her gift. The papyrus kept telling her to practice with the ball they sent her. How could it be a gift if that was all it said? She had never received a present and wanted this one as soon as possible.

She had the small object that came inside the papyrus between the sheets. It was deep black and, unlike the sphere, very shiny, like a mirror. It was shaped like a pyramid with four vertices.

Grumbling, she got up from the bed, looking for the orb. There it was, on the divan in front of the fire. Selena looked at it. It reflected no light, no glow. It was like a night without a moon and stars.

She took it between her hands. As if by instinct, her fingers found the holes. They fit perfectly.

She saw a red flame burning in the middle of the *Oxbius*. It was neither inside nor outside. She felt it in her own mind. The flame grew bigger. It surrounded her. It burned inside her.

Impressed, she withdrew her fingers and looked at her hands for burns. The sphere fell to the ground.

The darkness was calling her. She took it again.

# 29

He stoked the fire by blowing on the embers. The twigs he placed in a pyramidal shape transformed into a flaming tip that craved more and more. He waited a few more minutes before presenting it with a mossy log.

He watched the fire the same way he did in his old home. After dinner, he used to sit with his wife in front of the fireplace to talk, to be together. He missed her presence, her way of laying her head on his shoulder, her skin, her body.

He picked up a large piece of wood and threw it on top of the previous one. A hurricane of sparks flew up and scattered; they eventually died out and landed like hot ash on the ground.

A part of him tried to hold back, to keep his thoughts calm so as not to arouse her anger. The other part did not doubt that all his pantomime was useless. If he noticed the changes in Selena, she surely had tied up loose ends much, much, much earlier. He could have sworn she was even aware of all his conversations with Pamela.

However, it was there that his reasoning did not add up. She punished (punished, that sounded so light!) many others for much less. He should not still be alive; another right hand could be found among any of the other captains. He was not indispensable. So?

On the contrary, her manner began to become much more affectionate. Could he say more human? Could it be true? The answer could not be simpler. The answer was with him all along. How could he not have noticed it before?

Exactly, she was becoming more human, more of a woman. He couldn't understand why or even how someone could become more human. He thought of the orb the mages had sent her. No doubt it was an artifact to train her. They must have sent it to her to help her overcome this change, to make her stronger so that she could continue to influence others.

He had to avoid it; maybe there was still time. When he saw her different, dizzy, affected, she wasn't faking it. She was vulnerable. And, if she was vulnerable, she could die. He could kill her, finish her off, and end this tyranny and orgy of death and destruction.

He unsheathed his sword and made his way to the tower where Selena was. He swore by his dead wife that the queen's head would roll tonight.

## *30*

He stirred in his sleep and woke up screaming:

"Sofia!"

He was alone, as always. He curled up again, and fantasies began to cross his mind. Delicious and bitter, bitter because they were nothing more than reveries. He shook his head sharply, trying to deny them.

The sounds of the forest accompanied him and lulled him to sleep. No, mages didn't need to sleep, but he wanted to. Béldar settled down on the grassy mattress, looking up at the stars between the treetops.

He fell asleep.

# 31

He gently pushed the door open, his sword in his other hand. He saw its edge glint under the torchlight.

He stood on the threshold, ready to pounce on his prey and... He was stunned.

Selena was sitting on the bed with her back against the headboard. Her hair waved around her and gave off reddish sparkles. Sparks flew from her eyes. She held her hands out in front of her face, making fluid movements. He sensed they were to control the orb that floated back and forth across the room.

He cautiously lowered his weapon. She gave no sign of having noticed his presence. He stepped back.

He cursed his indecision that afternoon. Not a chance of him being able to finish her off with a simple sword; he was no one against such a force.

He closed the door and heavily descended the steps. He felt dejected. Fate was cruel.

# 32

She felt the power inside her again. She was recovering it. It was all hers. The sphere gave it all back to her. It was what she needed. Thanks to the mages, she felt whole again.

She controlled the orb, moving it back and forth. Her hair was waving from the buildup of magic. It coursed through her. It fed every fiber of her being.

Suddenly, a whiplash of pain ran down her back. Her hands stopped their magical dance, and her hair stopped moving. A trickle of blood spurted from her nose.

That could not be happening. No, no, no. She was powerful and strong. She was Selena.

He plunged into darkness.

## *33*

As she rocked her son to sleep, Pamela thought about everything Cedric had told her. It was very clear that they could not escape alive. And she was only a temporary help in raising the child. She didn't need to be very smart to know that, in a few months, she would be one more, without any privileges, and would return to the stable of females for the vile satisfaction of the soldiers, and that was if Selena decided to spare her life.

Suddenly she saw a way to subsist, so to speak, when her milk was unnecessary. She had to get one of the captains; that way, she could stay in the castle, and other soldiers wouldn't dare touch her, and it would always be easier to satisfy one than a whole troop. Yes, it would have to work.

She laid the child in the crib and prepared to go to bed. After a long day, she was tired. Her legs ached from walking on the beach.

Men soon get fed up with the same flesh, and more so these men, who were mere bridled beasts. When the child was taken away from her, she would also lose all her concessions, and, sooner or later, the man of her choice would get tired of her.

But there were exceptions, at least one: Cedric. However, his very status as unique made him a threat. Selena could do without him at any moment, and she would follow in his footsteps... to the grave. At least she would try to make the best of it until that time came. The image of Cedric on the beach came to her mind. He was quite a handsome man; maybe, he would like her with a little luck. And who said he didn't like her already? He responded to her kisses. Besides, there must have to be some more reason for him to risk telling her what was going on with him, and he had always been very nice to her.

She wanted to think that there were forces capable of overcoming the strongest bondage. And she ended up smiling.

## *34*

Selena could not believe her eyes in the mirror. She spent the whole night practicing with the *Oxbius*. Her eyes looked sunken in, the veins about to explode, and horrible black crescents stretched under her eyelids. Her hair was completely tangled and dull.

She also noticed the nauseating smell. It was the first time she had ever been bothered by any smell. She looked around for the cause. She found it.

Fat flies flew over and rested greedily on the mush that her dinner had become. Now she remembered that a mysterious force compelled her to expel the food from her mouth.

Something pressed her inside. It was a feeling she had never experienced before. She could identify it as fear. She saw it many times in the faces of her victims. Now it was her who was being tormented. She could think of only one explanation for what was happening. She was dying, and she had created her fate herself by killing Égnever. With him gone, so would her spells; it was only a matter of time.

Well, if she couldn't find a way around it, she would let it happen. It didn't matter. But the world would remember her. Of course it would.

She rummaged through the furniture, looking for a brush. Daggers, swords, little else, as she expected. After all, she never needed any.

She was interrupted by a knock at the door. She was about to yell an order but restrained herself as she remembered what had happened the day before.

"Come in, Pamela."

She saw her enter and wait by the entrance, quite scared.

"Come on, come in, don't be afraid."

"Your Majesty, I wished to make a request."

"A request? Fine, fine, what do you want?"

"I..."

"Wait. Tell me: do you have a brush?"

"Yes, Your Majesty, of course. Would you like me to go look for it?"

"Yes, we'll talk later."

# 35

She ran the brush over and over again through the queen's hair. Little by little, Selena's hair returned to its usual state.

"Well, what did you want to talk to me about?"

Pamela found it hard to believe that the warrior was the same person from a few days ago. The queen was being kind. Maybe Cedric had been wrong when he said she would kill her when she was no longer needed for the child's sustenance.

"Your Majesty, do you remember that you offered me the men I wanted?"

"Yes, I'm not stupid. Why would I forget?"

"I'm sorry..."

"Stop being and tell me already who you want. Hm... let me guess, Cedric for sure."

Unable to help herself, she blushed.

"So what your escorts say is true. He's been visiting you quite often. I guess you know who you're messing with. The scoundrel must have seduced you with his pretty words, protective attitude, and repressed desires as if he didn't want anything from you. Well, that's up to you."

"Is... is that true?" her voice trembled.

"Don't doubt my words; women must protect each other. I've heard stories about him and the tricks he's used to reach his goal. He even tried it on me, the bastard.

"When I met him, he was a hunter who drove the women of the town crazy with his muscles and manhood. I had little trouble convincing him to join my cause. He thinks I bought that he wanted to come to make things better when, in reality, all he was attracted to was plowing new fields. My campaign gave him a thousand opportunities to do so; it is very difficult to control soldiers during a war. One must turn a blind eye from time to time to keep them happy and prevent them from turning against you."

Pamela kept brushing the queen's curls. Her eyes were starting to sting. It was all a lie. She was being treated like an object again.

"But, well, I don't want to scare you with all that, just to warn you. I'm not saying he can't change, but I consider it very, very, very difficult. I'll talk to him at lunchtime about what you've asked for."

Pamela did not answer. She was trying to assimilate what she had just heard. Her heart shrank as she realized the deception.

"Well?"

"Your Majesty, on second thoughts, don't tell him anything. I may have been drawing conclusions about him."

"I just want you to feel comfortable here in the castle."

"Thank you, Your Majesty."

The wet nurse silently brushed the sovereign's auburn curls while cursing her 'friend' inwardly.

"Done, my Lady."

Selena stood up to look at herself in the mirror. She smiled at her.

"Thank you; it looks very nice. You can leave."

"Thank you."

The queen thanked her for combing her hair. She cared about her. She wasn't just a milk factory. She was her friend. Selena would watch over her, and she could raise her son. She would keep him safe. She wouldn't lose him again.

## 36

She hadn't wanted to see him for three days as if she was suddenly afraid of him again. What was going on?

He confronted the guards guarding Pamela's quarters.

"Let me through."

"No. The wet nurse has told us not to let you."

"I am Cedric, Selena's first captain. The wet nurse does not take precedence over my orders, and I order you to get out of my way, or you will regret it."

During the last few days, he saw Selena's face grow paler and paler, more and more tired. During breakfast, he thought he saw her drowsy, completely exhausted. He had to act immediately, not to give her time to recover and regain her strength. It was now or never.

The previous morning, he went upstairs to spy on her. He found her again on the bed in a similar position to that of the first day, when –may his wife forgive him for not complying– he swore to kill her.

Despite standing in the doorway watching her for several minutes, she didn't even flinch. He understood that she lost consciousness of her surroundings when she was immersed in practicing her spells. However, he couldn't get close enough to unload a definitive blow; an invisible wall surrounded her as if her magic was so powerful as to become tangible.

He was sure that, by now, she would be engaged in some other enchantment again; he could not wait for a better opportunity.

"Move away, I warn you."

Both soldiers unsheathed their swords, making him understand that they were unwilling to give in.

Before they had time to react, Cedric swiftly stretched his hands towards their faces. The blows crushed their noses and threw them back until their heads crashed hard against the wall. They subsequently fell to the ground.

He tried the door. It was locked. That bitch must have pulled the latch when she heard voices. He lifted his leg and kicked the wood decisively. He heard it creak, and specks of dust fell from the threshold. At the second kick, it gave way.

The third guard confronted him:

"Captain, stand back!" warned the man, drawing his sword.

"Nicholas, put down your weapon. I don't want to hurt you."

He looked for the woman. He found her crouched in a corner.

The soldier launched a thrust that he easily dodged while catching the man's wrist. He squeezed. Nicholas shrieked in pain.

Cedric threw a punch straight to the guard's jaw, leaving him unconscious.

He approached Pamela.

"I'm leaving; I'm taking the child with me. You can come if you feel like it. I'm not going to force you to do anything."

After much pondering, he concluded that the only way to harm Selena was through the child. It was the only thing that could really antagonize her. What greater pain than knowing that she could not fulfill the revenge he had sworn to his enemy!

His horse was waiting in the stable. Everything was ready. He was carrying a few liters of cow's milk for the child. If Pamela did not agree to accompany him, he would find a woman to take care of him. He had enough gold to convince anyone.

He wrapped the little boy in a blanket and held him in his arms.

"What? Are you coming or not?"

Pamela gave him a look of hatred before lunging at him. Cedric repelled her with a swipe, though he couldn't stop two of her nails from etching a souvenir into his neck. Blood ran down his chest, and a red stain made its way down his shirt.

"Damn you."

Angrily, he slapped her. The wet nurse fell to the ground.

"No, no, my son, my son, no," sobbed Pamela.

Cedric ignored her. Holding the baby, he ran out of the room. He was on his way up the stairs when he heard the girl's scream.

"SELENA! CEDRIC IS STEALING MY SON!"

## *37*

After dinner, Selena went up to her room. She sat down on the bed and reached out to take the *Oxbius*. As she did so, her fingers stumbled into the papyrus sent by Shao. A twinge of curiosity jolted her. She set the sphere aside and unwrapped her gift. She was surprised to read it and discover that the warning instructing her to follow the orb was gone.

She told herself that the wait was too long and considered that she was ready. She read the directions. She placed the small pyramid in the top hole and held the sphere with both hands. She followed the instructions and was now very close to the end, so close that she could smell it.

Unfortunately, something else was so forceful that it managed to pierce her concentration as a red-hot sword pierced human flesh. Pamela's scream warned of the captain's betrayal. To her mind came the image of Cedric stealing Triar's son, fleeing down the stairs after hitting the wet nurse.

She jumped up from the bed, but her knees did not support her. A warm liquid began to drip from her nose; she tasted blood, her blood, in her mouth. A whole constellation began to parade before her eyes, and her room seemed to grow larger and smaller simultaneously. She summoned all the courage she could and managed to get up.

Before leaving, she took her bow and quiver of arrows; it never seemed so heavy. She left her lair. From the corner of her eye, she could see that, for the first time, the *Oxbius* was glowing. She had no time to examine it; she had to kill a traitor.

## 38

Two soldiers passed him as he went down the stairs. He could feel Selena's presence; she was conscious again and was coming to get him. The edge of his sword slashed the chest of the two unfortunate men. He felt miserable for ending their lives. There was no other choice; he had to escape.

He ached at Selena's boots hammering in his brain as they approached him. Fear gripped his being, thinking that she could try to control him and thus stop him. He kept moving forward.

The castle looked uninhabited. As he stepped out into the courtyard, he heard the moaning of the wind and some distant thunder. No one else stood in his way. The queen was near, he sensed it, too close for his own safety.

Inside the stables, the animals were restless. Cedric jumped on his horse and spurred him towards the exit. Only two hundred paces separated him from the main gate. As fate would have it, the gates were raised. One hundred paces, fifty. He was about to be free.

"Cedric!"

Selena's scream chilled his blood. He turned his head and saw her on the main entrance steps. She was carrying a bow in her hand.

His hands were about to pull on the reins for brief seconds, less than that, to stop his horse's gallop. Instead, he frantically dug his boots into its flanks, forcing it to hurry up.

The queen drew the bow and placed the arrow in the shooting position. Her biceps suddenly contracted, and a grimace of pain appeared on her face. The dart flew swiftly towards the captain's throbbing viscera. It penetrated violently just a few inches above the heart.

The former farmer could see the sharp point protruding slightly through his shirt. Pain, never better said, pierced him from side to side. He almost let go of the infant, then pulled him tighter against his chest. He kept galloping.

"Damn it!" Selena shouted.

Cedric turned around. He saw the queen pick up another arrow, ready to shoot it, but it slipped through her fingers. Then, five horsemen came out of the stable to chase him. He could have escaped the warrior arrows, but the soldiers would soon hunt him down.

Just one more second, and he would have left the castle wall behind. Behind him, he heard the pounding of the horses' hooves speeding up over the cobblestones. It would be naïve of him to think he could throw them off, and, with that wound, he could not rely on defeating them with his steel.

Lightning flashed across the sky as if a crack had suddenly opened in the firmament. The fury of the discharge landed on the entrance portals, which exploded in a blast of rock, iron, and wood.

Cedric felt the heat of the blast on his back. Some boards flew next to him, and a boulder the size of an apple lacerated his kidneys. He thanked the clouds for giving him that advantage.

The entrance was destroyed behind him. He spurred his horse as he crossed the bridge to freedom.

## *39*

The detonation made her stumble. She watched as two riders were thrown through the air while the others struggled to control their mounts. Her vision blurred. She fought against the dizziness that threatened her. She knew she was going to pass out. It happened every night she practiced with the orb.

She fell to the ground. She tried to sit up.

A new flash of lightning illuminated the night. She saw a black shape approaching her. She wondered why she didn't hear footsteps. Before the glow was completely extinguished, she could appreciate beautiful green eyes lowering to her face. And, right then, she sank into her own black hole.

A black panther, not much bigger than a dog, started licking her face, trying to wake her up.

# 40

He leaned against a tree, looking for rest. He was very tired. Not only because he had been running for hours but also because of the loss of blood.

He checked the baby. He was fine. No injuries.

He achieved the first part of his plan: fleeing the castle. He was sure that Selena would send troops to pursue him. He had to continue escaping; get as far away as possible. He would leave the usual routes and go into the forest paths. He would return home. No! That would be the first place where she would look for him. He would go north to the Kingdom of Glastia.

He heard footsteps, bare feet approaching him. In just a few seconds, the figure of a man loomed before him. He distinguished that he was bald and was wearing a robe in the darkness.

"Bravo, my boy, you have done well. Your work is done."

"Who are you?"

"It is of no importance. Give me the child. I will take care of him."

Cedric tried to protect the little one in his arms. He surprised himself by holding him out to the stranger as if his will did not count in the least. In exchange, the stranger threw him a bag of wine.

"I'll leave you in good company," he said, walking away.

He first thought he was referring to the liquor. A few minutes later, he heard the first howls.

# III
# THE CHRONICLE OF KNOWLEDGE

# *1*

He was next to her. He looked for a secluded place in the forest to be alone. The moon tinged the treetops with silver and allowed him to see the face of his beloved.

He spent many sleepless nights preparing the words he would say when the time came. He remembered nothing and had to resort to the usual formula to make his feelings known to her:

"I love you. I have loved you for a long time."

He dared to stroke her forehead with the back of his finger. If she followed him there, it had to mean something, but... He was so afraid of her; his adoration for her grew too much over so many months, even though he thought one could never love too much, and he knew she could hurt him too easily.

He could not take his eyes off hers; even in such low light, her eyes glowed fabulously, and he felt like a moth flying tirelessly around a torch, closer and closer, until he hurt himself in the heat.

Her hands slid down his neck, and her fingers got lost in his brown hair. She pulled him close until he could feel her form clinging to his. He shyly reciprocated her embrace as if he was afraid she could evaporate in his arms.

"Soph..."

The rest of the words were lost between her lips. Her mouth opened over his, as appetizing as a freshly picked strawberry.

From that moment on, he did not hold back. He gave himself completely to the kiss, trying to merge with her. A slight shudder ran down his spine, awakening every cell of his body. Immediately, heat arose everywhere where he could feel contact with Sophia's body, a heat so suffocating and at the same time so delicious that it urged him to undress and strip her of her attire. He ran his hands down her back, wishing his nails were claws to tear her dress to shreds, to make his way as quickly as possible to her naked skin and melt into her.

She broke it off suddenly, so much so that Béldar didn't even manage to close his mouth. He looked at her disappointed; surely, it was nothing more than a game. She would turn her back to him and return to the town mocking him. It was then that she began to take off her clothes.

The vision in front of him was the one that most often seeped into his dreams. Today it was real. Again, Sophia approached him; she began to undress him. Béldar tried to focus on her eyes, which were fixed on his, but his desire betrayed him, forcing him to study her breasts and the confluence of her thighs.

She smiled. When their last garments ended up resting on the grass, she kissed him again. It was not just heated; it was as if a fire had broken out, and the flames would devour them at any moment.

He was willing to take the risk, and without realizing it, he made her lie down. His lips gently swept down her neck, barely grazing the feminine skin.

He breathed in the feminine scent that emanated from every pore. He savored it thoroughly and would never trade it for the most exquisite roses.

"Béldar."

Her voice caressed his ears like a nymph's song of pleasure.

"Béldar!"

It communicated urgency; he should not delay any longer. He sought her lips. The movement of his pelvis became more insistent.

"BÉLDAR!"

He felt a sting in his side, a very strong and real sting, unlike his dream. He sat up a little disoriented and ready to repel any further aggression with his magic.

He drove a knee into the ground when he discovered Shao only a few steps away from him.

"You disgust me as a mage. How long has it been? Eighty? Seventy? You are still acting like a teenager. Loving an image, because that is all she es. You know she is dead. You dream of a rotting corpse. You are pathetic. I would not be surprised to see you trying to resurrect her a hundred years from now to turn her into a toy for your whims."

"Mas..."

"Do not even dare to call me master; I would rather die than have a disciple like you. Even a peasant could have killed you. I do not know how many times I had to shout your name. Be thankful I only kicked you.

"I am sick of your pilgrimage. With that pace, you will not last long. But glorify yourself; I come to offer you the opportunity to gain a few steps in your ascent to wisdom."

Béldar did not reply. His face showed skepticism.

"Well, you may not be a hopeless case. Of course there is something behind it. Your assignment will be dangerous; however, you will be able to get something you want more than anything I can give you." Shao's eyes filled with anger. "No, no, stop thinking about Sophia! If you want her corpse, you will have it by your side in a second, and you will be able to do everything you were dreaming of with it."

He raised a hand to emphasize that he was not kidding.

Only for an instant did Béldar catch a glimpse of a cadaverous face hovering over the sorcerer's left shoulder.

"I'm sorry, Shao."

"Good. I hope you control yourself. You will have to go to the castle of your new queen: Selena. The poor thing needs a lot of help; she cannot cast a spell without being out of breath. You will have to teach her to use what she has. You will see that it is a lot."

"Nothing else?"

"Earn her trust. We need her in our ranks."

"Our ranks?"

"Someone with so much power must be on the side of the Council."

"I understand."

"Béldar, try to stay alive. Remember that Égnever died under her sword," Shao warned.

The young mage watched as the head of the Council turned his back to him. He was being given the honor of being Selena's teacher. What was the point of the...?

"I find my idea very amusing," Shao told him without turning around. "Take it. You can do whatever you want with it."

In front of Béldar fell a body reeking of decay. He had to put his hand over his nose so that the odor would not make him vomit.

"What's the matter? Don't you want to appreciate the aroma emanating from each of her pores? Ha, ha, ha..."

The laughter continued to hover in the air long after the mage disappeared as a reminder of his cruelty.

Béldar bent down to take a closer look at her. Her skin was worm-eaten, but there was still a faint trace of who she had been on her face. A moonbeam suddenly fell on the face of the corpse as if it had been conjured and revealed before him the worm paradise it had become. Never again would those eyes that had tormented him so much shine in those sockets, and those flabby forms would never again evoke desire in him.

He sighed and then sat up.

There was nothing left to cry or lament for. He took one last look at her, and thankfulness to Shao crossed his mind for helping him get rid of that last remnant of his past, which did nothing more than torture him, keeping him in a world where he did not belong, to which he would never return.

He was a mage, an entity above mortals who did not have to abide by any rules or feelings dictated by any other man or woman.

He pulled up his hood and began to walk towards the castle. May the forest dispose of the repellent remains he was leaving as it pleased.

## *2*

After much effort, she managed to open her eyes. Her eyelids were incredibly heavy; if they had been a little heavier, she could have sworn some reckless person had dared to sew them shut.

The first thing her foggy vision beheld were long, slender whiskers that started from a muzzle as black and smooth as forest moss. She immediately felt a warm tongue soaking her cheek and could see a kind of smile on her panther's face.

With a trembling hand, she stroked its head. The feline lowered its neck and raised its nose, closing its eyes to enjoy the affectionate gesture of its mistress.

*My little one, I finally have someone completely loyal to me,* she thought.

A purr, as if the beast's mind had grasped her thought.

"Your Majesty."

Selena looked away from her cub and focused her eyes across the room. Room? The last thing that flashed in her memory was Cedric's escape attempt and her strength faltering, causing her to fall to the ground.

"Your Majesty."

It was Pamela. She had just gotten up from a chair placed right next to her bed; she may have been watching her sleep. The torches were out, and the dim light came from only two candles, one sitting beside her bed, the other being held at that very moment by the wet nurse.

"Your Majesty, are you all right?"

"Yes."

She felt as if her tongue was an entity foreign to her body and had difficulty moving to form that syllable.

"Rumors are spreading through the castle. Soldiers are restless. Your captains guard the gate."

What was this girl talking about? Rioters? So much so that she needed to be protected during her sleep. She opened her senses, allowing her aura to expand again. Yes, they were beginning to think, but there was no danger yet.

She closed her eyes to focus better. She looked for the cracks she had entered through more than once and drove her pins again.

Screams reached the top of the tower. Selena smiled and looked gently at Pamela.

"There is nothing to worry about."

"Your Majesty, Cedric managed to escape."

She stood up from the bed as if it had suddenly started to burn. Her panther recoiled and turned its head towards the insolent girl who dared to disturb its mistress. It gave her a roar, and its teeth shone as only the full moon could shine.

"Easy, easy," her words caressed the beast's ears like water running in a stream, soothing it. "Now, Pamela, tell me we know about this traitor."

The young woman bowed her head in obedience.

"Lightning smashed the entrance, preventing your men from leaving immediately in his chase. At this moment, a patrol is following in his footsteps. There were traces of blood in the courtyard; your arrow was accurate..."

"Of course it was," she interrupted, "but I failed to kill him. He won't last long, no matter how strong he is, and he won't risk asking for help in the villages. He is cautious and has learned a lot during all this time. But they will find him, and they know they have bet their lives that they will."

Selena made her way to the terrace. She needed fresh air and that traitor's head on a platter.

"Tell my captains to stand down; I can take care of myself. You stay. We have a lot to talk about."

# 3

The wind swept the sand, creating sinuous shapes under the omnipotent sun. Shao cursed more than once as he walked the few yards that separated him from the dwelling carved into the rock. Even he (especially he) was not allowed to appear in the middle of her abode. He could stand the grass, the mud, even the steepest rocks, but he had never liked the terrible caress of those little grains under his feet.

The entrance was small and without a door closing its passage; only darkness kept the interior safe from prying eyes. Shao cursed that lost place in the world again.

"Nadia, it is Shao. Open up."

The only response was the howling of the wind over the dunes.

"Nadia, I am not alone."

He could feel her eyes roaming over his body and devoting deep attention to the bundle in his arms.

"Are you satisfied?"

Like a cascade of stars, darkness fell to the sand.

"Finally."

Shao had to stoop slightly to enter the dwelling. How childish! This was how she got people to bow before her.

"Welcome, Grand Head of the Council."

The voice still sounded sweet to him despite the heavy dose of irony.

"How are you, Nadia?"

"Now you see me."

"Yes."

Her silhouette was outlined against the glow of an oil lamp. So many years, and she still possessed such an appealing body. He felt a twinge in his lower abdomen. He forced his body to submit to his cold mind.

He observed the room, small and cozy, although it was no more than an entrance hall. Few furnishings, all made of fine wood, more than fine. There were four corridors with a certain slope lost in the rock's immensity. Not a chance that Nadia would offer to show them to him.

Shao tried to sit down; her voice rang out then, telling him not to. From the tone, he understood that it was better not to tempt fate.

"How long has it been since the last time we saw each other? One, two, maybe three centuries?"

"Four, because you wanted it that way. You have not attended any of the meetings, none of them. And you... No, let us leave it like that. I did not come here to discuss the past."

"Yes, it's easier not to."

"I have brought this boy for you to take care of."

"A boy?"

Nadia took the creature that Shao held out to her.

"He is the son of King Triar. I want him to grow strong and wise; I have a great destiny prepared for him."

"Our son could have had it too."

"Nadia, do not make the shadows come back."

Her eyes lit up with fury as if the gates of hell itself had just opened.

"That's so easy for you to say; it was I whose entrails the master tore out. A woman never forgets something like that."

Sparks flew from the furniture in the foyer, some of them lingering on the walls and marking them with rage.

Nadia took two steps forward so her face no longer was in the shadows and so he could see it clearly. There were no wrinkles on her complexion. Like a young girl, her skin glowed immaculate, smooth, and radiant. Her hair was the shade of sand in the sun, completely straight and untouched. Her brown eyes maintained the same young girlish glow that made him fall in love with her many years ago. The mage's vanity was struck. Nadia did not look young, as he tried hard to pretend to be; no, she was young.

Shao said nothing. He swallowed his pride, even though he had a thousand questions about how she managed to keep her youth. Yes, magic extended their lives, only that, but the passage of time eventually left its traces.

"You didn't dare to face the master and defend me. You were there by my side when Zerun took him from me. He banished me. He sent me away. You turned your back on me. You, who so often swore eternal love to me, did nothing. On the contrary, he forgave you; look how far you have come with his grace. He did not even grant me the privilege of baptizing me as a mage. I will forever bear my woman's name, marking my weakness. No, our weakness!"

"I gave you the chance to join us with honor when he died; my word has been the law ever since. You never agreed. You could have cleared your name and taken a chair at my side as a worthy heir to our master's wisdom."

"You would never understand. Now tell me: why did you think of me for this assignment? Others would have accepted your orders without question, others who would have had no choice."

"There is no one like you, and I wanted the best. What do you say?"

"Well... What happened to his parents?"

"Selena tried to eliminate both of them. She succeeded with the mother; the father is recovering from his wounds at my house. I may give him a second chance."

"Selena? Yes, I felt her birth. Your disciple was quite good."

"I must go. Many strings are waiting to be pulled."

"Tell me one thing, Shao, who will now take your place when you die? You know very well that you cannot name a successor if he has not been educated under your tutelage."

For the first time in many years, Shao felt a slight shudder in the supposedly solid structure of his reasoning.

"What are you getting at?"

"You know it very well. If our story had not happened, both of us would be the heads of the Council, and both of us would have taken a disciple under our hand. Yours is dead. Let this child occupy your chair if you truly intend to honor me. It is only fair."

"I will think about it."

"No, Shao, tell me now if you want me to take care of him."

"All right, but he will do so only if he succeeds in the tests I have prepared for him."

"You just made that up. Tell me what tests."

"No, my dear, you show him the path. Look at it this way. What more advantage than to have him from such a young age. Accept him as the son you never had."

"We never had, Shao, remember, we never had. Now go away and try not to show up here again for a long time. You are still the same coward you have always been."

The sorcerer put a finger to his lips in an attempt to silence her.

She just looked at him. The sand beneath his feet began to turn to glass. The sudden shock threw the head of the Council outside. Shao cursed as he felt the sand slip through his robe.

"You're right, Shao. I am the best."

The mage stood up, shaking off his clothes. He hated sand; he hated that place.

*The best? That remains to be seen*, thought the head of the Council as a smile laden with bitterness graced his features.

## *4*

A hundred yards away, the Lebassi Castle stood majestically. Béldar crossed the streets of the village towards the construction. Soldiers and villagers were engaged in various tasks. Some stores were open; others were destroyed or looted. Somehow, the inhabitants were trying to get back to normal.

A group of children, abandoned or orphaned, surrounded him, asking for food or coins, whatever he had. He knelt in front of one of the girls, who wore her blonde hair in two pigtails. She could not have been more than eight years old.

"What is your name, princess?"

"I am not a princess. My name is Beatrice, but all the other children call me Bea."

"Hello, Bea. My name is Béldar."

"Do you have any coins?"

"Me? No, I don't have any. Although I thought I saw one hidden in your ear."

The mage pulled a coin from behind the girl's head. The little girl's eyes lit up.

"Oh, you are a sorcerer!"

Béldar put a finger to his lips.

"Let it be our secret. Now go, play with your friends."

The girl showed the coin to her friends and walked away to a bakery smiling.

When he received Shao's order, he considered the option of appearing directly at the castle. In the end, he preferred to walk; he needed to reflect on what had happened, and he would never find a better way to do it than walking.

He set off again. He was close.

He removed the hood from his head and then put it back on. It would make a much better impression to be seen arriving covered.

He crossed the stone bridge. The entrance was in ruins, and many workmen were going back and forth carrying stones and mortar. None of them noticed him as he crossed through the repairs to the main courtyard. They did not, but the guards did.

He could still advance a few steps before a pair of spears cut him off. Then he noticed the dried blood on the stones. Some battle?

"Stop!"

He did not flinch and made the spears rise like an arc to allow him to pass.

The soldiers retreated and then attacked him.

He held both spears in his hands. With a twist of his wrists, he broke the shafts so that the guards held only two broken sticks.

His eyes showed an electric blue glow.

"Well, you have done your job. Now let me pass."

One of them turned his head as if looking for reinforcements. His companion was a poor brat standing a few feet away with eyes as wide as plates and more inactive than a frozen beehive.

Béldar advanced.

## *5*

Karl, a native of the Kingdom of Tolm and an accomplished drinker, watched the spectacle in the courtyard. The rest of the captains considered him the worthiest successor of the deserter. He walked, dryly placing his boots on the ground, and the little free will he had left was used to draw up plans. His eyes were bloodshot; he spent the night awake. Had he been able to trust anyone, he would have killed the queen during her fainting. He did not know why, but his head was filled with ideas, and many remained.

The stranger was dressed in black from head to toe, covered with some kind of robe. He broke the guards' spears as if they were toothpicks. A semicircle of workers surrounded him; he didn't know whether they were frightened or fascinated.

Now the guy was starting to walk towards the entrance. He noticed that he was barefooted. What kind of madman… Égnever was barefooted! It was ridiculous. This boy couldn't have been more than twenty-five years old.

He crossed the path of the black-clad man and waved off the crowd around him.

"Spread out, slackers, there's still a lot of work to do! Who are you? What do you want?"

The subject looked at him defiantly.

"I said let me pass. I spared your men's lives, don't tempt me to take yours."

Karl reached to his waist and drew his sword.

"You'll die, you bastard," the captain said.

He launched a quick strike aimed at the man's neck. His target dodged it by leaning back slightly.

He changed the attack. He raised the weapon over his head to unleash it from above. The stranger turned around. He thought he saw him move his hands.

He felt that time stood still and suffered from a strange sensation in his throat. He brought his left hand to his neck and withdrew it soaked in blood. He looked down and saw a piece of the spear sticking out of his stomach.

"He killed him, he killed him!" he heard people shouting as they fled in terror.

He retched and vomited a liquid that might as well have been wine but was not. Tears welled up under his eyelids and slowly blurred his vision. He fell to his knees and tried to stretch out a hand to avoid lying down. A splinter got stuck in his palm, and it was the blow he needed to finally be knocked down. He convulsed slightly before losing himself completely in the void.

The man in black continued walking towards the castle steps.

# *6*

Selena did not understand how they allowed such an event. She went down the stairs as fast as she could. A stranger in her abode. A stranger they let in as if he had been invited. That he had killed Karl; well, fantastic. Wasn't there a good handful of other men who could stand up to him? They would see her deal with him; they would all regret being around.

She saw the man lying on her favorite divan; he had only a few seconds left to live. No one, absolutely no one, no matter how strong, could surprise her and defeat her. That deluded man dug his own grave by coming to look for her.

She unsheathed his sword, and the steel sighed, feeling blood's proximity. Selva, her panther, stood next to her and roared with all the strength its small body allowed.

The queen stopped only two yards from the divan and looked at the man dressed in a black robe.

"You are going to die, whoever you are."

The mage slowly raised his hands; Selena thought he would give up, but instead, he pulled back his hood, revealing his face. The first thing she noticed was his shining eyes, of a purer blue than the August sky, and then she noticed his hair, so black that, depending on the angle of the light, shone blue as well. His hair was tousled, not unkempt, as if he cared little for them or didn't care in the least about the opinion of others.

So much for Selena's analysis; he was still an enemy after all. She raised her right arm to give momentum to her blow. Her steel cut through the air with a piercing hiss a second later.

The stranger's eyes bore into hers firmly; if she remembered correctly, he was the first person who dared to do so. That striking blue pierced into her green eyes and mercilessly analyzed the small red specks adorning her iris. From there, it slid down the rest of her body. He looked over each of the curls of her hair and compared their color to the specks in her eyes. Then he crawled up her neck like a snake. He immediately went down her sternum, then forked and turned his attention to her breasts. He followed each of her curves, concentrated on her tiny waist, and expanded across her hips. He traveled down her femininity, reaching the middle of her thighs, to then drip like warm oil down to her feet. When he had finished visiting her five-feet-and-three-quarter height, he turned his attention to the descending sword and immediately moved his eyes back to Selena's.

She stopped the blow and stepped back a little self-consciously. She had to look at herself to be sure she was dressed.

The stranger stood up and smiled at her.

"They did not lie to me. The queen is a beautiful woman, very beautiful."

The sword ended up pointing to the ground and the queen, who was never surprised, who was never defeated, felt a warmth light up her face until her white skin matched her hair.

"Who are you?"

But that was the least of it. It was the first time someone had praised her, and his words seemed sincere. What was the point of this? She was a warrior. Why should she care if she was treated like a woman? However, a strange feeling came over her.

"You called me; you said you wanted a mage. Here I am."

"But you are very young. Mages are old."

"Okay, I can come back in a couple of centuries."

He turned around and started walking towards the entrance.

Selena was both perplexed and irascible. Never before had she been addressed so brazenly and shown so little respect. No, no, it could not go on like this.

"Stop, I order you."

He stopped walking.

"You order me. Dare you order me?"

He turned to her with his eyes sparkling. The robe fluttered a few inches above the floor, and the queen could appreciate that her guest was barefoot.

"I am the queen; my will is done here."

She could not allow the first stranger, no matter how much of a mage he was, to stand up to her and attempt against her authority. After all, she had already killed a mage once. And she wanted to think that her father was very powerful.

She firmly gripped the sword and approached him, ready to cut him in half. Her opponent did not make any gesture to stop her. The blow came with the same fury the sky unleashes on Earth.

Her sword plunged just below the ribs and penetrated the flesh easily, too easily. In a tenth of a second, the steel appeared on the opposite side without meeting the slightest resistance. The queen spun around twice, and the blade of her weapon went crashing into the wall.

Her opponent looked at her in amusement.

"What, bad vibes?"

A black spot fell on top of the stranger. Selva's fangs sought his throat, and its claws tore at the robe of its mistress's attacker. Béldar squeezed Selva's neck with one hand and pushed it away from his body so that its paws could not reach him. The feline kept snorting at its enemy. A bit of saliva landed on the mage's arm. With a gesture of weariness, he threw the feline into a corner. A faint emerald glow emerged as the animal hit the stone.

"I will kill you," Selena hissed. She looked at him, radiating pure hatred. The killing had always been circumstantial; it now made real sense.

She stood before him and raised her unarmed hand; fire is fought with fire. A ball of light began to form between her fingers; he was about to know who she was!

The mage did not give her the pleasure of waiting; his hand projected at incredible speed and slapped her without her even seeing the blow. The queen's head spun in a frenzy, and her hair hid her face for a few seconds. When she faced him again, a trickle of blood emerged from her mouth, and her left cheek bore the unmistakable trace of a hand.

For a few moments, the queen felt like crying. Out of the corner of her eye, she saw Pamela cowering against the wall of the stairs. She could not let herself falter; if they saw her defeated, she would lose control, and her kingdom would crumble.

She clenched her fists until her veins were about to burst, each of her muscles tensed, and her fingernails left crescent-shaped marks on her palms. A red aura began to spread around her. Her hair seemed to come alive and began to wave. The divan was violently pushed aside until it shattered against the wall.

She saw her enemy; he was standing in front of her looking at her. Yes, he was a young mage; had he been more experienced, he would surely try to escape her attack.

"I'm waiting for you, Selena; show me what you can do," the stranger encouraged her.

If lava could have looked like a beam of light, it would have precisely matched what came out of Selena's hands.

Good, she got it; it was hers. And... the light faded halfway through with no effect. Her de-electrized hair fell straight, framing her face. Her eyes were veiled with a crimson film. Her head was lashed with pain so terrible it made her nauseous.

"Pam..."

She could not finish her call because her muscles gave out, and she started to fall. She did not feel the blow against the floor; Béldar took her in his arms, preventing her from hurting herself. She was unconscious.

## 7

He fiddled with the hair that hid Selena's forehead, and his fingers caressed a woman's skin for the first time. There was no lightning, not even small sparks, only a warm sensation that spread like a tide from his fingertips to the rest of his hand. It was pleasant, very pleasant. He breathed in the warrior's scent until it saturated his olfactory cells. He appreciated her features as only a sculptor could; he etched every pore and curve in his mind.

Béldar let the queen rest on her bed; she needed it. As he lifted her in his arms, he was surprised at how light she was. He noticed that her clothes were loose as if she had lost a lot of weight in the last few days. He ordered her maid, Pamela was her name, to prepare something to eat and told her that no one would interrupt them, quite sure that his orders would be promptly executed.

He went to the window and remembered the long, cold nights he had spent. For once, he thought things could have been otherwise. He raised his hand and looked at it. He took a slow breath, trying to go back a few moments and find the warmth he experienced. Yes, there it was; it was not an illusion. He tried to imagine what it would have been like to have someone by his side, someone to share with. He could not; no matter how much he tried, he could not. Those were dreams, nothing more. He chose his path, and now he was navigating the waters of his fate the best way he knew how.

He looked back at Selena's body. Her countenance was so peaceful. Whoever saw her like that would never imagine the horrible things she had done and ordered to be done. But was it her fault? She was just a toy, like everyone else. However, this did nothing to change the present, nor the past, but the future? He was there, next to Selena, not by her side.

*"You will be able to get something you want more than anything I can give you,"* and he was foolish enough to think Shao meant Sophia when he meant Selena, Queen of Lebassi and ruler of lands that stretched far beyond what the eye could see, far more than days on horseback, far beyond any mortal's paltry dreams of grandeur. Nevertheless, now he understood, and, for a mage, it was never too late. Béldar made a decision: that queen, that impregnable fortress, that star so far away in the firmament, but, above all, that woman, would be his.

He retraced his steps and leaned over the queen; it was still too early to call her his queen. He perceived her rhythmic breathing; for a few moments, he paid attention to the rise and fall of her chest. Then he focused on her closed eyes and saw them flutter slightly under her eyelids as if she could see him through the skin, and her dream was only a ploy to attack him unaware. He did not fear; he knew she was really sleeping, just as storms sleep in some lost corner before rising in a foul temper to sweep away everything in their path. He joined his lips with hers in a candid kiss, certain that this would only be the prelude to what their fate had prepared for them –because, together, they would have only one–.

# 8

Fire. Smoke. Reality came to her like screams through a pillow. It was hot in there, in her bedroom. She was in danger; she sensed it. However, she was so comfortable in the middle of the blankets that not even an army would have been able to lift her. It didn't matter now; she was so humiliated that she wished never to see the sunlight again. If she were not about to die, the result would surely have been different. That sorcerer's apprentice could not have treated her that way. But she was tired and wanted nothing more than to lie in bed. Death could wait for her to rest if only for a few minutes, nothing more. It wasn't too much to ask for; after all, it had served her well during her campaign. The creaking of bones reached her ears as if her guest was listening to her and stretching its muscle-less body preparing for the wait. That was good, very good indeed.

Fire! Smoke! That bastard wanted to burn her. He intended to make her go back to her roots. If that was what he wanted, then she would show him what she was made of. If she had to leave, she would take him as her lackey for all eternity, and, when she gathered her strength again, she would return, leaving him stranded, lost forever.

Her body felt heavy as if some buffoon had sewn her clothes to the bed. Her eyelids peeled back with no urgency. She managed to sit up. It was hard to see; her eyes could not pierce the darkness. Then she realized that it was night, and the only light was a small fire in the fireplace.

The fire, the smoke, was nothing more than a dream. She was in her room like any other night. She must have fallen asleep, not passed out, while practicing, just like other nights. She did not find the orb beside her. She supposed it should have fallen during her sleep; yes, that sounded reasonable.

Before she checked her theory, she could see a figure squatting in front of the fireplace. It was the stranger. He was stoking the flames with a branch, and, on the other hand, he held a skewer with a smoking piece of meat; she recognized by the smell that it was deer. Then she discovered that she was hungry and would kill for the most miserable crust of bread. She looked for her sword, but she could not find it. Damn, she was unarmed. At the other end of the enclosure, she discovered her bow. It would be impossible to get there without warning him, but she lost nothing by trying.

She got up with extreme stealth; an ant would have made no less noise. She checked the stretch ahead of her: nothing to trip over. She fixed her gaze on her host, looking for any aggressive movement. All she had to do was reach, take the bow, place the arrow, draw it, and...

"Are you hungry?"

Once again, he brandished the meat over the fire. The fat crackled and fell on the embers giving off an intoxicating aroma.

Selena wanted to keep her pride for a few moments and respond with disdain to his invitation. She couldn't.

"Yes!"

"What are you waiting for, then? Come closer. Who do you think I'm roasting it for?"

The queen approached and held out her hand.

"Sit down."

Then she saw the image clearly; as she tried to sit down, he would grab her and bury her face in the middle of the embers. Of course, she would not be foolish enough to fall into his trap.

"No, I don't need you."

"If I had wanted to kill you, I would have done it. Besides, I wouldn't ruin a face like yours by burning it."

Selena's eyes glittered just as an arrowhead gleams under the brightness of a bonfire. She extended her mental appendages, ready to rummage through every corner of the sorcerer's brain.

He did not stop watching her in amusement.

Just a few hours ago, he had marked her face with a slap; now, instead, she received the blow inside her head. She moved back her right leg to not be knocked down by the impact.

"Don't try that again, little woman. I will never be one of your puppets," the mage warned her.

Selena gritted her teeth and exhaled loudly through her nose. Then she sat up.

"Well, I'm sitting down."

"Here," he held out a piece of deer, "it will be ready in a few more minutes."

She looked him in the eyes defiantly, then focused on the deer, to again pin her gaze on him.

Wordlessly, she sank her teeth into the flesh, not because of how hungry she was, but to antagonize him somehow. Strands of blood ran down her chin and fell into her lap after a few moments of balancing on the tip.

"Do you like it like that?"

Selena moved her jaws up and down, trying to tear it apart. She turned her head hard and finally managed to tear off a piece. She chewed, trying to keep her mouth closed; it was impossible.

"Do you know that mages don't usually eat?" She didn't pay the slightest attention to him. "Yes, we don't need to. But make no mistake, we can do it; sometimes we even feel like it."

Selena was not up for conversation. The deer resisted, but the taste made up for it all; boy, it made up for it. She swallowed.

"You could do without food, too; you are pure magic, you know that?" He raised a glass of wine to her lips. She didn't even think to ask where he got it; she drank it greedily. "Your presence is felt from far away, worthy daughter of your father. I did not know him, but we are few, and it is difficult not to hear from each other, at least, especially when it comes to mages with a certain prestige."

Selena listened attentively, although she did not comment. It was the first time someone had spoken to her about her father. She watched as the sorcerer brought the cup to his lips and drank; she thought he was emphasizing his words about doing it when he felt like it.

"How was the meal? Feeling better?"

The queen gave him a doubtful look. She wiped her chin and mouth with the back of her hand, which in turn wiped on her pants.

"Who are you? Why have you come?"

"Thank goodness. I thought you were going to let me talk to myself all night. To answer your question, my name is Béldar and, as you can see, I am a mage, as I told you in the hall."

"You haven't answered my second question."

"You must still have a fever. I told you all about it downstairs. You asked for a mage; here I am."

"If you are here for me, why did you attack me?" Her question resounded like the outburst of a thunderstorm.

"Listen to me and listen to me well. I have not come here to put up with your pretensions as a newly crowned queen. Do not think that, because of who you are, the rest of us, without exception, must prostrate ourselves and lick your boots begging for clemency before your powers, great sovereign. We must..."

"Don't make fun..."

"And you..." if any emotion was above fury, it was precisely what Selena saw in the mage's eyes, "... don't ever interrupt me, ever again." His words were only a whisper. "Where was I? Yes, of course, your arrogance. You think that because you have a lot of lands, soldiers, and people scared to death, you can do whatever you please with whomever you please. If I were to take away your magic right now, you would be nobody. Do you understand me? Nobody."

Sitting on the floor next to him and with flames warming her, she felt cold.

"It is very late. You must rest, you will need it for tomorrow. Don't worry. I will watch over your sleep."

"No, tell me more."

"Tomorrow, little woman."

Selena watched as the mage reached out, intending to stroke her hair. She repelled the gesture by stepping aside.

"You don't have to stay with me for the rest of the night; you can leave."

The mage stood motionless next to her, staring at her.

Selena felt uncomfortable again. She was not a child who needed chaperoning. This was what the Council was sending her, a babysitter?

"What are you waiting for to leave?" asked the queen sharply.

"Your permission, Your Excellency."

Selena burned with the desire to poke him in the eye but restrained herself. It was better to wait until she possessed his trust before attacking him off-guard.

"You may leave."

Béldar's black robe remained tucked in the emptiness of where his body used to be for a few seconds and then fell, as what it was, a simple piece of cloth, on the ground.

# 9

She was sure she would find him in the hall when she came downstairs, as sure as she was that it was daylight at the moment: roosters had crowed long ago. As a sign of her freedom, she delayed as long as possible to make him wait.

The table was set for her, as usual. Pamela was standing beside her chair, waiting for her. However, Béldar was nowhere to be seen.

"Good morning, Your Majesty."

"Well, where is he?"

"I don't know, my Lady."

"Do you know where he spent the night?" But she immediately saw that her questions were leading nowhere. "I guess he will show up. Have you thought about what I proposed yesterday?"

Selena took a seat and began to enjoy her breakfast viands. It might be true that mages did not need to eat, but, at the moment, she needed to, and she also felt like it.

"Yes, Your Majesty, it would be a great honor for me."

The queen smiled. The wet nurse was still very young, but recent events had hardened her greatly.

"Perfect, look for Roland. Tell him to start training you."

"Thank you, Your Majesty."

Selena watched as the wet nurse hurriedly left the great hall. It would be a fun experiment to turn her into a warrior.

# 10

Pamela walked through the intricate corridors of the castle until she reached the parade ground. About twenty soldiers were practicing then. Under a makeshift awning, Roland was supervising the practice at one end. She knew very little about him. Around his neck, he wore a pendant in the shape of a hook. Rumor had it that he was a fisherman on the Great Salt Lake before being recruited by Selena. He had broad, calloused hands and long, honey-colored hair that he wore in a ponytail today. The few times they exchanged glances, his green eyes were cold, and his countenance was always marked by severity. With Karl and Cedric dead, he held the title of First Captain.

The thought that she could be his captain gave her a strange feeling in her stomach. Could she deny something to the queen? Had not it been her who had taken her under her protection, taking her away from that terrible fate that awaited her in that wagon? Selena had been good to her, and she would never forget it. Besides, this promotion would allow her to take revenge. She would take revenge on the men and try to find the one who had hurt her the most. Even if it took her whole life, Cedric's head would come to adorn her wall. He used her and the queen; he abused her trust, and, in the darkest part of the night, he abducted her son, her beloved little boy. Selena tried to stop him, but he had luck on his side. The queen almost lost her life to save the child. Pamela would never forget something like that, never.

Determined, she crossed the courtyard. Several whistles and compliments accompanied her. She didn't even bother to look at them nor to respond. Several of them she *knew*.

“Captain Roland, the queen sent me.”

“And what does the queen want?”

“For you to train me.”

Compliments were replaced by laughter. The man looked her up and down.

“You’re not soldier material,” Roland objected.

“The queen…”

“It will be done as the queen wishes, but we will waste time. Take a sword. Show me what you can do.”

Pamela approached the gun rack. Several blades were gleaming. She grasped a long, thin sword. She was surprised by the weight. She faced one of the men.

“Dolly, dolly,” joked the soldier.

Roland nodded his head affirmatively.

The young man launched a soft attack that Pamela could barely parry. Several more blows. She began to sweat.

The young man laughed at her. He raised his hands.

“Send her back to the wagon. She’s more experienced there!”

Rage lit up the wet nurse’s face. She would never, ever go back to that place. She began to throw blows violently, one after another. One ripped the soldier’s arm.

“Damn you, bitch!”

The man pulled her back with one hand. And launched a furious lunge seeking to pierce her chest. Roland's sword got in the way.

"Enough. You will train with me, Pamela."

She caught her breath before answering.

"Thank you, my Lord."

## *11*

Without any sound having alerted her to his presence, hands rested on her shoulders and proceeded to massage them.

Selena stood up and threw the chair back to push him back and face him. She didn't need to see him to know who he was.

"Don't do that again."

"You gave me an order again." Béldar smiled mischievously at her. "I'm sorry, Selena, but it's hard to resist you."

"What do you mean...?"

"I see you've finished your breakfast," he interrupted her. We have a long day ahead of us.

"I can't leave; I have things to do at the castle."

"You misunderstood. It's not about whether you can or cannot come; if you don't come, I will leave, and I assure you that no one else will come to replace me."

"Are you unique?"

Selena noticed that her words affected the mage. Did he think only he knew how to use his tongue to hurt? She was no fool. She may not have been able to read and control his mind, but she was certainly capable of intuiting.

“You are. That’s why I’m here.”

“Where are we going?”

“To see your work, my Queen. Come with me.”

For a few seconds, Selena assumed he would hold out his hand to her and would have loved to turn him down, but the gesture didn’t happen. It might have been a mistake to think so; last night showed her how easy it was for him to be one step ahead of her.

## *12*

“I want to kill her. I don’t give a damn about the kingdom and my subjects; I just want to kill her. And, if what you tell me is true, taking her life will be too little punishment.”

The King of Lebassi turned to face Shao. They were outside his hut. The sky was becoming cloudy; it might snow again today.

“You are still too weak to think of revenge. Be patient; the time will come.”

Triar clenched his fists, forgetting about the wounds on his body.

“How can I be patient!”

"Give her time, let her be overconfident, and then you will be able to get back at her for what she has done. You should go inside, it's cold out here, and you're not in your best shape."

"Yes, I will."

His feet did not move from the spot.

Triar waited until he heard the door close before walking away from the cabin.

The old man was very kind to him, but, even so, he didn't want to trust him. And they were in the mountains; he had traveled a lot when he was young, but never to such a place. The snow was so compact that it might as well have been there for all eternity.

His eyes scanned every spot around him, looking for a way to get away from there. Nothing, absolutely nothing, only snow, trees, and mountains. Not a road, not even the smallest path.

And most interestingly, all the trees looked intact, with no stumps, yet the chimney never lacked logs.

The only thing he knew about the old man was that his name was Shao, and the only thing he sensed was that he was a mage, one with much more power than Égnever. He had picked him up in his land and had brought him here without the slightest inconvenience, and, despite the distance, he was well aware of everything that had happened.

His wife had been dead for days, as well as his son; Selena did not keep her promise. Triar thanked the gods that this was so; a man could only live as a man.

He stopped when he heard a howl brought by the wind. *Wolves,* he thought, *here they are again.*

He returned to the hut feeling completely helpless; never had he wanted a sword as much as he did now.

## *13*

All she saw in front, behind, and beside him was pure and utter misery. And maybe she was even a little lenient in making that judgment.

"What are we doing here?"

"Shut up and watch, little woman."

The mage was leading her as if he knew the town perfectly well. They passed by a fountain in the middle of a square. Although the water was pure, the water in the basin had a slight pinkish hue.

Selena saw red stains on the cobblestones of the square. Some weeds made their way through the stones, and mud accumulated around the fountain. She also noticed the fleeting glance that Béldar gave it as if he expected to find something or someone there.

He took her there on foot. It was a town near the castle; it took them a little less than two hours to get there. It was one of the last villages she had razed before facing Triar. The vast majority of the houses were still standing, although some with newly repaired roofs. It looked much better than the last time she had passed through.

Selva accompanied them all the way. Taking pity on her cub, she allowed her to go and look for something to eat in the forest.

The mage stopped in front of a ramshackle building. The walls were stained with soot as if flames had licked the rock trying to wear it down, and the door, made of solid oak wood, was scratched and somewhat moldy, yet Selena thought it might well hold many more years before its owner would have to replace it.

He reached out his hand and pushed on the surface with only two fingers. To Selena's surprise, there was no squeak. Instead, the sound of voices came to her ears, and her nose was filled with an aroma of spices, wine, sweat, and evil.

It was a good time; the tavern was full. There were fifteen men, a plump waitress, and the barkeep; looking at him, one could imagine his kinship with the waitress: his belly was as prominent as one of his wine barrels; it was hard to believe he could fit behind the bar. The men were rough, and none of them used their belts only to hold up their pants.

As soon as they crossed the threshold, the conversations stopped. An uncomfortable silence reigned in the place. Eyes were on them, assessing them. Some hands grasped their knives. Selena watched as a blind man sitting at the bar inhaled deeply through his nose and then muttered, "Female."

The murmur caught the attention of one of the men, who got up from his table. They nicknamed him 'Bear', not only because of his size but also because of his smell. The mercenary looked at the two visitors. He laid his eyes on the stranger's bare feet. Those bare feet reminded him of stories about mages. When you traveled a lot, you heard all kinds of stories about the powers of sorcerers, some perhaps made up. They said they dominated time, could live forever, conjured mythical animals, and threw fireballs; they allied in the shadows with kings to maintain power. Stories. Each village had one, each one different. Two elements always repeated: firstly, they went barefoot, and their feet were always clean; secondly, they were old. This man was barefoot, yes, but he was young. Some of the women he was with had more hair on their faces than this boy. He couldn't be a mage. He ignored him. But the woman, no, the female; beautiful and delicious. He always liked redheads. He longed to see how much of a redheaded she was. He let out a loud laugh.

Selena was fed up with her mage. She didn't understand what she had to learn in a tavern if you could call it that. It was a disgusting hole in the middle of a repellent little town for her.

"WHAT ARE WE DOING HERE?" she was more than angry. Right now, she could be supervising Pamela's learning or practicing with the sphere. This way, she was just wasting time. If she didn't want to leave any loose ends before she died, she had to start weaving her shroud, her legacy.

Béldar moved slightly to his left. Bowing and making an arc with his arm towards the lowly individuals before them, he said, "I present to you the scum of the realm."

The eyes of the man, focused solely on her before, gave off brief sparks of rage. Selena heard steel sliding on leather sheaths: knives, no swords.

"Everyone freeze. They are mine!"

Bear's voice was firm, powerful, a voice that would not have calmed wild beasts but would have cowed them back to their dark dens.

The innkeeper seemed to realize that he needed to take stock or dust or simply shelter from the impending storm. He called his daughter, and they disappeared together through a door in the back.

The queen looked at the big man who stood in front of them. Cedric was a big man; this one was huge. His features looked roughly sculpted, and he had incredibly clear sunken eyes. A dark, tangled mane of hair fell to his shoulders. And he stank as if his body had never known soap and water.

The giant approached with a crack of his knuckles.

"What are you looking for here? Are you looking to hire a service?"

"Oh, no, my good friend! She doesn't need to hire anyone to, you know, take care of others. Besides, you guys don't even hold a candle to her."

Bear burst out laughing:

"Don't make me laugh, you wretch. Did she kill them with pleasure? I'd like to taste that pleasure under the blankets."

"There are many kinds of pleasure," said the mage.

Selena took a step forward.

"You don't know who I am, do you?"

The big man shook his head left and right without wiping the smile off his face.

"Where were you when my soldiers razed this village to the ground? Where were you when I allowed them to take all the women they wanted?" She used her fingernails to dig through his gray mass. "Where were you when your mother died?" One more touch. "I hope that slut was worth it."

The smile disappeared from Bear's face. The sound of his breathing was heard throughout the place. He didn't say a word. The air that rushed out of his lungs said more than a chatterbox at a fair.

Selena saw how the mercenary grabbed the knife attached to his left leg. She understood that it was just a ruse. She played along by lowering her gaze. The man drew the steel with a rehearsed slowness. The real attack came from his right hand. The bandit threw his fist straight at her nose. Possibly that trick had worked for him on many occasions. Any other opponent would have had trouble stopping such a mass of flesh and bone. To her, her attacker's movements were slow, as if they were fighting inside a colossal basin of water.

The warrior received the huge fist in her hand and wrapped it as best she could with her delicate fingers. Those delicate fingers ended in nails as sharp as those of her panther. She drove them mercilessly, so well that they pierced two veins.

His adversary did not scream, nor did he bat an eyelash. At least, she had to give him credit for having great strength.

Selena swiftly threw her free hand towards her opponent's elbow as the nails continued to sink into the flesh. First, there was a slight resistance; instantly, the joint gave way, and the queen let her opponent's arm fall useless.

"You're fast. Damn you."

Selena drew her sword, and, before the surprised bear cub could do anything, she ripped his belly open. His intestines peeked out timidly as if towards the light.

The assassin's healthy arm tried desperately to hold them back, but he could not restrain them. They ended up scattered on the ground. Bear followed them.

Selena wiped her sword on the dying man's shirt.

"Well, does anyone else want to play with me under the blankets?"

The warrior heard a few coughs, and most of those present stopped paying attention.

"I still want to try you in bed, and I'm sure there are many more who share my desire."

The voice was as cold as a river in winter. It came from a wiry individual sitting on a stool in front of the bar. His back was to them; he had only turned his head to look her straight in the eye.

"You may have taken one down, and I'll give you credit for that. Bear lived up to his name, but very few lights shone in his head. You may be fast, you may even be strong, but I don't think you can stop us all together; I'd bet my life on it."

"I accept your wager," the queen proclaimed.

Selena watched as daggers and knives were pulled from their sheaths. The mob stood up, waiting for the signal. The guy at the bar turned on his buttocks to get a better view. He was stroking his neck with a very thin stiletto.

"You may begin," the thin man encouraged the mass while still remaining in his seat.

The mage leaned against the door, perhaps to get a good spot to enjoy the show or prevent some coward from escaping.

Sword in hand, Selena waited for their attacks.

## *14*

A shiver ran through his entire body. His legs momentarily lost their strength, and he had to cling to the table's surface to keep from falling.

Fortunately, the king was asleep. It was not convenient for him to see him in a moment of weakness.

Shao pulled up a chair and sat down. His hands reached for the cup of mulled wine. His impatience to drink caused a few drops to run down his chin and fall on his robe.

The attack was slowly passing. Only it was not a proper attack; it was a warning. It was the warning of death. He closed his eyes, trying to concentrate. Unfortunately, he saw no images, as if a much more powerful force was pushing them away from his recognition.

Only the essence of what had happened reached him: Terwa was dead; one of the members of the Council was dead.

The next scent was much more disturbing: he had been murdered.

## *15*

Béldar watched the fight with critical eyes. The queen did not waste any movement, her control over her sword bordered on perfection. However, it was barely a graze, and they were many more. The mage praised the queen's cunning; she used her magic on no occasion. A single moment of weakness would be enough for the swarm to fall upon her and absorb her.

"You need help, my Queen."

He noted the scornful response inwardly. The queen was a stubborn woman.

"If you say so."

She stood by. She would never forgive him for giving her support when she didn't need it. Even if she did need it, it would be quite possible that she would rather die than accept him as an ally.

So far, counting Bear, nine bodies littered the floor. The air smelled of sweat, blood, and manly rage.

He would continue to wait and enjoy the combat demonstration.

## *16*

Crouched on the branch of an elm tree, it watched its prey: a medium-sized boar with juicy meat; it could taste it. It allowed it to come closer. It sensed it was fearful. Maybe it sensed that something was wrong.

Rather than jumping on it, it let itself fall, just as water slides down a waterfall. It tensed its forelegs and extended its claws, ready to dig them into its neck.

The victim discovered with a glance the fate that was falling upon it; it was too late to escape. The panther was not much older, but in its green eyes, the unmistakable sign of a predator gleamed. The boar ordered its hooves to get it out from there.

Selva managed to tear the boar's side, and its nails were stained red. It planted its anatomy on the ground, ready to finish it off. Its prey rolled over in pain and turned its face to the feline; it showed its long, curved incisors as if telling it would put up a fight. It lunged at the panther with a deafening shriek, hoping its bravado would intimidate it.

Selva didn't even bother to roar. It propelled itself with its strong hindquarters and soared with the characteristic grace of its breed. In midair, it turned its body, completely reversing the direction of its trajectory. It dug its paws into the beast's side and immediately clamped its jaws around its neck. The boar's warm, life-giving liquid drenched its tongue, giving it appetizing prospects.

It forced the animal to lie down and sank its fangs even deeper. A brief period of agony passed. Selva gazed into the glassy eyes of its prey; before it died, one of its hind legs flailed frantically for a few moments, then the body went quiet.

The panther dragged its food into some bushes to eat in peace. It buried its snout into its belly and tore skin and flesh. It slowly tore its carcass to shreds, dyeing its black fur crimson.

# *17*

The stiletto flew swiftly and accurately until it stuck in the queen's left shoulder. The man who challenged her looked at her with fascination; he was the only one left to face her.

"I must admit that it was a wonderful exhibition."

Selena answered by ripping the weapon from her body without uttering a whimper. Then she closed her eyes.

"Don't tell me you're giving up; it will be a pleasure to accompany you to my abode. It doesn't have the luxury of your palace, but I assure you that you won't be cold."

He got up from his stool and walked toward her. He stopped walking.

The queen's hair began to flutter. The blood gushing from the wound began to bubble and then disappeared completely, leaving the skin free of any damage. Within seconds, the tissue also recomposed itself.

Selena opened her eyes.

"You have lost the bet."

She threw the stiletto with strength and saw it go into the knee of her adversary, shattering it. The tall man fell to the ground.

"Come to me, Selva," Selena mentally commanded.

The tall man's gaze was clouded, and threads of sweat ran down his face.

"Come on, bitch, kill me."

"You're not worth it." Selena's face lit up with a smile. "But I think a good friend of mine will like you. Béldar, open the door."

The mage obeyed immediately.

"Selena, your legs are shaking."

"Did anyone ask you? Shut up!"

"Little woman, you don't need to impress me; you're sweating too much. I bet you have a fever. If you want, when we get home, I could massage your body to get you to relax."

The man with the stiletto took advantage of the discussion to walk away from the storm in the form of a woman.

"Shut up! And stop talking to me as if I were a child or as if we were married."

"All right, majestic sovereign. However, in a few seconds, you are going to faint."

"First, I will see him d... die."

In front of Selena's eyes, an infinite number of constellations of stars began to parade.

She heard the echoing of Selva's paws as it approached across the plaza.

"Your friend is here, my Queen."

Selena looked at him with hatred, only to fall down faintly.

"Well, Selva, I think your mistress wanted you to take care of that crawling creature." The panther's muzzle was stained with blood. "Wow, I'm sorry I interrupted your lunch; I hope this one is to your liking."

He reached out his hand to try to pet it. The feline roared and bared its teeth.

"Okay, we're not friends yet."

Selva turned its gaze between the mage and the body of its mistress lying on the floor. It approached the queen without taking its eyes off the sorcerer. The animal roared as it lunged at the fleeing man.

"No, no. Get her off me, please..."

The panther began to eat.

Béldar leaned over Selena and moved away the hair covering her face.

"Well, little woman, you may really need my help now."

The mage took the warrior in his arms, and they disappeared, ignoring the chewing of flesh.

## *18*

The Kingdom of Iluran was fertile. Famous for its large vineyards and productive vegetable and fruit plantations, it had an enviable position: to the north, the Kingdom of Kasnia, so it had a barrier against the northern kingdoms; to the east, the Great Salt Lake, a beautiful surface that rivaled in extension with any sea; Lebassi stood to the south, while the Ocean of Desolation washed its shores to the west.

Omar had explained all this to him as they rode towards the territories of Sabilo the Right-Handed. Now, at last, the great castle stood before them. Whoever the builder was, had excelled in their work. The fortress stood at the edge of the lake. It was constructed with large light-gray blocks. The roofs, almost flat, had a greenish hue, similar to the mold that grew in the dungeons of his own castle. Above the sea, a long breakwater, beside which nearly two dozen fishing vessels were anchored. Fish was another of its many advantages.

Gregor and his entourage entered the village. Hundreds of houses and businesses lined the edge of the castle. The daily routine contrasted with the stories circulating from Lebassi and Tolm.

"Nothing is happening here, Omar," Gregor proclaimed.

"It seems so, Your Majesty."

"Let's go on. Attention, everyone."

Children ran through the streets. Shopkeepers were advertising their wares. It was a normal day.

Winding through streets and alleys, they approached the castle. A beautiful building, a huge stone esplanade patrolled by less than twenty soldiers armed with spears and swords, but no moat, no gates, only a few puny wooden doors. What kind of warrior would not protect his stronghold? The young man began to doubt the old man's sanity. They kept pace directly towards the king's dwelling.

Patrols did not notice them. They were less than fifty paces from the entrance when a trumpet sounded. The doors opened.

Gregor pulled on the reins, slowing down his horse, and motioned for his men to stop.

A beautiful girl came out accompanied by what appeared to be two huge black mastiffs with leathery fur and eyes alight with a yellow glow. The animals had small dark spikes along their backs and showed their long fangs.

"Who are you? What are you looking for here?" she asked.

Gregor found the voice enchanting. The damsel had blonde hair so lustrous that it could rival the sun. Her eyes were large and beautifully almond-shaped. She wore a long vermilion-colored skirt and a white blouse with sleeves folded at her elbows.

"Be cautious, Your Majesty," Omar murmured in his ear.

The boy raised his right hand to clarify that he did not need his advice.

"My name is Gregor, son of King Triar, heir to the throne of Lebassi and regent of the coalition of the four kingdoms. I come to see King Sabilo, the Right-Handed, who fought alongside my great-grandfather, the Peacemaker, for the honor of Lebassi and the southern kingdoms."

The girl, not much older than him, looked at him in amusement. She threw her arms up in the air. The creatures roared, leaving a trail of spittle on the cobblestone.

"Gregor. Archers," warned the captain.

So it was. Not only archers appeared in well-concealed loopholes, but the square's guard was also on the lookout for combat. Surrounded!

"You understand that we can't let any little boy pass just because he says he is the king of everything and everyone. What proof do you have of what you say?"

Damn foul-mouthed girl! He had been sleeping in the open for two weeks. He had fought outlaws and beasts on his pilgrimage from the Iron Mines. And now this! Stupid child. Who did she think she was?

He dismounted. He did not listen, he felt several dozen bows tighten. He walked towards the girl, who did not flinch or back away.

The animals furiously bit the air.

"Your Majesty, be careful!" emphasized Omar.

"Captain," Gregor commented calmly, "if they wanted us dead, we'd be dead by now."

That said, he extended his clenched fist towards the maiden's face so that she could see his ring. Emeralds glittered against the black color of the dragon.

"Where did you buy that trifle? If they charged you more than a dog, they deceived you. Do you think I'm going to let you pass because you have a...?"

"Enough, Agatha!"

A voice boomed from inside the castle. It was followed by an old man with completely black hair who walked leaning on an iron cane with a carved snake from hilt to tip.

The mastiffs backed up and fiddled around the old man. The man stroked both of their heads.

"Easy, easy. Go home!"

The animals ran away.

"I'm sorry, grandpa," the girl apologized.

"We have an important visitor." As the girl lowered her head and stepped back, he continued, "Welcome, Gregor. I am sorry about your mother. I am sorry about your father. What happened in Lebassi is a tragedy."

The old king's condolences touched Gregor's heart. It reminded him of his pain. He held it inside. He could not allow himself to falter.

Then, King Sabilo, who fought alongside his great-grandfather, let go of his cane, which clattered against the ground and hugged him with his one arm. The boy felt tears running down his cheeks. He let himself be overwhelmed by the octogenarian's warmth and appreciation lavished on him.

"Thank you," Gregor muttered.

When the embrace was over, the young man noticed the king's cane and gestured to pick it up.

"No, my King!" objected Sabilo. "I can still do it."

The man began to bend down. Instead of holding the cane, he placed his hand on the ground and placed one knee on the stone.

"Hail King Gregor!" cried the old subject of Lebassi.

Gregor was startled when the soldiers in the square, his own men, and the insolent girl mimicked the gesture of honoring him.

After a few seconds of surprise, he helped the king to his feet.

"Come on, come on, you must be tired. We have a lot to talk about, young Gregor."

## *19*

The gigantic cavern was reached by innumerable tunnels excavated in the rock. Three quarters of the enclosure were covered with water that constantly flowed through the tunnels. The dry area was covered with a thin grass carpet, and the walls were hidden behind a tapestry of vines. Golden light glowed and sprouted from the ceiling, enveloping the atmosphere with a mystical aura.

Sitting at the edge of the pond, Nadia cradled *her new son*, so magnanimously given to her by her *former love.*

"You know, you mean nothing to me. I could throw you in the water, and I wouldn't experience the slightest remorse. You wouldn't protest either, would you? Your first lesson will be to learn how expendable you are.

"The sun does not cease to rise, nor does the wind stop blowing when someone dies. A city may be destroyed, a famine may sweep away thousands of people, but flowers will still grow, and trees will still bear their fruit. No matter how hard you try, you can never stop nature's slow, ponderous advance. That is where our power lies.

"We are only as strong as nature allows us to be; nevertheless, we are as strong as nature if we succeed in becoming one with it, a whole."

The warmth of her words plunged the baby into a deep sleep, close to that which an unborn baby immersed in amniotic fluid can experience. The sorceress continued talking and playing with those virgin neurons.

## *20*

Selena woke up with the smell of the forest tickling her nose. Her shoulder ached terribly. She brought her hand to it, finding a plaster made of leaves and a bluish ointment.

"The wound has been reopened, little woman. You have been greedy and played with fire too soon. You should let me help you. That's why I came."

"Can I stop you from doing anything? You have taken me on an excursion and made me face a party of thieves and murderers for some strange reason."

"Damn it, Selena, you're so blind you can't see it. Stop thinking of me as an enemy or someone you have to show how much you can do. Think, think, use that little head of yours for more than just showing off that beautiful hair. I give you as much time as you need; use it to surprise me with your intellect."

She looked at him defiantly, and her lips mimicked the line of the horizon. She tried to calm the desire to scream at him and slit his throat, to focus on the young mage's words. According to him, everything he did had some meaning. The only thing she realized was that he was wasting her time.

She tried to get up, but thick clouds threatened to cover his mind.

She watched Béldar close his eyes.

"Let me show you," said the young man.

Instantly a root fresh out of the ground caught her right ankle. She moved her leg forcefully, breaking the vegetable chain.

The queen smiled at the mage; she was not as helpless as he thought. He smiled back. This time, Selena found it impossible to count the number of roots that emerged around her and immediately held her. Within seconds she couldn't move. Her smile turned into a grimace of rage, impotence, and hatred, infinite hatred towards that being that never stopped humiliating her.

"Feel, Selena, feel," the mage murmured.

"You feel my hatred and my..."

One of the roots began to squeeze her throat; she was forced to contract her muscles to avoid being deprived of precious oxygen.

"Close your eyes, little woman, close them and feel the touch of the earth, of the grass, of the infinite life."

The pressure on the warrior's neck decreased, and, for once, Selena followed a piece of advice, not an order. She closed her eyes and tried to empty her mind, searching for those sensations that Béldar indicated to her. She felt that she was on the ground, she felt the hard touch of a stone, and she felt the tender blades of grass in her hands.

Feel, feel.

The sun's rays that filtered through the treetops slightly warmed her face. The warmth was pleasant, and she felt she could relax. Images crossed in front of her, memories of her short and hectic life. Again, that immeasurable burning when she stepped on this Earth and breathed this air. Oh, yes, lava licking her body and filling her with life, the warm breeze gliding over her skin for the first time, the black clouds covering the sky. She saw, relived, felt, and enjoyed each of her campaigns pursuing the King of Lebassi. She searched and found doors that held more and more details and continued to rejoice at her experiences. And, back in the forest, she heard the faint twittering of a sparrow, hundreds of yards away; she perceived the crashing of waves beneath the castle, and even conversations from villages miles away reached her. Her fingertips tingled at the touch of the grass. The roots that held her were no longer shackles but mere extensions of the underground through which she began to venture into these domains. She sank into them, seeing with her mind, not with her eyes, and reached so far that she felt the warmth of that incandescent center from which she emerged. The softness and damp smell of the earth enveloped her as she returned to the surface, and there she began to spread out on the grass and climbed the trees, prying like a newborn squirrel. She felt it, by all the gods, she felt it; she felt an incredible force that enveloped every entity, no matter how minuscule. But no, it was not enveloping them; it was inside them forming a single being, a single flame, linked to hundreds more, so many that she found it impossible to imagine a fire so huge and devastating; a fire that was there, at her fingertips, just waiting for an energetic voice to tell it what to do. And Selena knew that she had the right voice to carry out such a task; that was her mission in life, and, even if she had little left, she would devote it to spread her mandate throughout the world, her desires… Her desires? Were they really her desires? Doubts camped in her head, and she felt that link with the earth shatter, leaving her alone again in the forest with the mage. She tried to retain the sensations, but they slipped away like water through her fingers.

When Selena opened her eyes, she was surprised to see that the roots were not imprisoning her. She thought that her visions, to call them something, lasted only a few seconds; however, the sun was quite low and tinged the clouds with a light-orange tone edged with violet. Nevertheless, the spectacle of the sunset seemed puerile compared to what she had just experienced.

"And well, my dear Queen?" said Béldar.

She sat up lightly.

"I felt it, I felt it..." She paused, weighing his words. "I felt it. It was as if every being spoke to me, as if every speck of dust, every branch, every stone told me, communicated their existence to me," the words came rushing out of her mouth, like a little girl telling her father about her encounter with a fawn in the forest, "and shouted how alive they are. Everything, absolutely everything, was there; they reminded me of who I am, where I came from, and what I must do. They showed me the light, the way to go on. And they showed me the strength, the purest energy. You have to teach me; you have to tell me how I can use it. I promise to learn; I promise to obey you in everything you tell me. I will be the most dedicated pupil a teacher can have. And so..."

"So you can get revenge on all my insults once I have shown you how to make your own what you have only been allowed to intuit."

The illusion was erased from Selena's face.

"No, you can't refuse."

Béldar looked at her in amusement:

"And why not?"

"Because you have been sent to help me, and I..."

"You order me? It is funny that, a few moments ago, you were about to beg me; I knew it wouldn't last long. You weren't born to grovel; anyone would notice." Selena watched him perplexed; never had he spoken to her with such frankness in that direction. "You are made of the best dough a mage could wish for, so good that they would not only want to mold it but would envy it for themselves because they know that, no matter how much they control the magic forces in this world, they will always be a million steps behind what you can achieve."

"Béldar, I..."

"No, little woman, let me continue. I know you've always known you were different. No, don't make that face, I know it's quite obvious, but do you really know what you are? There is as much strength, as much power in the flutter of a single one of your eyelashes as in the most furious of cyclones. You are part... you were born of the purest of magic, and when you manage to re-establish that link with it, you will bend the world with your gaze alone." He paused. "And now, are you ready to learn?"

Selena's face was tinged with disbelief and contempt. She turned her back to him sharply.

"Why are you lying to me? Go away. I don't want anything to do with you."

The queen felt the mage's hand on her shoulder; with slight pressure, he invited her to turn around. With her watery green eyes, she faced Béldar again and listened to him:

"I have not lied to you."

"No? Tell me, then, why am I dying? Why?"

It was then that the indomitable warrior known as Selena experienced crying. Salty drops ran down her face, framing her features and giving her a human appearance that she never had before. She was put on this Earth with very few ideas, without a past, without a life, only with one disturbing idea in her head: to destroy Triar. Her father, so to speak, created a powerful entity but, at the same time, empty of personality and history. The few months of her life dragged her into a maelstrom of destruction, death, and desolation. And all this without question, without a doubt, as an unconscious puppet of the strings.

She took refuge in the embrace that Béldar offered her, thinking, for the first time, that she could trust someone; maybe the mage really was sincere to her.

"Selena, Selena," he whispered in her ear, "who told you that you were dying?"

The queen did not answer, as if she did not hear him or did not want to; she only clung tighter to Béldar.

"No, you don't need to talk, little woman. Let me see what worries you."

She felt the mage's caresses between her fiery curls. The gliding of his fingers, soothing her, as a warm presence, entered her head, not as an intruder but as a protective friend concerned for her good. Selena gave him full access to her mind, allowed him to wander through her innermost thoughts, see her most hidden fears, and, as an excellent hostess, took him by the hand through all her memories. Together, they explored her birth, pilgrimage, battles, and thirst for blood and destruction. Deep, deep inside, in her innermost depths, together they found the remains of Shao's manipulation that destroyed her connections with Panameria, that cursed her by depriving her of everything, of almost all of her power.

"Selena, listen to me," said Béldar in a gentle voice, "you are not dying."

She stepped back far enough to look him in the eye without losing the safety of his arms.

"You are under the powerful effects of magic that turns you, little by little, into an ordinary woman. That's why it's hard for you to do what you used to do so easily," he added. Selena looked at him in disbelief. "I assure you, Selena, you are not dying; you are just becoming like any other human being. I know it's not wonderful, but it's not so terrible either. And I can assure you that, with my help, you will soon leave all those inconveniences behind."

"You promise?"

"Yes, little woman, I promise. You know, I'm beginning to like you; I like this new side of you: so fragile and sensitive."

Selena backed away like a cat caught in the middle of a kennel, leaving Béldar hugging the air. Her countenance became as rough as a marble quarry.

"I knew it could not last long. Well, my Queen, do you think we should head for the castle? The night will soon fall, and you may be tired."

Selena was about to answer when the roar of her beloved Selva came from behind her. She turned to her and smiled.

"It's still too early to go back," she said without turning her face to Béldar, "and I'd like to spend the night learning everything you want to teach me."

"It will take us more than one night."

"Then we'd better get started right away."

## *21*

The figure advanced on the loin of a black-winged horse through the shadowy tunnels. It was clad in armor as opaque as a tar pit. The electric gleam of blue eyes could be seen within the helmet.

The horse stopped when it reached a grassy plain overlooking a magnificent pond.

The rider dismounted with a leap, despite the armor, unhooked a leather bag from the saddle, which seemed to contain a good-sized melon, and advanced towards the woman sitting at the edge of the water. He stopped respectfully, only a couple of yards away from her.

"So?" the woman asked him.

The warrior responded by taking a man's head out of the bag. Nadia recognized who once was a mage named Terwa, who as a man was nothing more than a fisherman of the northern seas until a storm caused his ship to dock on the island of the mage Talcris, who took him under his tutelage and gave him, upon his death, his seat on the Council.

"Did you have any problems?"

"No, my Lady. The armor has protected me, and the sword could not be sharper," the man's voice sounded bitter.

"I know you deplore what I command you, but it is the only way. To destroy her, you must first destroy those who support her. Now go and rest."

The man bowed his head and then turned around.

## *22*

Pamela dined alone. The castle seemed immense and empty when Selena was not walking around it, saturating it with her magical aura. She knew the cause: the mage. And the mage was a man, and men could bring no good. He would try to turn Selena against her to make her see that her presence was a hindrance now that she had no child to care for.

She let the remains of her meal rest on the table. She lost her appetite. She headed for her room with a weary step and flames of vengeance engulfing her heart.

Once there, she looked sadly at the crib where her son was not resting. She breathed in the scent of the baby still floating in the air. And she tried, she tried with all her might, to listen to his cry. A tear ran down her left eye, and a sigh squeezed her heart.

Too many memories were accumulating there. She needed to air out the room to remove those ghosts. She opened the windows to allow the night breeze to wander as it pleased. And she saw them, down on the beach. Selva was resting on the sand, and both Selena and the man were looking out to sea.

Pamela could also see a mass of water rising in the shape of a prodigious dragon. It had long wings and legs ending in claws. She expected a breath of fire to burst from its snout at any moment. The creature rose a few yards and then fell to merge back into the ocean.

## *23*

"It was good, quite good."

"How could it have been good if it faded away?" Selena replied angrily.

"Your problem is that you don't know how to pace yourself. I told you how to form a pure water being, and, instead of daring with something small, you thought of trying it with a dragon. Just because you know how to hold a dagger doesn't mean you can defeat a tiger; do you understand me?

Selena frowned but nodded:

"I'm going very fast."

"Yes, little woman. Come on. Try it again, and, this time, make a pigeon for me."

"A pigeon? Pigeons are stupid. I'd better surprise you."

Béldar liked to see the smile on the queen's lips.

"All right, but try not to faint on the sand."

## *24*

The king without a kingdom moved silently inside the hut. He could see the thick snowflakes falling incessantly from the clouds through the panes. He held an oil lamp in his hand to get some light. On the hearth, like cat eyes, a few embers were still glowing.

Triar was determined to find 'something' that would help him get out of there. The old man could promise him heaven and the queen's head, but he was unwilling to wait. It was madness to face the blizzard; of course, it was also madness to remain isolated in that lost place, knowing that a woman ruled his kingdom far away. That face was so stuck in his mind that it was impossible to get it out of his thoughts. Every night, he dreamed the same thing; every night, he saw how his son and his wife died under the sword of that woman, of that woman who was the most primal fruit of his dreams.

It was logical to expect the old man to have some sword hidden among his things. He opened one of the cabinets and began to take out jars filled with strange substances one by one. He stepped back as a sort of winged snake stirred inside one of the containers and fixed its yellow eyes on his.

Triar was about to put everything he had taken back into storage when the front door burst open, and an icy breeze blew into the hut. Flames leaped from the fireplace and lit up the room. The sorcerer's green robe was silhouetted against the black night, and two wolves accompanied him. Two wolves accompanied him. What wolves! They were much larger than normal wolves. The ruler of Lebassi expected lightning bolts to emerge from the old man and turn his existence into ashes.

"What are you doing?"

Triar stood to his full height and faced the mage:

"I'm looking for a way to get out of here; I'm not going to wait any longer."

"You could have asked me. I'm here to help you." However, Shao's face remained stern.

"I want my kingdom back. I need a sword and a horse to get out of here. I know that you are a mage and that you can give me what I ask for. I don't expect you to understand what I feel; I know you are above human emotions. Spending so much time with Égnever was useful..."

"Shut up. You don't know anything about us. You haven't the faintest idea who I am. It was I who sent Égnever to you; it was I who taught him everything he knew." Triar watched as the wolves began to show their teeth. "Who do you think you are to come here and order me around? I could rip your heart out without even extending my hand. You want a sword, and you want a horse? You'll get them, I assure you. I had a good future prepared for you. From now on, you are no longer under my protection."

"I never asked for it."

"Without me, you would have died."

The king did not dare to reply in any way. The mage's eyes gleamed, and he was no one to confront him.

Triar watched Shao approach him, drawing a sword from his robes, so shiny that it hurt his eyes. The hilt was gold and smooth as a mirror.

"Take it. Try to tame it. The last time it tasted blood was two centuries ago."

"Is it a magic sword?" asked Triar as he held it up.

"No, you don't deserve something like that, but it's very tough. A horse is waiting for you outside, and my wolves will escort you until you leave the mountains. From then on, you will be on your own."

"Thank you." Triar bowed his head in front of the sorcerer and fastened the sword to his belt.

"Now leave. I don't want to see you again. By the way, your son is alive, but you will never find him; I have made sure of that."

The king gritted his teeth, restraining his desire to attack the mage.

"That's good," he continued, "it would have been stupid to try to kill me. You would have lasted much less than with Selena."

Triar's boots soon met the snow. He walked without looking back and with his eyes fixed on the brown horse that awaited him, a horse that remained calm despite being accompanied by a dozen wolves.

## *25*

"Tell me about you. How does it feel to know that other people are inferior creatures?"

Selena sat on the sand with her legs tucked up and wrapped by her arms. Her head was resting on her knees, and she was looking at Béldar to her right.

"How did you get the idea to become a mage?"

Béldar picked up a shell and threw it into the water. The ghosts of memory began to dance around him, and some of them stung him with their spears, causing him terrible pain.

"That is boring, little woman, and I don't want you to fall asleep while I'm telling you about it," said Béldar.

"I promise I won't."

The mage observed the gleam in the warrior's eyes and understood that she would not break her promise. She might be tired, she might have fainted twice so far this night, but she would stay awake until he finished his story.

A shooting star left its trail across the sky, and neither of them missed a detail, like two people paying attention to the small miracles of life for the first time in a long time.

Selena stroked the black fur of her panther. The feline had curled up next to her and was sleeping peacefully.

"So?"

"I was born and raised in the town we visited today."

"I knew it. You looked at the fountain in a very particular way, as if you were looking for something in it or hoping to meet someone there."

"Do you want me to tell you or not?" threatened the mage.

"Yes."

"That fountain was the beginning of it all," Béldar said bitterly.

Selena lived up to her promise, and although her eyelids were heavy, she didn't yawn once.

## *26*

Having finished his story, Béldar rose to welcome the sun shining in the distance over the waters.

"I don't understand."

"Little woman, that's the interesting thing about the game; no one knows what's going on in their minds," said Béldar without looking at her.

"Do you think that I could..."

"I don't know; I really don't know. Next to him, I'm like a mouse next to your panther, and I may be falling short."

"But you said I'm pure magic. We could..." and Selena fell silent. The mage faced her with a smile on his lips.

"See, little woman? You're not the same as before. A day ago, you would have given anything to cut my throat, and now, look at you," he pointed at her with his hand, "sitting on the sand listening to stories, like a teenager who has run away from home and wants to postpone punishment as long as possible."

The Queen of Lebassi jumped up and pointed her index finger, ending in a sharp fingernail, at her "master".

"I am me; I will always be me. No one will take away what I have. The Council may be powerful, but no one is like me," Selena exclaimed angrily. "And you will help me sweep all those old men from this land."

Béldar crossed his arms and shook his head negatively a couple of times.

"Maybe that's what Shao is expecting. I could tell you where his abode is, I could even take you there, but then I would have to bury your body under the snow. You are vulnerable, Selena, very vulnerable. Yesterday those men in the tavern could have killed you, so how do you plan to resist the attack of the entire Council? It's impossible, little woman, get that in your head."

The queen closed her eyes. The mage waited.

The tide stopped, and the waters receded to form the body of a gigantic creature. The dragon rose above the sea and spread its wings. It opened its jaws and spat out its fiery breath, hiding the sun's brightness for a few seconds.

"See? I've done it. It only took me one night."

Selena's words caused the huge mass to scatter over the sea as what it was: pure and simple water.

"See, little woman?"

The queen turned her back to him and stormed toward the castle.

## *27*

Béldar stood alone on the beach while Selena returned to the fortress. *"You will be able to get something you want more than anything."* He could not deny that the queen was a fabulous woman. The opportunity Shao gave him could not and should not be wasted. He, a modest mage, had the chance to take as a disciple the greatest creation of Panameria since the time of the Battles of Creation. He dismissed the idea immediately, seeking not to attract the gods' attention.

He turned his mind back to Selena. She wanted to challenge the Council, destroy them, and finish them off, his brothers, or supposed brothers. The mages did nothing but treat each other cordially the few times they met. Some of them lived as ascetics and others as gourmands of earthly pleasures. It could not be said that they were above the rest of the humans; yes, they could be longer-lived and perhaps wiser, but, deep down, and not so deep down, they were no better.

Destroy them! It had been years since he had seen his own master cast any spectacular spells. For all intents and purposes, he could see the mages as forgotten monks who had no power, no ambition... No power, no ambition? If that were not so, power was intrinsic to them. Living in seclusion on mountains or islands didn't reflect much ambition. How old was Shao? How old was his master? And the members of the Council? Rumor had it that Shao was around six hundred years old, that he had been Zerun's apprentice, the first head of the Council of Mages in history.

Why was Shao interested in Selena? Why weaken her? Why send him to train her after casting a spell on her? Why? What was his and the Council's game? Controlling her? Using her power? And if so, what for?

Béldar's mind kept playing with the possibilities. Of course, he was nothing but a pawn, but Selena was a queen, and pawns must sometimes sacrifice themselves for their queens.

It would be impossible to fight against the Council. She was still weak; she had almost been killed in the tavern. And he, with all his doubts, his weaknesses, would he be able to face his mage brothers? No, they wouldn't stand a chance, not even if they used Selena's entire army; after all, they were just men. Besides, was he a military strategist?

Béldar looked at his hands. He formed a pair of fireballs and threw them into the sea. They melted into foam and steam.

Could he? Could he use his magic to attack another of his own? Would he break the mages' code?

He looked up at the tower where Selena had her quarters. *"You will be able to get something you want more than anything."*

If he chose to accompany the queen in her madness, it would be suicide. When the world turned its back on him, he turned his back on the world. Now, sixty years after that, he was still alone. Perhaps it was time to change that, make his mark, or die trying.

Béldar smiled.

# IV
# THE CHRONICLE OF THE ALLIANCE

# 1

Dawn was breaking when Perlion appeared in front of Shao's hut. As always, he wore a gray robe that wrapped his wiry body; his long white hair was loose as a reminder of his youth in the northern kingdoms, those that Gregor the Peacemaker was unable to revolt, thanks in part to him. Mages sometimes did take sides. After Shao, he was the oldest mage, with just over five hundred years of wisdom.

Like the others, he was summoned to discuss the recent threat. Terwa's death was not an accident but an assassination. And not only that, Terwa's departure opened the way for his disciple, Aliana, to ascend. He wished he could agree, but that girl was no more than fifty years old. While Talcris was well known for his sobriety and hermeticism, Terwa was anything but. It was rumored that his island in the north was a microworld of pleasure and that he chose that girl to satisfy his lust. Terwa's death would weaken them doubly if they allowed her to occupy one of the ten chairs.

Without knocking, Perlion opened the door to find that every seat at the table but his own was occupied. Undeterred, he arrived exactly when he was supposed to arrive. He repressed a gesture of disgust at the sight of the new member, just a girl with a rounded face, black hair, and fleshy, the prototype of the vicious Terwa's tastes. The girl, because that's what she was, nibbled her nails to Shao's right. To Shao's right! What was that bastard up to?

"Brothers," he greeted them cordially, "I am glad to see you. Lady Aliana, welcome," he gazed at Shao.

"Welcome, Perlion," Shao exclaimed. "We are all here. We can begin."

Perlion looked around at the rest of the members of the Council. Most of them he had known for over two hundred years. The Council had always had its intrigues because mages loved to play politics more than courtiers, but it was nothing more than silly power games. Something different was happening now. In the last five years, tension had escalated until it culminated in Terwa's murder. His instinct was screaming at him that Shao was responsible for everything.

"What happened to Terwa is very unfortunate, and we trust that Salmur will take care of his soul," Shao said.

Netrés, guardian of the Creation Mountains Pass, lover of wine and good food, let out a chuckle:

"I don't know about Salmur, but, given the stories I've heard about his island, I'm sure Rumlas got his soul." His own witticism made his ruddy face burn even brighter.

An awkward silence settled over the hut as Shao continued:

"As our laws dictate, Lady Aliana takes the place of our fallen brother, and that is why I summoned her to this conclave. Brothers!"

Perlion repressed a smile when Shao rose abruptly from his chair and banged hard on the table.

"We are at war," said the head of the Council.

"Nonsense, Shao," interrupted Lady Cilux, who had her abode in the underwater caverns of the Great Salt Lake. "This is no war. Yes, we all lament it, but surely Terwa was killed by one of his sex slaves who finally rebelled and got tired of being his plaything. We all know that Terwa's powers were rusty; any mortal could have ended his life."

Perlion stared at Cilux. Her statement made perfect sense; however, he agreed with Shao for once.

"It is hard for me to admit it, but Shao is right."

"Thank you, Perlion," Shao said. "You see, there is no doubt. There is a war against us."

"Who is our enemy?" asked Lady Aliana in a whisper.

"My dear, I am glad you asked because that is what we need to find out so we can defend ourselves. That is why I thought that you could be the one to find out as a token of your devotion to the Council."

As Shao took his seat again, Perlion watched the young woman blush and then turn pale, rivaling the snow outside. Mages may have liked to play politics, but Shao was a true master at that game.

"What do you say, *sister?* Will you accept my offer?"

The mages faced the young woman waiting for her response.

"I... I accept," Aliana murmured.

"Well, wonderful, I knew the Council could count on you. However, I know that the rest of my brothers have doubts about your abilities because they have not yet met you. I know about them all too well because of your teacher's good recommendations about you. Therefore, the fairest way to support you in your challenge is for each member of the Council to place their disciple at your disposal. What do you think, brothers? Would you feel more comfortable this way?"

Inwardly, Perlion could only applaud Shao's maneuver. While his intentions remained a mystery, the way he duped Aliana and the Council was brilliant. Having concluded, no, having supported the war theory himself, no one would dare deny the support to safeguard them all from the threat.

"I agree," concluded Perlion. What other choice did he have?

One by one, each member of the Council ratified the decision.

"Brothers, I expect your disciples here in my hut tomorrow at dawn. Lady Aliana, I have prepared a room if you wish to stay here today. Then we can both get to know each other better."

Perlion bowed his head in assent. The other mages imitated him, and, one by one, they left the room to communicate the new mission to their disciples. He took one last look at Shao before stepping into the snow and disappearing.

# 2

When Béldar returned to the castle, he found Selena in the great hall accompanied by Pamela. The former wet nurse was dressed in fatigues. The queen had commissioned one of her captains to train her for combat, and the young woman was making good use of the lessons. The mage was not sure if Pamela's loyalty was real or induced by the magic of the lady of the palace.

"We need to talk," said Béldar.

"Then speak," Selena replied curtly.

"My Queen, I would prefer privacy for what we must discuss," added the mage.

"Nonsense, I trust Pamela unreservedly."

As if on some kind of signal, the jet-haired girl smiled at Béldar.

"As you wish. I will support you in your attack against the Council."

As he said this, Béldar sat down opposite Selena, at the other head of the superb table.

The queen's green eyes lit up, and a smile framed her face.

"Well, but you said it was impossible, a suicide, that I was not ready."

"And you are not, my Queen, but as a former subject of Lebassi, I owe obedience to my sovereign," exclaimed Béldar in amusement.

"Ha, obedience? I know I was almost born yesterday, but I don't buy that story."

Béldar could not suppress a laugh:

"That's why I like you so much, Selena. Like you, I think that I've discovered that I don't want to live under the rules and influences of others anymore. I'm not lying to you, it's not going to be easy, but we can have a chance if we play our cards right."

"You said that the two of us alone could not..."

"And we can't," the mage interrupted her. "We can't do it alone; that's why we need allies."

"I'm listening."

"My master told me a story, a legend, but he swore to me that it was true. Shao was a disciple of the great master Zerun. This great master was feared and revered and was an important pillar during the second half of the Age of Enlightenment, guiding the tribes of men. It was he who established the Council of Mages and who created our rules two thousand years ago. There were mages before him, but there was no organization as there is today. The story goes that Zerun took in two disciples, only he had the power to break the rules: Shao and a woman. It is said that the two fell in love, and upon discovery, Zerun expelled the woman while allowing Shao to continue as his disciple. Shao then inherited the position of head of the Council. My teacher told me that, upon Zerun's death, Shao tried to vindicate her and let her become a mage, but she refused the offer, or, perhaps, refused him."

"And does that help us?" asked Selena, bored of listening to stories of frustrated love affairs.

"Think, Selena, think. If Égnever, Shao's disciple, had the power to create you, can you imagine the power that she, who learned directly from the great master Zerun, may have? Besides, my master told me that, after being banished, she took refuge in the Resandian Lands.

"Resandian? I've never heard of them."

"Of course not. Some people even consider them myths, but Resandians are older than men, elves, or dwarves. They were spawned during the First Age to participate in the Battles of Creation. Once the twins got bored of their "games", Resandians settled south of the lands where the greatest battles were fought, in an area greatly affected by magic, and magic became part of their daily life. They are very different from us because they are not mages but magical creatures. And that mage not only continued to learn with them but also was immersed in the power of that region." Béldar saw that Selena was now paying attention to him. "If we manage to ally ourselves with her, I'm sure we could challenge the Council. What do you think?" finished the mage.

Selena looked at him without blinking. She reached for a bottle of wine and slowly poured herself a glass. After draining its content, she wiped her lips with her sleeve.

"How do we get in touch with her?" asked the queen calmly.

Béldar sighed. He stood up, placing both hands on the table.

"That's the problem: no one knows how."

# *3*

The first thing Netrés saw when he materialized in the dining room of his fortress was the decapitated body of his disciple: Caltros. The young man he had known for about a hundred years was lying on his back on the table while his albino head rested on a silver tray placed on the Council member's seat as if it were a cruel offering. Caltros did not deserve such a thing. He was always a good apprentice, a faithful apprentice. His white hair and pale skin earned him hatred in the village where he lived a century ago. He picked him up, accepted him, and trained him.

The second thing he noticed was the silence. An uncomfortable silence reigned in the room, a silence that made him feel that danger was still latent, waiting for him, hidden in some corner.

"Guards!" he shouted.

Since Shao gave him the responsibility of guarding the Creation Mountains Pass, the best-known overland route to the Kingdom of the Dwarves and the Resandian Lands, he had set up a guard of stone trolls. The trolls could not be called the brightest, but they could be counted on to obey faithfully, and he avoided getting his hands any dirtier than necessary.

No one answered his call. Silence came back to haunt him.

Anyone who saw him may think he was too fond of wine and delicacies. His inflated belly and ungainly jowls may make him look helpless, but Netrés was in the prime of his powers at less than four hundred years old.

"Show yourself!" he ordered.

Silence.

A bead of sweat appeared on his left temple and slowly slid down his cheek. He blinked, and his hands caught fire with a red blaze. This was not the best place for a fight; the dining hall was on the fourth level of his fortress, so his contact with earth was limited. It didn't matter; a mage of his level could absorb energy from mere crumbs of breakfast.

He fired a volley against the doors of the dining room. Cut more than half a century ago, the oak wood exploded into a thousand splinters. Among the reddish magic fire that licked the entrance, Netrés could make out the lifeless bodies of two of his trolls.

"You bastard, show yourself and fight!"

In response, the mage heard a fluttering behind him. He launched another blast towards the windows facing east, towards the Creation Mountains, without thinking twice. The windows and part of the wall disappeared with the magical explosion.

Then, Netrés saw it. A figure, clad in black armor, on the back of a winged horse, also black, surely brought from the Liamen Archipelago, where the dark elves were famous for creating hybrid creatures.

Without wasting a second, the guardian of the pass unleashed another volley on the stranger, certain of thus wiping him from the face of Panameria.

Without flinching, the black knight absorbed the impact of the magical flames.

"You bastard, your armor is made of dwarven steel," Netrés said.

As the only response, the black enemy drew his sword and jumped down from his horse, landing on the dining room floor.

The mage's hands went out. He stretched out his arms, and two spears hanging from the north wall flew towards the stranger, who repelled them with blows of his sword.

Netrés then turned his attention to the floor beneath his feet. The stone began to bubble and melt, dragging the rider down.

As good as his armor was, he was a mage, one of the best mages in all of Panameria. A little dwarven steel was not going to stop his attacks. Now he understood Shao and Perlion's words; they were at war, but the war would end today. Who the hell would it be? Why was he attacking them? Generally speaking, mages were fairly neutral in Panameria; nothing could motivate an attack of these proportions.

He saw with delight that the knight was sunk to his knees. When his hands were imprisoned, he would interrogate him to understand his motives and then bring his life to a happy end.

The warrior raised his arms and held the sword with both hands. Forming an arc, he violently buried the steel in the stone in front of him. The impact caused a loud explosion that destroyed the entire dining room floor.

The attack completely surprised Netrés, who was plunged towards the library between stones and wooden beams. Through the dust, he could see the knight fall gracefully. He found a long splinter of wood piercing his right thigh when he wanted to get up. Putting a hand on it, he made it disappear. Then he put pressure on the wound and cauterized it with the same reddish glow of his first attack. She stood up and faced him:

"Why are you doing this?"

The stranger swiftly lunged at Netrés. As he ran towards the mage, he crossed his hand, holding the sword in front of his chest to strike backward.

Netrés parried the blow with his bare right hand and squeezed the sword until it broke. He smiled at him; it would be a piece of cake to finish him off without his sword. Only a few inches away, hidden inside the helmet, he could appreciate his bright blue eyes, blue eyes that gave him the impression that they were also smiling.

It was then that the mage understood that the attack represented a feint. The stranger's left hand went deep into his chest until it pierced his heart with what he sensed was a cryol dagger.

Netrés, guardian of the Creation Mountains Pass, fell dead in the rubble with a frozen smile on his face.

While the winged horse flew to fetch him, the warrior decapitated Netrés. Then he placed his head in a canvas bag and tied it to the beast's saddlebags. Afterward, rider and mount flew out to the southeast.

## *4*

Perlion felt it instantly. He was sure that the others had sensed it too. No, there was no doubt: they were being hunted one by one. That put pressure on Shao's plan, which put pressure on the Council to find the culprits and stop them. Their disciples were powerful; Lady Aliana could be young, but she would have learned something. The idea was not bad, a group of ten mages was a colossal force, but two members dead in such a short time emphasized the great power of their enemies.

Panameria was extensive; while they searched for those responsible, the rest of the members of the Council would still be in danger. Would they have to summon the rest of the mages? Would it be better to unify forces? He was sure he could defend himself; however, wouldn't Terwa and Netrés have thought the same?

"Megania!" he shouted. His disciple had been with him for a little less than two hundred years. She had only left him for about forty years to roam Panameria and continue learning, but, in the end, she went back "home". He was proud of her and loved her like a daughter.

Perlion had chosen to live in a beautiful enclave on the northern coasts. Unlike Shao, who enjoyed the cold climate of the mountains, he loved the icy sea wind. So he took possession of an old temple dedicated to Salmur and made it a comfortable place to live.

"Master, you called me," Megania greeted as she materialized. She was a beautiful young woman with dark brown hair, which she wore loose at shoulder length. Her olive skin matched her bright black eyes.

"Yes, my daughter. I must tell you something; the Council and I need you."

They both took a seat, and the mage began to tell him everything that had happened.

# 5

Under the sands of the Resandian desert, Nadia could not conceal her joy at seeing that her faithful servant was fulfilling his mission.

She glanced at a pond where a basket made of splendid emerald-green vines was floating. Inside, Magnus, son of Triar and one of Lebassi's heirs, was sleeping.

The sorceress left the area. Her walk took her through several tunnels to a room that glowed with a blue color that inspired tranquility. In the room, a little more than half a dozen small black marble pilasters held dark indigo amphorae made of cryol with wide openings and filled to the brim with what appeared to be water.

The legends said this was the metal with which the twins Salmur and Rumlas armed the colossal creatures that participated in the Battles of Creation. Aside from weapons, Nadia discovered that its properties could be exploited for something else, and for several years the amphorae had allowed her to see and hear in the distance; she only needed to have something from the place she wished to spy.

The sorceress selected the third one on the left and leaned over it while holding the handles with both hands. She closed her eyes, and a kind of electric current ran up her legs until it was transmitted to the metal. Slowly, very slowly, the image of a great hall began to materialize, and the enclosure filled with voices that became more and more familiar to her every day.

"You don't understand what I'm saying, Selena," she heard the young Béldar say.

"Of course I understand," the new queen replied angrily. "You're presenting me with a stupid choice. You intend to ally yourself with a forgotten mage, who might as well be just a legend. And that is your great plan to defeat Shao and the Council."

"My teacher says..."

"Your teacher says... Let's see, what does your good teacher say?" Selena mockingly interrupted him.

The mage's eyes flashed with rage; he clenched his fists, turned, and headed for the stairs.

"Such beautiful lovebirds!" commented Nadia in the distance.

Having said this, she plunged her head into the liquid. Her head was immediately filled with lights and colors, and her ears absorbed a thousand sounds until the distance separating her from Triar's castle was shortened.

The mage appeared floating above Triar's large dining room table like a ghostly apparition. To all intents and purposes, she was not there, but, to anyone else, she was. This way of 'traveling' had proved undetectable because her physical presence never really moved. Her body remained safely tucked away in her beautiful desert.

"I believe you were looking for me," was her greeting as she appeared.

## *6*

Triar calculated noon was near. No sign of the wolves remained, and their descent from the mountain, though complicated, ended smoothly. The eternal snow gave way to the green grass of a gently sloping hillside that ended in a forest full of majestic pines.

He had never traveled that far, he never really went beyond the boundary of the four kingdoms, but he recognized the place from his grandfather's tales. Undoubtedly, he was in the territory of the northern kingdoms, the only lands that Gregor the Peacemaker could not annex. He was sure that no one would recognize him there, but he would need to keep a low profile.

When he was closer to the forest, he could make out a path and smelled a faint odor of burning wood. There had to be a town or village nearby. He and his mount deserved a rest. They had a long way to go until they reached Tolm or Kasnia, the nearest kingdoms.

Once there, he would regroup the surviving troops and launch a counterattack against Selena. That damned witch might have won the first round, but he would bring her down. He would make her pay for what happened to his wife and son. It was all her fault. He looked up to the sky.

"By Salmur, I will not die until I destroy her," cried the king without a kingdom and spurred the equine to make haste.

## *7*

Béldar watched Nadia, or whatever it was, floating in the middle of the room. At the other end of the table, he could see Selena draw her sword and face the apparition.

It couldn't be that simple. It was too easy. A mage who was the stuff of legends appeared in front of them because... Why were they looking for her? And this apparition? The woman looked like a body sculpted from indigo glass. Perhaps, if she had been still, they might have thought she was an ice sculpture, but no, she moved, she spoke, they could see how she breathed. She was the presence, but she was not there.

She watched with amusement in her eyes as a hawk played from the heights with two small mice. He cursed not remembering her name, though he doubted his master ever mentioned it.

"My Lady," Béldar dared to pronounce as he dropped to one knee on the cold ground, "you honor us with your presence. Yes, we were looking for you. We would like to propose something to you."

Then she looked directly at Selena and fixed her gaze on the flaming sword. She hoped the redhead understood that it was not a good idea to threaten a mage, THAT mage.

The figure continued to smile as her feet approached the ground. Béldar stood up and approached her to offer her a chair.

"Thank you, boy, but it's not necessary," Nadia stopped him. "As you understand, my physical body is not here. I heard your call, and I wanted to check that you were trustworthy people."

The mage sighed as Selena sheathed her sword and took a seat at the head of the table.

"We thank you for your presence. Selena and I had in mind to travel to meet you."

"And did you know where to look for me?" Nadia questioned softly.

"No, we..."

"Of course not," the apparition interrupted him. "Few know where my refuge is. Tell me, then, how can I help you?"

"I want to destroy the Council!" Selena shouted, hitting the table so hard that she broke one of the planks.

"I love your enthusiasm. Continue."

"If what Béldar says is true, you are very powerful. I am the daughter of a mage..."

"Égnever," said Nadia.

"Yes, how do you know?"

"Because Égnever worked for me."

"The Council condemned Égnever," said Béldar.

"Yes, for trying to kill Shao, because that was my wish, and Égnever fulfilled all my wishes." Then, Nadia looked directly at Selena. "You may feel that he was your father, but I am your mother. It takes more than a mage locked in a dungeon to give life to someone like you, so perfect, so magnificent, so powerful, or, should I say, such a powerful woman.

"You are my daughter, Selena, my real daughter! You were torn from my womb by my ill-named master when you were not yet born. Your body was destroyed, but I was able to rescue your soul from the very realm of Rumlas. I protected you for centuries until the golden opportunity arose to bring you to life."

Béldar could see the confusion in Selena's eyes. He did not understand what was happening. Looking for an ally, they found Selena's true progenitor, not the one who created through magic but who conceived her in her entrails.

"No one has returned from the Rumlas' domain," muttered Béldar.

"That's right, boy, no one, only me. It took years of study in the Resandian Lands just to find clues on how to descend into that terrible realm. Once inside, it took even more years of fighting and defying the nightmarish creatures that populated it. Until I was finally able to free you," concluded Nadia as she approached and held out her hands to the warrior.

Selena stood up and took the mage's translucent hands.

Béldar suffered a fit of suspicion for a moment, thinking that it was all a trap and that the queen was in danger. However, no attack occurred. On the contrary, the sorceress gently embraced Selena, and, little by little, her true self began to materialize.

No longer an apparition, an entity made of crystal or ice. Nadia was there.

## *8*

Dusk was approaching when Shao watched as Perlion and his disciple materialized and walked towards the door from the window of his hut.

"Welcome," Shao greeted them.

Perlion and Megania bowed their heads and entered in silence.

"Shao, we have to talk," said Perlion.

"Let's sit by the fire."

Shao pointed to wooden armchairs lined with bearskin. The visitors sat down.

"I explained to Megania everything that is happening. We both came to the same conclusion: Selena."

"That can't be. We took care of Selena. We cut her natural connection to magic. She will soon be our puppet, and we will be able to use her for whatever we want."

"Are you sure?"

"Perlion, friend, brother, you collaborated in the spell to cut that perfect bond yourself. Yes, she has power, but she is no match for us. Now, with Béldar, she is just rediscovering how to do carnival tricks."

Shao watched as Perlion nodded. He considered it then; it was too much of a coincidence. He mentally reviewed everything that had been done to him, and there were no doubts left: Selena could not be behind the attacks.

"The mage Terwa, in the north, then the guardian Netrés, in the Creation Mountains Pass. What if it's the dwarves?" Megania dared to bet.

Shao looked at her carefully. The young Megania might not be so misguided.

"The dwarves!" exclaimed Perlion. "It cannot be. What could be the reason? The great matriarch Alsuria the Forger has never had anything against us, and we have never conspired against her; have we, Shao?

Shao sighed.

"Shao! Right?"

"Of course, of course, of course. I give you my word that I have done nothing against them or any other tribes. There is no reason for them to attack us now."

"What about Triar?"

"Impossible. He left the hut just a few hours ago. The last report from my wolves says he is heading east, to some village in your kingdoms. And he was here when Terwa was murdered."

"I have never had a good feeling about the dark elves, but your assessment, Megania, could rule them out. They would have attacked from the west. The Kingdom of Lebassi would have been the most logical point."

"Master, what if that's what they want us to think?"

"No, my daughter, no. These attacks are not an invasion..."

"Perhaps they are a prelude to an invasion," the young mage interrupted him.

For once, Shao was intrigued. That possibility he had not considered.

"Explain yourself, Lady Megania," asked the head of the Council.

"We think they are attacking *us.*"

"That is what they are doing!" said Perlion.

"They are doing it, I know. But let's imagine for a moment that we are not the ultimate goal, and, if we are not the ultimate goal, perhaps we are an obstacle for them to achieve that goal."

"Conquer the human kingdoms," Shao muttered.

"My dear. It makes a lot of sense; it is a possibility. When King Gregor wanted to conquer the northern kingdoms, I took sides and prevented it. If there is a war of conquest going on, we could tip the balance. What do you think, Shao?"

Shao shifted uncomfortably in the armchair. He leaned his torso, resting his elbows on his thighs, and then intertwined his hands and rested his head on them.

"A war of conquest?"

Young Megania would be a worthy successor to Perlion. Shao had tried to find some explanation for these attacks that made sense. He found none plausible enough. Even if it was a bit far-fetched, this option fit quite well for him. Damn dark elves! Why start the attack with Terwa and Netrés? Why? Why?

"Perlion, you have a very wise disciple. Young Megania, you have my respect. Your hypothesis may be the explanation for the evil that stalks us."

"I suggest that we speed up tomorrow's mission this very night. Let's summon the disciples. Let's separate them into two groups to check both places where our brothers perished. Lady Aliana can lead one group and Megania the other. That will buy us time."

"I will also convene the Council today. I will also summon the Council today. Perhaps we should visit the regents of the tribes to..."

"Let them intuit that we know something is happening that may lead them to commit some indiscretion. Very well thought," said Perlion enthusiastically.

The head of the Council glimpsed that his 'brother' was enjoying this discovery; perhaps Triar was not the only one eager to relive past glories. He felt his blood flowing even more strongly. A war of conquest was not in his plans; his idea had always been to convince the mages to take control of the human kingdoms; now, with this saving action on their part, it would be much easier to convince them all that they should be the rulers. There is nothing better than a mage to ensure tranquility, security, well-being, and absolute prosperity. And, of course, as head of the Council, he would be the absolute ruler of the human kingdoms. Then he could think about how to enslave the rest of the tribes.

Shao closed his eyes and contacted his brothers and sisters to call them to the meeting. The Council was decimated but still powerful.

"They are summoned. Let's get ready."

## *9*

The first stars of the night illuminated the Resandian desert. The rider and his mount glimpsed the entrance to the cavern where Nadia had her abode. They descended with alacrity and in complete silence.

The warrior dismounted and led his winged steed to a cave where the greenest grass he had ever seen grew. The noble animal devoted himself to replenishing his strength by grazing and drinking from a small trough.

Holding the canvas bag where Netrés' head rested, the man walked through several tunnels, subtly illuminated by iridescent moss with a faint blue hue. Nadia's errand was done, and he was bringing her the proof she requested. Even if he had not carried the mage's head, he was certain that she would know perfectly well that his life was forfeit.

After a few minutes, he found her. She was coming out of that strange room with vessels.

"My Lady, the head of the mage Netrés."

"Perfect, Cedric."

It was the first time she had called him by name after picking him up when he was dying in the woods.

"Thanks to your services, the Council is getting weaker and weaker. Selena trusts me and has asked me to be her ally in destroying the mages. All the stars are aligned for you and me to get our revenge."

The former queen's captain nodded silently. Memories flew into his mind, images of all the death and destruction. He remembered his wife and daughter. He was in a trance when he saw them die; he did nothing to save them. Now he could only mourn them and follow the designs of the sorceress to put Selena's head in a bag.

"When can I get my revenge?" the words came out with hatred and expectation.

"Soon, soon. You will have to be strong because now we are Selena's 'allies'. You will have to fight by her side, help her achieve victory, and then take your revenge. Will you be able to do it?"

Cedric clenched his fists in anger.

"I can do it."

"Good. Rest. At dawn, we will travel to Lebassi to finalize details with the queen."

Without a word, the man nodded and headed for his quarters. Revenge was near. The moment to make amends for his past and honor his beloved family's memory, everything was approaching. He would have to pretend; he would have to fight alongside the woman who murdered his life. The price could seem very high, a sacrifice he was willing to assume to give peace of mind to his soul. Soon he would bring Selena's down to Rumlas' realm.

## *10*

The king without a kingdom could feel eyes on him. After a couple of hours of riding, late at night, he found a shabby village called Calgranio. In his saddle, he found a pouch with some bronze coins; they didn't have his grandfather's effigy, but he guessed that they would do in these kingdoms. The damned mage thought of everything. He used some coins to rent a room and get himself a miserable meal in a stinking tavern called *The devious dragon*. That surely was what dragon dung smelled like.

Maybe because they didn't know him, maybe because of his southern accent, maybe because of a thousand other things, he felt that everyone was watching him. So, as he raised a mug of beer with his left hand, which tasted like deer piss, he kept his right hand on his sword. He had to be cautious. To him, the northern lands had always seemed like wild wastelands; much to his regret, he now realized that they were not so different from his own kingdoms.

When he put his hand on the hilt, he felt a warm tingle, like a subtle invitation to draw the sword. The mage told him that the blade was not magic; deep down, he hoped that it was and that it would help him destroy Selena.

He took the last sip of his beer. He quickly put the mug down and banged the table loudly as a reflex action. If he thought everyone was looking at him before, now he was sure they were.

The innkeeper, who was busy wiping the bar with a black cloth, gave him an angry look as if reprimanding him for disturbing the peace of such a distinguished establishment. He cursed his indiscretion inwardly, he had to go unnoticed, and he was not succeeding.

"May I join you?"

The sweet voice brought him out of his reverie. Lifting his head, Triar found beautiful gray eyes, light-brown hair, and a well-proportioned body. The woman had left her youth behind, but not her beauty. She wore a brown skirt and a tight white bodice that left little to the imagination.

"Of course," replied the king.

The woman took a seat across from him and leaned on the table to emphasize her generous breasts. Triar found it hard to look her in the eye.

"I don't know you, and I *know* almost everyone around here."

If her tone had been sweet before, now it oozed lasciviousness.

"No, I'm not from here."

"Ah! That doesn't tell me much. Where are you from?"

"From the south."

"Ah! There are lots of places down south. Are you going to make me ask you where you're from all night?"

"No, no, of course not. I am from Tolm."

"Ah! A subject of Lebassi. You're very far from your homeland. What brings you here?"

The woman's breasts were having an effect on Triar, who could barely concentrate on the conversation.

"Uhm, I am a merchant."

"Ah, a merchant! I've never *met* a merchant from Tolm before. And what do you trade?"

"Uhm, wine."

"Ah, wine! I like wine. Would you buy me a glass?"

"Of course."

Before Triar could make any gesture, the innkeeper placed two glasses and a bottle of wine on the table. The woman took the bottle and pulled out the cork with her teeth; then, she spat it on the floor.

"We won't need it," she smiled mischievously.

Triar forgot his mistrust. In that woman's company, he would not arouse suspicion, and he could have some time of peace to help his mind clear of the tragedies of the last few days.

"What's your name, beautiful?"

"Oh, honey, I thought you'd never ask. My name is Paola, at your *complete service.*"

The northern kingdoms were not as uncivilized as he had once imagined. He just hoped they were a bit *wild.*

## *11*

Selena could not fall asleep. At some point, Béldar had told her that mages didn't need to sleep or eat or anything like that. She was just beginning to regain a little control of her powers, although that was not what was troubling her. She had met her mother, the true architect of her life. So, she was the daughter of the two most powerful mages in the world: Nadia and Shao. Did Shao know that she was his daughter? And what did it matter? She still had to finish them all off, especially him. Shao did not fight for Nadia's love and allowed Zerun to snatch her from her mother's womb to send her to the realm of shadows, where a hateful god and a court of evil beings guarded… no, imprisoned souls. Now, she and her mother would claim their revenge.

She got out of bed and started playing with red fireballs that she materialized in her hands and threw through the open door of the tower into the sea. After about ten throws, she began to sweat. She was barely on her twentieth when she couldn't summon any more.

"Damn it! You are weak," she scolded herself.

She focused, and small flames glowed between her fingers. She couldn't materialize the spheres, no matter how hard she tried. The mage had also explained to her that it was easier to use magic when in direct contact with the earth. The magical energy that populated everything *hated* to be separated from Panameria or, at least, far from it.

"Damn it!"

How was she going to fight inside a castle or a palace if that was so? She remembered that it was a matter of concentration and practice; the most experienced mages could draw energy from anything. Training also helped to avoid fatigue. Being a channel through which magic flowed could be exhausting. To think that, in the past, feats used to come out at the snap of a finger.

Her thoughts went back to the Council, to how they took everything from her, leaving her in that shell as just another mortal. No, it would not be like that anymore, and she would see that it was so.

She clenched her right fist tightly until the crimson glow appeared. She felt it grow. She recalled the first time she communed with Panameria and freed her mind of thoughts and emotions. She let the energy flow, let it grow, and channeled it. She reached out her hand to release it and blew up a large part of the outer wall.

"Good!" she congratulated herself.

She felt something warm gushing from her nose. She brought her fingers to it to discover a trickle of blood leaking from her left nostril as a reminder that she was not yet ready.

Just as she was about to curse again, there was a knock at her door.

Who could it be at this hour? Surely Pamela was worried about the explosion and the fireballs and came to see what would have happened. She wiped her fingers on her nightgown and approached the door. She thought about opening it with magic; better not take any chances.

Upon opening, she was surprised to find Béldar.

"My Queen, I was fascinated by the shooting-star show, and it suddenly stopped. Are you all right?" he asked with a sarcastic smile on his face.

"I was practicing. You don't have to make fun every time something doesn't work out for me."

"I would never dare to make fun of you."

"Come in and help me; you may be useful."

"You know I am at your service."

Selena loved the glow of the fire. Even though the night was not cold, she had the hearth lit with thick oak logs. The dance of the fire mesmerized her and helped her relax.

"Sit with me, Béldar."

She guided him, and they sat on the bearskin spread out in front of the fireplace.

"What do you think of Nadia?" asked the queen suddenly.

"What do I think about what?"

"About the alliance, her help against the Council, and her being my mother."

Selena gathered her legs and hugged them. She bowed her head on her knees and looked expectantly at Béldar.

"I don't know. Sometimes it seems too perfect. We wanted her help, and she showed up. Égnever worked for her. And, besides, she's your mother. A mother who fought fiercely against Rumlas and his army to rescue your soul. That may be hard to believe."

"What do we do?"

"It may be hard to believe," Béldar repeated. "We have no choice. We can't do it alone. If what she says is not true, at least we will get support to attack the council."

"And then?"

"And then we'll see. All in good time, little woman."

Selena sighed. It was hard for her to admit, but she liked it when he called her 'little woman'. She didn't know if it was because of the Council's spell or why, but her desire for blood or destruction had been decreasing for a few days now. Perhaps it had to do with Triar's death or her having fulfilled her purpose, the only purpose for which she was created... Created? She was conceived as the fruit of a love affair between two aspiring mages. She was destroyed before she was born. She was rescued, and a lava body was formed for her. All very convenient, all very calculated.

"What are you thinking about?"

Béldar's question brought her out of her reverie.

"Nothing. It's nice to be here with you."

"Nice? My Queen, you seem to be getting soft."

The queen lifted her torso suddenly and raised her right arm as a red flare enveloped her hand. She hurled her fist in a fury at the mage's face. Finally, she was going to make him pay for all his insolence.

Selena could feel the power in her hand. Time seemed to pass very slowly, allowing her to appreciate a million details. The mage smiled in amusement. She listened to the crackling of the fire. The roar of the sea reached her ears as it crashed against the castle's foundations. Distant murmurs of soldiers camped on the outskirts of the village. She felt it. She was in perfect harmony with all of Panameria. She would harm him so that they would settle the score, and he would see, at last, that she was up for the feat before them.

It was then, in that magical synchronization, that she saw Béldar's quick gesture. The palm of the mage's left hand moved swiftly, enveloping her fist, absorbing the energy. The impact was greater than expected; Selena managed to invoke a lot of power and made Béldar lose his balance. Both rolled on the bearskin struggling to gain control. They knocked over one of the tables, and a bottle of wine crashed onto the stone floor, soaking everything with nectar distilled in the vineyards of Iluran.

The fight went on for several more seconds. Selena was determined to defeat him. She managed to free herself from the initial grip; she tightened her grip on the mage's wrists, pinning them to the floor, stopping him from turning and straddling the man. Now, he was helpless, at her mercy.

"I beat you!" she exclaimed, victorious and radiant with happiness. "I finally beat you. You'll pay for this."

"As you wish, my Queen."

Selena watched him closely. The hood did not cover him. His black hair was in disarray, covering part of his forehead. His gray eyes sparkled with amusement. His smile remained resplendent. She focused again, and both hands were flooded with crimson energy. She was sure that if she let go of her prey, it would scramble and strike back. She spread the flames across her arms, reaching out to embrace them completely. She was born of lava; she could withstand all the heat. She was sure he couldn't. She would only burn him a little to teach him a lesson and show him that she was Selena.

Why was he still smiling? He should be suffering from some kind of burn. No bead of sweat appeared on his peaceful face, and she felt that she would soon lose her grip on the flames.

"My Queen, now that you have burned our clothes, what do you intend to do?"

The comment completely broke Selena's concentration and made the flames disappear. Instantly, Béldar raised his head and kissed her. She felt the warmth of the mage's lips, felt the taste of his mouth, his scent. She pulled back, thinking of escaping from him. No one had ever kissed her, no one. A strange sensation ran through her. Her heart raced. Her mouth parted, and she let herself fall softly on top of him, seeking his lips, and allowed desire to flood her for the first time.

## *12*

"Brothers. The war has claimed another victim. As you know, Netrés and his disciple were murdered today. Perlion and I have discussed the matter, and we have an idea of what may be going on. One of the tribes wants to conquer the human kingdoms, so they intend to eliminate us first.

"We have always been wary of the dark elves, but the attack on Netrés makes the pass through the Creation Mountains vulnerable, so it could also be the dwarf tribe. We must advance the missions and reinforce the mountain pass."

Shao paused to take a breath and look at them all. They were only nine now at the table for ten, and one of them was just a girl. They had no time to name a successor to Netrés; the Council and the mages' survival was more important. Lady Megania had been allowed to sit behind her master out of courtesy.

"Lady Cilux," he continued, "I need you and Égredor to guard the pass. We can't risk an invasion."

"Understood," agreed Lady Cilux.

"Lady Aliana and the first group of disciples will accompany you."

"It's not necessary," replied the mage. "Égredor and I can take care of checking if there are..."

"NO!" Shao exclaimed authoritatively. "The passage is now vulnerable. I trust… we trust you to protect us."

Lady Cilux nodded silently.

"Lady Megania will go with the other group to Terwa's abode. Hopefully, one of them will find something to help us identify the threat."

The head of the Council had his doubts about what they might find. The attacks would have to have been planned well in advance. They would have left nothing to chance. They had to exhaust their options and prepare for battle.

"Anything else?" asked Landros, who lived in the easternmost part of Lebassi, very close to the Creation Mountains.

"Yes. We must visit the leaders of the tribes."

The table was filled with murmurs.

"Brothers," this time, Perlion intervened, "We must let them know that we suspect them as subtly and forcefully as possible."

"Who will go?" Landros asked.

"You and Perlion will visit Lord Ak Ma Tion. Lady Fergissa and Lady Odalia will contact the great matriarch Alsuria the Forger. I will visit Selena."

"Selena?" exclaimed Perlion, doubtful. "We have already discussed that she is not behind this."

"No, but her power can be of great help to us if we come to war. The magic of the dark elves rivals ours, and the dwarven weapons make them invulnerable to our spells."

"Maybe, maybe," agreed the mage with the long white hair.

"Will someone visit the Resandians?" suggested Lady Fergissa.

"No, I don't want to talk to those assassins. They live isolated from Panameria; they are just hired killers who offer themselves to the highest bidder. We will leave at dawn. The others will remain in my cabin. Needless to say, they must be alert.

"Should we warn the human kings?" questioned Landros.

"Not yet. We are still the target if it's as we believe," Shao said.

## *13*

The sun's rays entering through the destroyed wall awakened Béldar. Next to him, Selena slept. He did not remember when they had left the bearskin to settle on the huge bed. He smiled indulgently, reveling in the queen's scent. He would remember their first union forever, though that *forever* might be short-lived considering they would soon face the Council of Mages.

He took the opportunity to stroke Selena's forehead and leaned over her for a kiss.

"Good morning, my Queen."

He watched her wake up and snuggle up next to him.

"You don't expect me to start calling you my King, do you?"

Béldar could not suppress a loud laugh.

"Of course not. You can even try to kill me from time to time."

Now it was Selena who laughed.

"What if I succeed?"

"You are the queen; no one would do anything to you."

"But I would lose you, and I would have to fight Rumlas himself to get you back."

"I'm sure you could beat him; it runs in your family."

"Do you really think she...?"

"No, I don't know yet. Let's wait and see how events unfold."

"You keep waiting. I'm going to get ready; my *mother* is coming at dawn."

Béldar watched her get up. He delighted in her exquisite, shapely form as she dressed. He reminisced about every moment of the night. He dared to fantasize about running away with her, forgetting about this madness, and growing old together until the end of time. He knew that would not happen. He pledged his word to Selena and would honor that promise, and she would not cease until she accomplished her goal or perished trying.

He wrapped himself in the white sheets and transmuted them into a black robe very similar to the one Selena had evaporated in the night.

"I am ready."

"Let's go downstairs," Selena smiled at him.

## *14*

Selena saw that Nadia was true to her word in the dining room. The mage was seated at the head of the table, and standing beside her stood the superb figure of a tall knight clad in black armor from head to toe.

"Good morning, Selena," greeted Nadia.

"Good morning, Nadia."

She never said someone would accompany her. Who would it be? Why did a mage like her need an armed warrior?

"Sit down, daughter. I see the concern on your face. You are probably wondering who is with me."

"That's right."

"He is a faithful friend who has helped me annihilate two members of the Council."

"Impossible!" exclaimed Béldar.

"Impossible? My young mage, you underestimate my power and the power of determination. Killing two mages is easy. Killing the rest will be difficult. I'm sure Shao must have activated some plan to protect himself or track the assassins. The surprise factor is gone. That's why we must plan our next moves precisely."

Selena then realized that Nadia was a worthy ally, and, with her by her side, they would have a good chance of achieving their goal.

"Come closer," Nadia invited them.

The mage moved her hands on the table, and a map of the human kingdoms appeared. The mountains and forests, even the various cities and castles, were clearly visible.

"We have three targets to attack simultaneously: Shao, Perlion, and Lady Cilux. They are the most powerful members of the..."

The queen watched as Nadia made the map disappear and turned to the right. She looked in that direction and saw it. Shao had just appeared in the dining room and was glaring at them.

"Conspiring against the Council. You will pay dearly for this treason."

"Cedric, attack!" ordered Nadia.

Cedric! That damned traitor was Nadia's ally. The mage had a lot of explaining to do.

The warrior tried to jump towards the old mage when chains imprisoned his legs.

"I smell dwarven steel from here. Is this how you defeated your brothers?"

"They are not my brothers," spat Nadia.

"And I am not..."

"You are nothing to me, only a coward who allowed our daughter to die. Our daughter that I have recovered," said Nadia pointing to Selena.

"Lies. No one can..."

"I CAN!"

Selena could feel the ground shudder. Her *mother's* feet hovered over what looked like a melted gray rock, and she saw Nadia's hands charge with white energy. The discharge destroyed the entire wing of the castle it impacted.

"He escaped," Nadia lamented. "Not only that, now they know our plans. We must act fast."

"Wait! What is Cedric doing with you? That traitor ran away from here and wanted to kill me."

"Sometimes alliances make strange bedfellows, don't they? "

"That's not an answer!" said Selena.

"What answer do you expect, my daughter? That I am not omnipotent? That I need help to carry out my plans? That I will seek to ally myself with whomever I deem necessary to achieve our goals? Are those answers good for you?"

Selena extended both hands towards Cedric. The warrior was still chained and would be easy prey for her magic. She focused her powers on the tips of her fingers, creating light crimson tendrils approaching the man. A fireball would be too quick a death; she wanted to see him suffer and writhe in pain.

"Stop," interrupted Béldar. "It's no use fighting among ourselves. Selena, I beg you, stop your attack."

The queen heard him and kept on. The tendrils continued to approach Cedric. They would penetrate his veins, run through his entire body, paralyze his heart, and tear at his every fiber.

"My Queen, please, I beg you."

The mage's hand rested on hers, squeezing it gently. She turned to look at him and saw the pleas reflected in his gray eyes. She would wait. She ceased her attack and faced her *mother* angrily.

"Strange bedfellows, daughter, strange bedfellows," Nadia repeated.

## *15*

"It's Nadia! Damn witch," Shao communicated to the rest of the mages. "There is no war of conquest. Your disciple has wasted valuable time, Perlion."

He gathered them all together again. He glared at Perlion and cursed himself for agreeing to the idea.

"Fortunately, we already know who our enemy is: your beloved girlfriend. I still remember when you wanted us to accept her in the Council, and she despised you," exclaimed Perlion angrily.

"Shut up. We don't know what their next steps will be. We must attack Lebassi."

"You're crazy!" interrupted Lady Cilux. "Nadia has Selena's backing and her army. We are not enough."

"Lady Cilux is right," Landros said. "We need an army."

"The northern kingdoms," Perlion said. "I can convince them."

"Their leaders are weak; they won't be able to lead them," Shao commented.

"Let us grant the king his wish," Lady Fergissa smiled.

Silence reigned at the table upon hearing those words. Shao looked at her carefully. Fergissa was a young witch of barely two hundred years who had been in the Council for little more than fifty years. She had slanted eyes, pale skin, and an enigmatic cerulean hue on her hair as if she wanted to stand out from everyone else. She dwelt in the very Iron Mountains in Lebassi. Shao admired her intelligence and listened to her the few times she spoke.

"Triar will not accept," concluded the head of the Council.

"Nonsense. You underestimate the king's lust for revenge. Nadia is holding his son prisoner, has taken control of Lebassi and will use Selena to conquer all human lands and then all Panameria."

"We don't know..."

"He doesn't know either. You just have to convince him and, if necessary, beg him."

"Beg him? The head of the Council…"

"The head of the Council has never been in a situation like this before," Perlion interjected. "The whole Council is in danger. We will all support you, Shao."

Shao put his fingers to his temples, massaging them in circles to appease his thoughts. An army of humans and mages led by a king with a lust for glory; a king who could unify the missing kingdoms; a king he could manipulate and through whom he could rule as absolute sovereign.

He watched as Lady Fergissa searched through her clothes for something.

"I have something that can serve as an offering to the king." A broad-bladed sword in shades of violet with a black steel hilt gleamed. "The last sword wielded by Salmur, forged by Nobulka himself."

Shao marveled. Lady Fergissa was a true master. Give a king the sword of a god. Who could refuse such a thing? No one. Triar would see his deepest wish fulfilled. With his tenacity, the sword, and the best mages in Panameria, victory could not resist them. Nadia, the traitor, would pay for it. To think that he once loved her filled him with disappointment. She hated him for not intervening when Zerun discovered them. She hated him for not defending her and preventing her master from ripping the child from her womb. She hated him.

"It will be done as you wish," Shao said.

# *16*

The sun was high when Triar woke up. The woman, Paola, was still sleeping beside him. He remembered the night and part of the dawn. He was pleased to have his full strength back. When the woman questioned him about the recent scars on his chest, he lied about a bandit raid last month.

He sought the warmth of the female under the sheets. He thought the payment had to include some extra morning service. She didn't refuse and wrapped her arms around him. This was how all awakenings should be. That's how they were with his beautiful Katrina... That's how they were. The image of his dead wife took over his mind: his wife, who must have suffered under Selena's sword. Now he was betraying her memory by sleeping with a common harlot in a tattered town. Where were his honor and pride? His son was lost somewhere. That damned mage told him he would never find him. He didn't know how much determination he could show. First, he would finish off Selena, then beat the prince's location out of the old man in the green robe.

He turned down the woman, who also did not protest too much.

"Get dressed and leave. I must leave."

"Ah, they're all the same. Once they get what they want, they throw you away."

Triar watched her rise shamelessly, giving him a glimpse of her generous flesh. The king had to suppress his desire to throw her on the bed and possess her again.

Without turning her back to him, Paola dressed, delaying deliberately. Once she had put on the last of her clothes, she turned around and headed for the door.

"It was already paid for, so it's your loss," she commented, slamming the door.

Left alone, he stood up and wielded the sword with the golden hilt. He stretched out his arm, admiring the length of the blade. It was undoubtedly good steel. Forged with exquisite simplicity. The edge without a nick.

"Have you finished admiring it?"

With a bold gesture, Triar turned towards the voice source to find Shao wearing his usual green robe with the hood covering his head.

"We have not been formally introduced," he said as he uncovered his head. "My name is Shao. I am the head of the Council of Mages of Panameria, and I come to you with a proposal."

The king looked at him sternly, showing the loathing he felt for his supposed savior.

"I prefer to talk to you when you are more presentable. I'll wait for you at the tavern," he added as his body dissolved in wisps of green smoke.

Proposal? Council of Mages? They were up to something. His departure from the old man's cabin was not on good terms, and, only a few hours later, he was looking for him to offer him something. No doubt all those old men were devious and kept a thousand

and one secrets. His grandfather never told him about a Council of Mages. He did tell him that, during his northern campaigns, mages conspired against him, siding with his enemies. It was no coincidence that he was currently in the lands denied to Gregor the Peacemaker. Surely, they would have their settlement and plot against his kingdoms here. He opened the doors for them himself by accepting Égnever and letting him work on his 'wish'.

A feeling of anguish overwhelmed him. Should he run away? Turn his back on this Shao? He immediately dismissed that possibility. The powers of magic surpassed his skill with a sword, of that he was certain. Trying to flee was futile. Trying to attack was suicide. He had no choice but to listen to the damned mage's *proposal.*

He angrily grabbed his clothes and proceeded to get dressed. He girded his belt and placed his sword in the perfect position to quickly unsheathe it. If anything happened, he would be ready. He would put up a fight. He buttoned the cloak around his neck and left the room.

As he stepped out into the hallway on the second floor, his warrior's sense of smell warned him to be careful. The room he had rented was near the staircase leading down to the tavern. The night before, the revelry that could be heard almost prevented him from concentrating on Paola. Now, absolute silence reigned. It was not normal. He proceeded cautiously, slowly descending the steps without taking his hand off the hilt of his sword.

The tavern was not empty. The barkeeper was there with several early drunks, and two or three tables had diners. The beautiful silhouette of his nightly partner was silhouetted against the door.

Everyone was still, transfixed. He drew his steel. Then he saw him. The mage occupied one of the tables in the back. On it, there were two burnished silver goblets and a bottle with a golden liquid inside. He guessed it was mead. The drink was not to his liking because of its sweet taste and the little alcohol it contained.

"Come with me, Triar. Let's drink," greeted the old man as he poured glasses of the liquid.

The king sat down at the table and took one of the glasses.

"Let's drink," added the mage with an enigmatic smile on his face.

"Why?"

"For an alliance that will last for centuries."

They both drank. Yes, it was mead. He detected the taste of bee nectar. The sweetness was tempered by a high alcohol content that warmed his throat and whole body.

"It's from my personal stash. Do you like it?"

"It's good and kicks like a crazy mule. Tell me your proposal."

## *17*

In her hundred years as a matriarch, Alsuria the Forger never received human mages. Men did not meddle in her affairs except to trade, and she did her own thing; if gold changed hands, she had no problem selling items to other races. That morning was different. Only a few minutes after her breakfast, two mages visited her; as a gesture of courtesy, they said, and to warn her that someone was murdering mages, but she should not worry, as this threat should not affect dwarven lands. Courtesy! The two women kept looking in all directions as if searching for something. They were also looking worriedly at her double ax; she wasn't sure if they were struck because a huge diamond-shaped dagger topped it or because it was made entirely of cryol. She did listen to them out of politeness, not because she was interested in the intrigues of sorcerers. She also listened to them because they amused her. Human mages thought they were the best. Today's retinue was nothing more than a desperate gesture to pry information out of her. She listened to them. She wished them luck. She even promised to let them know if she heard anything suspicious. They thanked her. Once they left, she called her most trusted advisor.

The Forging Hall was made entirely of gold with a circular structure. The throne of Alsuria attested to the might of the dwarves. It was a great work of art with a high back and seat lined with white bearskin. Following the contour of the circumference, nine more seats for the four generals and the five holy mothers. The floor was a huge mosaic made with an infinity of precious stones where a mythical scene of the Battles of Creation was recreated: Salmur, the light twin, and Rumlas, the darkness twin, fighting with their armies of creatures.

The elderly counselor entered the hall at a slow pace. Alsuria smiled warmly at her and urged her to sit on the throne so that she would be comfortable. The old woman greeted her by placing a calloused hand on her cheek and stroking her smooth beard.

"Tell me, mother, who is killing the mages?"

# 18

The afternoon was waning as Béldar rode alongside Selena. Behind them, Cedric followed. They left the castle around noon to visit their army's camp. The horses kept a smooth trot, and it should not take more than half an hour to arrive.

The mage wanted to think that the plan would go well. After Shao meddled, everything was rushed. Tomorrow they would start the campaign to destroy the Council. They did not yet know where they would ride to. Nadia assured them that she would reach the final objective tonight and finish sharing the details with them. He knew the sorceress had something up her sleeve; the attack could not be that simple. She vanished the moment she finished with the explanation. She had issues to solve, she told them.

He turned to look at Cedric. The former captain wore a serious expression, and his eyes glittered with hatred. Another ally he didn't quite trust.

He heard a fourth horse approaching them. The rider must have spurred hard to catch up with them. Pamela's graceful figure stood to Selena's left, but not before giving Cedric a spiteful glance.

Fabulous! The team was now complete: the exiled traitor, the scorned wet nurse, the daughter rescued from hell, and the mage in love with the lava woman. In the distance, a nest of vipers with fangs in the shape of magic. What more could one ask for? He forgot someone else: the self-sacrificing mother, destroyer of gods. He was dying to hear the songs bards would compose about their heroic deeds.

He saw the tents. A group of soldiers gathered from various kingdoms. During her advance toward Lebassi, Selena added more and more men to her army. No matter what age, no matter what creed, it only mattered that they were fit to fight, and even that was a contemptible requirement.

The commotion of the troop ceased when they saw the queen approach. Selena's four captains came out to greet her and kneeled on the ground to show their loyalty. Béldar was not sure how much control the queen maintained over her men. He could attest that this army would follow her to the end.

"Stand up," Selena greeted them.

All four did so and bowed their heads to the warrior.

From his horse, the mage could see a large number of tents. The smell of filthy beast hit his nose. What struck him most was the stillness that reigned on the esplanade. Every man was watching the red-haired sovereign. Terrified or anxious, he could not tell.

"Your Majesty. Two thousand soldiers at your service and ready for combat," reported Roland, the first captain in charge of the army.

Béldar and the rest of the entourage dismounted. He stood to Selena's right and the other two to her left. He noticed a gesture of disgust from Pamela for having Cedric at her side.

He watched as the queen advanced toward her men. The woman reached to her waist for the hilt and drew her sword. She raised it above her head, pointing it at the sun, a red flare engulfed it, and a crimson flash of lightning pierced the air, accompanied by a roar.

"The battle awaits us!" she exclaimed as thunder.

The cry of the army, two thousand throats turned into one: "For Selena".

That was how it all began. Nadia promised them that they would overthrow the Council and eradicate any mage who opposed them tomorrow. The task was difficult. No matter how unversed, any mage could put a dozen men in check. Trying to imagine what a member of the Council could do was beyond his imagination. Two thousand men would help as a distraction. Would they be enough? Tomorrow they would know.

Selena turned her back to her battalions and walked the short distance to her horse.

Before she mounted, Béldar sensed something. The queen was walking on the muddy ground, resulting from rains or who knows what liquid. Her boots were spotless. Although mud splashed her, it was instantly repelled.

Inwardly, the mage smiled. It was a good sign.

## *19*

The king without a kingdom was pleased, very pleased. The mage gave him a generous gift: the Nobulka sword. Legend had it that Nobulka was the most gifted of Salmur's blacksmiths. The god commissioned him a weapon, and the vassal devoted himself with care to what would be his last creation. Forged in cryol, Nobulka knew that only a sacrifice would make the power of the metal extreme. As a last gesture, he thrust the weapon into his chest until it pierced his heart, tempering the blade with flesh, blood, and soul, a soul that imbued the sword and strengthened the inner grain.

The sorcerer also made him a promise: his son's freedom. He assured him that the child was resting in a safe place and, if he fulfilled his duty, he would give him back to him. Shao stretched out his hand and shook his as a seal of the oath. Triar could feel a tingling in his palm. When he looked at it, an emerald-colored letter S glittered. "Symbol that my word is pledged," the mage told him.

Finally, as he could not do it alone, he offered him the armies of the north. The training of the soldiers left much to be desired. A leader was what they needed. He could be one. He would be one.

The sword, the soldiers, his son, all in exchange for something he would have done for free: wiping Selena and all her allies off the face of Panameria.

Yes, he was pleased. And now he was here, in the castle of King Aremis, accompanied by him and King Ivanivok. Aremis was a decrepit old man who might as well have fought against his grandfather and who could not stop coughing. Ivanivok, on the other hand, had inherited the throne only three months ago; he must have been half his age, and, although he had the muscles of a sickly sparrow, his gaze was intelligent and penetrating.

The three of them sat in the war hall, which might as well have been a sewing room in the castle, discussing the battle. Shao and another long-haired mage watched them without saying a word.

"I've had it!" Triar spat. He masterfully unsheathed Nobulka and hit the thick walnut table, splitting it in half.

He focused his anger on the elder Aremis.

"You are a weak king. A nuisance. Your battle plans are a joke."

He watched the sorcerers for a second, thinking they would intervene. Perhaps he had gone too far. None of them made any gesture to stop him. On the contrary, he thought he detected a nod from Shao.

He tightened his grip on the hilt and threw a blow against Aremis' neck. The royal throat offered less resistance than the wood, and the sovereign's head rolled to the ground.

"I claim this castle and this kingdom. Any objections?" he asked in a mocking tone to the young king.

The monarch of the Kingdom of Glastia stared at him and then bowed his head.

"None, Your Majesty. What plan do you have in mind?"

"Perfect. Now listen to me."

He had the weapon of a god, a new kingdom, an army of soldiers, and a solid alliance with the mages. The actions to achieve his desire and purpose were in his own hands. Selena would succumb at his feet. He would reclaim his kingdom and annex the northern kingdoms, the same denied to his grandfather. He would not appoint kings as his grandfather did. He would be the only king, and his son would succeed him upon his death if he ever died. As he wielded the blade, he felt his strength renewed; a sense of invincibility swept through him, intoxicating him with power. Today Triar the Conqueror was born to bring a new era to Panameria.

Yes, he was pleased.

# V
# THE CHRONICLE OF WAR

# *1*

Selena watched her mother seated at the other end from the head of the table. The table was set with several platters of roasted deer and wild boar. Several platters of boiled potatoes and chard completed the garnish. Glasses overflowed with red wine. On the hearth, thick logs warmed the room.

To her right sat Béldar and, to her left, the traitor Cedric. Pamela, standing behind her, stared, with what she imagined was hatred, at her former love.

"You know that neither you, nor I, nor that young man, need to eat, don't you?" commented Nadia.

"Yes, *mother,* I know."

The fiery-haired warrior kept her gaze fixed on the one who claimed to be her mother, who said she descended to hell to rescue her soul and then, centuries later, breathed life into a body created from Panameria's own entrails.

"I perceive a certain... anger, my daughter."

This alliance couldn't have started any worse. Allying with a powerful mage appeared to be a good plan, but when she brought in the biggest traitor, she couldn't help but think that something else was hidden under all these plans.

"Not at all. It's just anxiety about tomorrow's attack."

It also didn't help that her ally had materialized about a hundred Resandian assassins just outside the castle less than an hour ago. She was with Béldar when they appeared. She had never heard of them; it was he who told her. Of the four tribes, the Resandians were the only ones who fought in the Battles of Creation. According to the legends, since then, they lived south of where the battles were fought in a barren and inhospitable land, a great desert. Trade routes did not reach that place. The myths about the Resandians gave them a great magical prowess innate in them. They lived in small settlements on the sands. A life of sacrifice and resignation. They were famous for their assassins, able to move at will through Panameria and infallible when attacking. That was the force that now joined the alliance.

"Tell me, Selena, what are you worried about then?"

Trust! There had to be trust for an alliance to prosper. What would Nadia's next move be? Allying with the Council? Bringing their own heads in bags like Cedric's executioner did with two mages? There was no trust here or anything like it. She told her that alliances also created strange bedfellows.

Selena sighed.

Alliances were also coming to an end, and she would end this one herself if something else did not please her.

"Nothing, *mother,* I'm only thinking about tomorrow's attack. I am worried about dividing the forces into two fronts."

"You must not worry about that. We will leave at dawn. I feel that, before the end of the day, we will have destroyed the Council."

"What about Triar?"

"Triar will fall by your sword. We have already discussed that. He was the vehicle to allow me to bring you back; your fates, in a way, are linked. You must end his bloodline and rise as ruler of the human tribes," the mage said.

"And that is my fate."

"Daughter of magic, daughter of the Earth, lady and mistress of this world. Then, when men are molded under your rule, the tribes of the dwarves and dark elves will fall. Panameria will be our... your playground."

"What about the Resandians?" Selena asked.

"The Resandians are faithful friends and magnificent instruments of destruction. To rule their nomadic tribe brings neither power nor glory. They are simple creatures that do not hinder, but they can unbalance. Believe me; it is better to keep them calm and on our side."

"What did you promise them to help us?"

"Peace, I promised them peace."

"Just peace?"

"Peace and all of eastern Panameria, the lands of the Battles of Creation and the dwarven realm. They welcomed me into their domain when Zerun banished me. I am grateful to them for allowing me to live and learn with them. With this, I reward them for their kindness."

Selena let out a loud laugh.

"Ha, ha, ha. Kindness! Half the world because they took you in."

"Yes, half the world, but not because they asked for it. I am going to give it to them."

"And what are those assassins going to do with all that land?"

"The same as today: nothing. Just living in peace, honoring their ancestors, and living in harmony with Panameria."

"Peace? Harmony? I see no peace or harmony in mythical assassins used by kings and mages."

"Because you are blind, my child, blind. Resandians may look like criminals for hire, but they only accept an assignment if they see a benefit to them."

"But they are murderers!"

"Yes, they are, like you and me, like your dear mage and the one you call a traitor, but with an honor that transcends centuries and an existence of communion with the magical forces that any mage of the Council would envy. The same Council they will help to destroy tomorrow."

"Are you so certain?"

"I am, my daughter, I am."

The queen remained silent for a few moments, pondering her next words. They still didn't trust each other, and she was sure that the plans her *mother* told her hid something else.

"Béldar, are you ready for tomorrow? New developments changed the plans; everything must be executed to perfection."

"Yes, my Queen," the mage replied. "I will lead the Resandian forces to attack the Council of Mages. According to Nadia's information, they are entrenched in Shao's hut in the mountains of Isolia, on the border of the kingdoms of Glastia and Bretia. Nadia will join us once she has recovered from opening the two portals to transport the Resandians, me and you, and our army to King Aremis' castle. By attacking together at both locations, we will undermine their chances of victory."

"You, Cedric, will go with me as captain of my army."

"At your service, Your Majesty," replied Cedric.

"Don't try to ingratiate yourself with me, you bastard. Once this is over, we'll settle the score."

"I also look forward to that moment; until then, my sword is at your service."

"Majesty."

Pamela's voice surprised Selena.

"Your Majesty, I too have a score to settle with this traitor."

"Yes, Pamela, I know. Don't worry; I'll leave something for you when this is over."

"Thank you, Your Majesty."

"Now, even if we don't need to eat or drink, let's do it. Let's celebrate together the night before the victory. Pamela, pull up a chair, join us."

"Thank you, Your Majesty."

Selena raised her glass and, without taking her eyes off Nadia, raised it and then drank it down in one gulp before wiping her mouth with her sleeve. Tomorrow would be a great day.

## *2*

Perlion accompanied Shao to the highest tower of the castle of the late King Aremis. The afternoon was falling, and the sun would set in only a few minutes. The last rays were passing over the ancient Plateau of the Gods, illuminating the area around the castle and reflecting the last glints of the Great Salt Lake.

The head of the Council held out a cup to him as he leaned against one of the battlements. They both drank.

"What do you think, Shao? Will we emerge victoriously?"

The old man smiled.

"Of course."

"Are you that confident?"

"Nadia and Selena are no match for the Council."

"Your former love has proven to be resourceful."

"But now there are no more surprises. We are ready. Triar and his army will decimate Selena's human forces."

"Several mages have been killed. By your own account, they were executed by a simple knight, not even by Nadia."

"A simple mistake. That will not happen again."

Perlion approached the edge to admire the beauty of the waters. Only once had he visited the abode of Lady Cilux. The view from the surface was as beautiful as from the mage's caverns.

"I would be very sorry to see these waters stained with blood. Our sister would not be very happy about that," exclaimed the mage from the northern shores with resignation.

"Tomorrow, Triar will march to Lebassi. The battle will be far from here, probably in the lands of Tolm or Kasnia. Our sister can rest assured."

"And we, shall we go to your cabin tonight?"

Deep down, Perlion was stung by that part of the plan: to take refuge like frightened rats in Shao's home. Yes, it was the safest but also the most cowardly thing to do. They were mages, about twenty between the members and their disciples. Together they were an unstoppable force. Nadia would be no match. Selena would be no match. The apprentice they sent to the queen would be no match either. Why the caution, then? Why the fear? Why the feeling that they were overlooking something?

Shao appeared confident. He was sure that inside he was gnawing with fear, no matter how much the head of the Council tried to conceal it. Would Nadia rival him in power? They both had the same master. Perhaps she could not be baptized as a mage. But does the ceremony make the mage? Does the new name make the mage? Or is it the power and knowledge that truly defines the mage?

He didn't need to think about it much: it was the power. The power.

"Let's finish drinking and leave, Perlion, old friend."

"Without saying anything to Triar and Ivanivok?"

"They know what they have to do. Triar will not sleep tonight. This has been his lifelong dream."

"His dream has already destroyed him once."

"In that case, round two," he muttered as he lifted his glass to his lips and tasted the mead he loved so much.

Perlion imitated him.

## *3*

Before dawn, the Lebassi Castle bustled with activity. Béldar stepped out onto the parade ground to find a ten-by-ten formation of Resandian assassins. Fabulous! That was the troop he would command to wipe out the members of the Councill. He, barely an apprentice, would have to stand up to mages three times his experience. "You'll do fine," Selena whispered in his ear in the early morning. *I'll do fine,* he repeated to himself to build up his courage.

Seeing him, the two warriors at the front corners took three steps forward. Crossing their right arm over their chest, they genuflected.

"Resandian warriors at your service," they both exclaimed energetically.

"Steel and fire on our enemies," shouted a hundred throats.

"Steel, fire, and honor!" replied Béldar. The night before, Nadia repeated the greeting to him like a mantra to ensure that he would gain the respect of the assassins.

The Resandians were dressed in tight-fitting jackets of what looked like blue leather. Their pants were gray and tight-fitting, the fabric resembling velvet, but he could sense that it was the skin of some animal from their deserts. Their boots were black and without heels. They hid their faces between what might as well have been indigo bandages, exposing only small eyes that resembled turquoise flaming stones. Not an inch of their skin was visible; even their hands were encased in cerulean gloves.

The mage would have expected to see them covered with swords or knives. On the contrary, no weapon was in sight. Moreover, he did not sense enough space to hide them in their clothing. Perhaps their skill consisted in the use of their hands or their magic.

He did not understand what they were. The gleam in their eyes did not seem to belong to that of a common creature that suffered and bled. Undoubtedly, a desert devastated by magic would have to have created beings with unimaginable characteristics, who, for him, until today, were nothing more than a myth.

The two warriors, who he sensed were their leaders, returned to formation. Arms behind their backs, right hand holding the left. A hundred warriors were acting as one.

The sorceress explained to him not to ask for names because they would not tell him. Looking at them now, he could have done little with names: Resandians were indistinguishable. Same bearing, same size, same clothes. He could have sworn the voices seemed one.

Trust! Selena repeated that word the night before. He could not say that he trusted these assassins as he would trust a friend or a brother. He could only trust their abilities; he had to start somewhere.

"Where is Nadia?" asked Béldar.

"Lady Nadia is behind you," replied the one hundred Resandians in sync.

Béldar did not notice her arrival and felt like a fool in front of his troops.

"Good morning, young Béldar. Are you ready?"

"I am. When do we leave?"

"Let's not keep the mages waiting; they've lived long enough," Nadia said happily.

The mage could not suppress a smile.

"Then let's go."

The sorceress walked towards the Resandians, who broke formation, forming two groups and a corridor, which Nadia crossed.

"Wait!" Selena shouted.

Béldar's heart was racing. He had spent the night with her, perhaps his last night. The queen glowed in a crimson armor matching her hair. She came up to him and embraced him. The mage could feel her heart beating through the cold steel. Even with the metal in between, he sensed her warmth. He kissed her. They kissed.

"Come back to me in one piece."

"As you wish, my Queen."

She turned her back to him and followed Nadia, who seemed amused by so much sentimentality.

The sorceress walked to the north wall of the parade ground. She stretched out her arms and began to swing them softly. Only a few seconds later, where moments before there were stone and bricks, the image of a snowy esplanade surrounded by pine trees and a hut in the background appeared. The portal was complete.

Béldar crossed and stepped aside to let his troops pass through. Then, he looked to his queen in silent farewell as the last soldier crossed and the gate closed. Where he could once see the castle and Selena, there was nothing left but the sight of a snow-covered hillside.

He turned towards his target. The hut was a few hundred yards away. The Resandians put one knee on the snow and rested both hands on the ground. Their clothes were dyed white until they became almost invisible, camouflaged with the environment.

"Good idea," Béldar concluded as he dyed his robe with frost. "Steel, fire, and honor," muttered the mage.

## *4*

Selena watched them cross and then disappear. She could feel the cold of the mountain, and small snowflakes settled at the foot of the north wall. The attack would begin shortly. She faced her mother and was surprised to see a smile on her face.

"What is it?" asked the queen.

"Look at you! A warrior like you longing for her man. You gave your heart to that sad mage, like an orphan begging for love in the streets."

Selena's eyes swelled with rage.

"Let's go. MY troops are waiting."

And without another word, she went to her mount. This time she chose a mahogany-reddish mare that still kept a wild spirit. She stroked its neck reassuringly and mounted it with agility when she reached the animal.

"I'll see you there," her *mother* replied.

She was joined in her riding by Cedric and Pamela. The traitor wore black armor. Béldar had explained that it was undoubtedly dwarven steel. Pamela wore a light mesh coat covering her chest and thick brown leather breeches.

Galloping, they left the castle behind. Selena looked askance at the fortress, thinking that there was a possibility of not returning. The feat they were beginning would be more than challenging, and, regardless of the outcome, the bards would compose a thousand and one songs that would narrate the events of the coming days.

In a gesture unbecoming of her, the queen turned to the wet nurse:

"Pamela, I release you from your obligations. You can return to the castle and leave. This war is no place for you."

"Your Majesty, this is what I want."

Selena nodded in agreement. While she still held dominion over her troops, it had been days since Pamela had been under her control. A sense of pride washed over her, infusing her heart with even more warmth. This little girl would risk her life for her and fight by her side as her equal, not as a puppet. In the last few days, Selena watched Pamela train with passion, ignoring pain and fatigue, rising again and again as she fell defeated to the parade ground. Girded about her waist was a long, light sword, so sharp it could be used to slice cured pork hams.

They were only a few minutes away from the camp. According to their orders, the troops were formed in front of the Silvan River; forty platoons of fifty soldiers each, armed with swords, axes, and maces, clad in light jet-colored leather armor.

She could see Nadia in front of the soldiers. She was facing the calm current of the river waiting for her.

"We're ready," Selena announced.

The mage did not respond, did not even look at her. She stretched her arms out in front of her, and two large water tentacles rose and zigzagged towards her hands. The liquid enveloped her palms first and then rose to her shoulders. A bluish glow illuminated the watery appendages, extending all the way to the caudal. As the glow spread, the flow of the water stopped. Slowly, a wall of liquid rose, as high as two men.

"Go ahead," exclaimed Nadia.

Selena sensed the effort in the sorceress' voice. Across the water, she could see a plain of green pastures and a village with a castle in the background, the castle of King Aremis. She drew her sword, not because she expected to fight instantly, but as a simple gesture to her men to indicate that the fight would begin shortly.

She urged her horse forward. The riverbed was strewn with fish writhing in agony while drowning at her feet. The equine hesitated for a moment before the strange wall. Selena ran her hand through its mane, soothing it. The animal's flews dilated, sensing the moisture. The mage dug her boots into the mare's sides to drive it forward and crossed with resolution. Behind her, she could hear the sound of advancing troops.

When she reached the other side of the portal, she was surprised to be completely dry. She kept walking to make room for her men to cross. Within seconds, the first brave ones accompanied her. Proudly, the queen watched them draw their weapons in unison as they crossed the wall preparing for battle.

Suddenly, a thunderous war horn resounded in the stillness of the morning. She followed the origin of the call to one of the village watchtowers. Only a few seconds passed before a second horn added to the warning of the first. Then another. Then another. And, still, her troops did not finish crossing.

"Quick," ordered Selena.

The soldiers advanced with alacrity to give rapid passage to their comrades following them. Thus, in a few minutes, the troops were complete.

Through the water, the warrior could see Nadia kneeling on the riverbank. As she warned her, the effort to open the passage was enormous, and it would take her some time to recover.

They may have lost the surprise factor, but her *mother* fulfilled her part of the plan by leading them to the gates of the fray, thus saving them many days of travel. Now, it was up to her to achieve victory. She led her mount to the front. She was joined by Cedric, Pamela, and her four captains, who were also on horseback.

She turned around to look at her troops. In her rise to the Kingdom of Lebassi, they fought by her side; they bled by her side. To them, she was not just their queen; she was their leader, their battle companion. She trotted through the first platoons, clashing her sword with those of her soldiers, first in one direction and then the other, until she returned to the starting point. She stared at them and raised her sword.

"Today, we will face the last bastion that separates us from achieving the peace of the kingdoms. Today we will unify the tribe of men to prosper. Today I ask you, once again, to place your swords and your hearts at my service. Our allies will subdue the mages. We will make Triar and his henchmen bite the dust. We will fight together until our last breath and rise to victory, and all of you, my men, my brothers, will be heroes, and troubadours will narrate your exploits until the end of time. To victory!"

"To victory!" they all answered excitedly.

*To victory,* Selena repeated to herself before starting to move towards the castle.

# 5

Shao observed the arrival. To summon a portal of that caliber required an indescribable magical level, only within reach of the most skilled mages of the Council. Undoubtedly, that snake Nadia conjured it; it could not have been anyone else.

He felt the agitated breathing of some of his younger comrades. Terwa's disciple was stifling a shriek that was driving him crazy.

"Get a hold of yourself, Aliana, or I'll sew your mouth shut myself!" he shouted in exasperation.

The newly-promoted mage put her hands to her lips to mitigate the noise.

Better. He kept watching. That third-rate mage, Béldar, appeared, followed by a hundred soldiers. No, they were not soldiers. They were Resandians. Resandian assassins, to be more precise. Or weren't all Resandians assassins? Consummate masters of stealth and annihilation, created by Salmur or Rumlas (it didn't matter now) to fight alongside them in the Battles of Creation. Then, when the twins were beyond jaded, they abandoned them in those desolate lands. They imbibed the purest magic and prospered for centuries as entities of change without ideology but with fee. A good sum of gold could tip the scales of a war, a king, or a kingdom. Now, Nadia hoped to tip it in her favor with magical entities that could rival the power of the Council.

The scales would tip; yes, he did not doubt it. The scales would tip; they would tip in his favor because where there was a will, there was a way, and he embodied the will of the Council and, therefore, he would show them the way.

Lady Aliana's suppressed shriek became a disconsolate cry.

"We're going to die," whispered the woman who, until a few days ago, had been the mage Terwa's servant.

Shao stared at her. His eyes glowed. Aliana's black hair extended to the front and, as if they were threaded needles, began to go in and out of the mage's lips until her mouth was completely shit. From where he stood, the head of the Council fanned two fingers and knocked the woman down, leaving her unconscious on the hut's floor.

Peace of mind, at last. He scanned the esplanade.

Their enemies, the enemies of magic and Panameria, dyed their clothes snowy. They intended to escape his eyes. He laughed. As assassins, they were accustomed to attacking from behind, blinding lives at request, dehumanizing their victims, and seeing them as targets, as moving bags of gold. Camouflaging themselves with the environment would not serve them well; the mages, his brothers, were not frightened deer in the woods where hidden hunters could shoot them down with accurate arrows. No, no, no, no. Their eyes were not human; their hearts were not human. They were…

While he was watching, each of the Resandian assassins disappeared. Each of them was out of sight. Each of them was becoming a threat.

The only imbecile (he had no other name) who was still *there* was Béldar. His figure stood out in the middle of the snow. He dared to think that the Resandians might be using him as a decoy.

The time of hiding was over. Shao opened the door and led his brothers into battle. He walked a few steps away from the hut. The rest arranged themselves in a crescent formation around him.

"Perlion, Cylux, watch your backs. The Resandians are treacherous."

The howling of several wolves tore the stillness of the morning. A dozen of these animals emerged from the forest and ran towards the mage. These beasts were half a man's height, with strong legs and long fangs. Their fur was shaggy like an old rag, with half a mane at the neck and a thick white tuft at the top of the back. Shao nuzzled the two that flanked him, and they licked his fingers affectionately, like docile puppies.

"Brothers, let us go into battle. Do not lose heart. May Salmur guide your minds and let us emerge victoriously," he exclaimed confidently.

Shao did not expect retorts or battle cries. He only expected the focus of the Council and his apprentices. For his part, neither fear nor defeat had any place in his thoughts, only the resolution to finish as soon as possible.

Suddenly, what could be about ten Resandian warriors materialized less than fifty paces away. They seemed to have jumped out of a tree, although the nearest ones were about a hundred yards away, as they fell with one knee bent and the other leg outstretched. Their hands were behind their backs, and, when they brought them to the front, they wielded scimitars.

The weapons were not made of steel or any metal. The blades seemed to be made of pure magic. Magic! If that was so, why put their hands behind their backs? Why didn't they just make them appear? It was not the time for reflections.

An indigo glow flooded his hands as he focused Panameria's energy. Two beams of energy burst forth, and as they advanced, they fragmented, seeking the targets. He smiled. That would be ten less.

The assassins masterfully moved their weapons, deflecting the attacks into the forest, where several trees fell down.

Shao heard the snow melting beneath the Council's feet. A subtle vapor rose from the earth as magic flowed towards them, feeding them, filling them with power. Assassin tricks were just that: tricks. Magic was not a trick; magic was everything, and they controlled it.

The head of the Council allowed himself a smile as he watched his wolves run swiftly towards the Resandians. He mentally connected with them, transferring more than just strength to them. The animals advanced in random leaps, mindlessly dancing a strange dance, to pounce on their prey in rage at the last moment.

Reddish arrows emerged from the trees, arrows that pierced the canids, spraying their blood on the unpolluted snow.

"No, no, no!" shouted Shao as fury grew inside him.

He stretched his hands out in front of him. Those bastards killed his pets. They wouldn't live another minute.

# *6*

Triar drew Nobulka. Selena's forces were advancing across the plain with the firm purpose of taking the city. The capital of Bretia, Perennia, received its name after stopping his grandfather's advance. Since then, it extended around the castle of the late king Aremis and created a defensive structure consisting of a moat and a stone wall about six yards high. In the barrier, every fifty yards, a square keep could hold up to forty archers spread over two levels. The access to the interior was limited to two points: the eastern bridge, in front of which the invading troops had appeared, and the harbor on the Great Salt Lake. The harbor was protected by an extension of the clamp-shaped fence, leaving only a narrow space through which a maximum of two medium-sized vessels could approach. The tips of the pincers housed turrets armed with crossbows and catapults. It was rumored that Bretian gunners were able to hit barrels the size of sheep. In short, an impregnable fortress.

Stationed from the barracks above the entrance gates, he could see that the soldiers of his *wish* were less than five hundred yards away and advanced towards the bridge. He estimated that his archers could take down a minimum of three hundred soldiers before they reached the gully's edge flooded with water and pitch. That might be a tenth of the invaders; there would still be hard work left to do.

It was then that he spotted her. She wasn't wearing a helmet. He would recognize those hairs at any distance. Damn it, Selena! She led her men marching without hesitation towards the village.

He heard a shout: "Charge." The riders, fewer than ten, spurred their mounts. The fighters began to trot. A winged horse reared up and charged mercilessly, steel in hand, towards the gate.

A red glow caught his attention. A ball of fire, as big as a foal, was heading for the base of the fort to his right. Impregnable! Yes, it was against human onslaughts, not magic.

A few seconds more, and the archers would have them in range.

"Prepare your arrows!" the king commanded. Triar heard the drawing of eighty bows.

His heart was pounding with excitement. Blood flowed through his body, and his exalted senses turned him into a war animal. He burned with the desire to come down from his settlement and cross swords with those heartless men. Arrogance defeated him once. He had to be smart and act cautiously and strategically. Success would be his if he played his cards smartly; he did not doubt it. For this, he trained for years. Although, at one time, he cherished the idea of retiring and leading the peaceful life his father led, that alternative perished with his beautiful Katrina. *My wife died because of my pride*; the phrase exploded in his mind bringing him back to reality.

The fiery sphere detonated on the stone. The explosion gnawed away at the foundation and set the liquid in the ditch on fire. Likewise, the king heard a crackling sound, and the ground shook beneath his feet. *Help us so it can resist!* he implored Salmur.

They were in range.

"Archers, fire!" he ordered in a thunderous voice.

His legions did not hesitate. The arrows flew swiftly. The sky was filled with a hissing black cloud.

Turning to his left, Triar addressed the soldier accompanying him.

"Now, give the signal."

The underling lit a dart and fired it in the direction of the zenith at the same moment that a second magical discharge was approaching them.

"Damn witch."

The first soldiers fell, hit by arrows. The mob did not stop. He expected nothing less. Soon, the second volley would again wreak havoc on the assailants.

And the base of the keep exploded. "Hold on." A crackle... Then another. And another. The floor not only trembled; it roared as if it felt wounded. The mortar of the stones lost its function, and the fortress walls cracked. Screams of agony added to the cacophony of destruction. The defenders were trying to escape from the granite trap that the fortress was becoming.

The attacking squadrons stood watching the chaos, waiting for the promised entrance. In their midst, the king could see his enemy, surrounded by a scarlet aura. He swore she was smiling at him in the distance.

The sound of hoofbeats to his left startled him. *Hooves?* The explosions and the magic made him forget the rider on the winged steed.

# 7

The forests to their left and right burst into bright indigo flames. The Council's counterattack was atrocious, devastating pine and fir trees in seconds. The heat oppressed his face and forced him to squint. Béldar was amazed and, at the same time, frightened. So much power, so much devastation.

The attack happened the instant accurate arrows shot down the wolves. He sensed that not one but several mages were behind such a feat. The Resandians were cunning. The frontal attack was meant to divert attention and thus fulminate several members. The appearance of the wolves delayed the maneuver.

He heard the cries of pain. A score of his allies was burning in the blue fire. This was not good, not good at all. He had always sensed that the power of the Council would be hard to overshadow; now, it was confirmed.

A thunderous explosion brought him out of his thoughts. Shattered branches flew through the air. Where more than sixty century-old trees once stood majestically, only ragged stumps remained, resembling charred fingers sticking out of the earth.

A few yards from him fell the inert body of a Resandian. He quickly approached him, looking for some trace of life. The eyes that once shone, imbued with magic, were not only dull but completely black. There was not even the faintest spark of existence left, only death. The burnt clothes exposed part of his skin, a skin that, although scorched, had silver tints similar to the glow of the stars. A slight crimson glow caught his attention. With cautious gestures, the mage removed the pieces of cloth so that he could see more clearly.

An intricate network of lines crossed the warrior's body. He did not understand the design. He followed the outline of one of them with his finger, and a tingle climbed through his hands. This produced a certain reaction, and he could perceive how a group of strokes shone with more strength. He drew back in surprise. He looked around him. Now he understood. The protruding stripes formed the outline of a small, straight-bladed sword. To be sure, he repeated his movements on another part of the skin... A dagger. A double-bladed ax. On the arms, arrows. They were their weapons. The objects were not hidden among his clothes; no, everything was there, at the surface of their skin, as one would say.

He put his fingers to his nose. Behind the soot and the smell of burnt flesh, there was a very particular whiff, ancient magic, in pure essence, primordial magic, cryol.

Somehow, the assassins tattooed their weapons with cryol. A magnificent trick that turned them into true legends. A powerful, undetectable, and deadly arsenal. As far as he could tell, space was not a constraint. The drawings crossed each other and overlapped. What a masterful technique! What other secrets did this millenary race harbor? How much of that knowledge did they pass on to Nadia? She assured them that they would win. Would she have the power to tip the balance?

He stood up. Reflections like these added nothing to the battle. He scanned the battlefield with his eyes. An amber dome surrounded the mages and the hut. The Resandian perpetrators of the first attack were nowhere in sight. The fire, its mission accomplished, was beginning to dissipate.

He thought he caught a glimpse of two of the mages disappearing or perhaps moving; the protective dome did not allow a good view. And, if so, where had they gone?

"So young, so naive, so easy to kill!"

The female voice came from behind him. The words were cold, icy, loaded with a hint of superiority, and, above all, so threatening that he did not doubt that his life would end in a few seconds.

Guided by his instinct, Béldar raised his hands.

"Come on, honey, turn around."

The mage began to move slowly in anticipation of an attack that would bring his life to an end.

"Don't be stupid. Turn around at once. You'd be dead if we wanted you to."

Turning around, Béldar realized that it was not one but two mages who had cornered him. The one who spoke to him was wearing a long emerald-colored dress with silver trim and a wide neckline that revealed generous breasts. Long, curly black hair fell to her hips. Although her ebony-colored skin looked smooth, he sensed that she was one of the oldest mages on the Council. Her companion was much younger, no doubt her disciple. Broad backs and a chest like a barrel made his crimson robe tighten at the top. Unlike his teacher, he was almost an albino with a face covered in freckles and a clump of short reddish hair.

"I am Lady Cilux, and this is my disciple, Égredor. Of course, you are the sad traitor, Béldar. It seems civilized to me that those who are to die should know the name of their executioners. Having said that, a few last words..."

He saw them clearly. Four Resandian warriors emerged from the snow like spirits. The bluish gleam in their eyes was gone; instead, crimson flashes illuminated their faces. Perhaps fury, rage, or a further invocation of ancestral powers.

They materialized behind Lady Cilux and her disciple. Each quartet member drew from within themselves a battle-ax and a strange crescent-shaped blade that turned their fists into a true meat grinder. In unison, they began to run toward their targets.

A violent magical thrust threw Béldar several yards backward. It was so surprising that he barely managed to block it, preventing all his ribs from fracturing.

"Then I'll deal with you, traitor," exclaimed the mage as she turned to repel the Resandian threat.

Lady Cilux and Égredor faced the assassins.

The first of them raised the ax to unload a deadly blow on the woman. The attack was quick, but Cilux was even quicker. The blade tore the air, just that. Before he could overcome the failure, a whitish beam coming from the lady hit the neck of the attacker, whose head fell heavily on the snow.

"I am Lady Cilux, Mistress of the Great Salt Lake! You are vile murderers, and today you will die."

Her words did not intimidate the henchmen. The three crossed their weapons in front of them in a defensive gesture and approached their prey. Two attacked the lady in synchrony, and the third one focused on her disciple.

The Resandians interspersed merciless ax thrusts with rapid arcs of curved blades. Their weapons seemed to come to life, and the gleam in their eyes infected the blades, giving them a crimson tinge.

From the ground, Béldar watched the fight. No one was giving an inch. The hitmen's movements were so fast and precise that the mages had to concentrate on repelling them.

He observed a faint cloud of vapor rising from the female's feet. Perhaps the exertion of battle required her to focus her strength. Ignoring the pain that afflicted his left side, he stood up.

The cloud grew larger; the snow had completely melted under her feet. Lady Cilux stretched out both hands and threw them to the ground as she did with him. A smooth frost mattress did not greet the two assassins; instead, sharp stalagmites rose from the earth, impaling them in their stomachs. With choked sighs, both perished in seconds.

Béldar advanced. He felt the blood running down his waist. He discovered that a splintered rib had pierced his flesh. He placed his right palm over the wound, concentrating on stopping the bleeding.

In front of him, the last Resandian standing inflicted a wound to Égredor's abdomen, which caused him to buckle under the impact. Instantly, the assailant's body exploded into pieces. Lady Cilux approached her disciple to help him. She bent down to look at the wound with a mother's skill.

Béldar took advantage of that moment to attack. He would not have another chance; he would not have a better chance. Many Resandians perished. The initial plan failed, and no member of the Council would fall yet. He owed this opportunity to Selena. He extended his left-handed arm towards the mage, concentrated all his strength, and felt the connection with Panameria, with magic. His being was flooded with energy; he felt it flowing; he owned it. When his body, mind, and spirit felt filled with the very essence of creation, he projected a bluish lightning bolt straight toward Lady Cilux.

It was as if seconds were lengthening. He clearly saw the beam emerge from between his fingers. The tiny tendrils of energy gathered together to create a single zigzagging beam that advanced towards his target. His nose filled with effluvia that reminded him of the smell of rotting fish. The distance grew shorter and shorter. He controlled the lightning to strike directly at the mage's head. A little more.

Égredor's eyes widened in surprise at the attack. He hugged his teacher tightly and spun her around, roughly safeguarding her from the vicious barrage. The attack struck him mercilessly in the middle of his spine and pierced him through to the sternum.

"Mother, are you all right?" was the last thing the mage could utter. His mouth filled with blood, and he exhaled his last breath.

Béldar tried to focus. The wound and the attack exhausted his last reserves. He felt faint and was sure that the mage would not only kill him but would make him suffer. He would face death with courage; that was all he had left. He thought of Selena, his queen. Selena, his beloved Selena. Unfortunately, his happiness was short-lived; his old longings and dreams were fulfilled, which filled him with joy. As he supposed, it had been fun, short, but fun. Selena would prevail, no doubt. And maybe their souls would meet somewhere, sometime. He could die in peace.

The Mistress of the Great Salt Lake embraced her disciple's lifeless body for a moment. Then she gently laid him down on the snow. She closed her eyes, crossed her arms over his corrupted chest, and kissed him lovingly on the forehead.

The mage felt his blood run cold when she looked at him. There was no trace of humanity left in those eyes, only fury, hatred, and a relentless desire to destroy. The sorceress's aura became visible, a manifestation of violet hues giving off tiny sparks of energy. It augured that he had mere seconds left.

The mage walked towards him. One step, then another, until she grasped his neck tightly with her right hand. Effortlessly, like someone picking up a rag, she lifted him.

"You killed him!" said the mage angrily. "You don't deserve to live, and you will NOT live."

The pressure on his throat became greater. The air was not circulating, and his lungs screamed in agony. His mind was beginning to darken. He saw tears in the lady's eyes, but he knew they were not for him. They were not for what she was going to do; they were for what he had done.

The mage's left hand clenched in a fist, surrounded by deep darkness. It was impossible to describe it in any other way. It was the prelude to his death. He accepted it. He closed his eyes and waited for the scourge of vengeance.

## *8*

The knight in black armor got off his horse. Just a few steps away was the former ruler of Lebassi: the dethroned Triar. He gently placed the sword he was holding on the wall.

"Majesty, let us stop this madness," Cedric offered. "Our forces are superior. The Council of Mages conspired against you and is dragging you into this senseless power struggle."

"Your offer is that of a coward," said the king. "You stink of fear and treachery. Do you think I'm afraid of a little magic?"

"I know that fear does not dwell in your heart, Your Majesty, but my Lady wishes to avoid further bloodshed."

"Your Lady! You can tell your Lady that this will not end until my sword spills her blood. It will not end until I have separated Selena's head from her body."

"I do not serve Selena, Your Majesty," announced Nadia's emissary.

After his words, he could see uneasiness on the monarch's face.

"If you don't serve that damn witch, who do you serve, then?"

"Lady Nadia is the most powerful of the mages. She proposes a deal."

"I'm tired of deals. Everyone offers things; everyone makes promises. My patience has a limit, and you're reaching it," he shouted while pointing his weapon at him.

Cedric brought his hands to his forehead and pressed his palms together in a reassuring gesture.

"You can end my life if you wish, but first, let me make you an offer."

The king lowered his sword. "Continue."

Nadia instructed him to perform this last trick against Triar. She sensed that the combat against the mages would not be easy. Selena was not yet fit for a magical confrontation, which could cause the army of men from the northern kingdoms to take advantage. Including one more distraction would help buy time. Of course, the idea had many risks. The king was not a naïve man. The prize would have to be good, tempting enough to plant a doubt in his mind.

"My Lady offers you not only to recover your kingdoms but also to take control of the northern kingdoms."

The monarch's threatening gesture subsided. A faint smile began to form.

"Also Selena's head," Cedric added.

Cedric felt that he not only heard him but also listened to him carefully. He took off his helmet.

"My name is Cedric, Your Majesty. I was Selena's first captain when Lebassi was attacked. Like you, I lost my loved ones under the blade of that assassin. I was under the control of her magic. Thanks to Lady Nadia's power, I managed to free myself from her evil influence. The atrocities I committed came back to my mind when that happened, almost making me lose sanity. For days I meditated on what to do in silence. I tried to kill her. I failed. I do not forgive myself for failing. But something good came out of that night; I managed to escape taking the prince, your son, Your

Majesty. Thinking you were dead, my Lady took care of the baby and still cares for him. So, my Lord, she will return your son to you so that he can grow up healthy and strong."

Cedric finished his story and watched him.

"Did you save my son from the clutches of that harpy?"

"It was the only thing I could do to atone for my sins."

The king switched his sword to his other hand and extended his right hand to the knight.

"Thank you. Let me shake the hand of the one who saved my son. Thank you.

He felt the king's firm, sincere grip. The king's little smile widened, and his eyes sparkled with excitement. Cedric succeeded. He smiled too, pleased. His lady was getting her way with the ruse. He would soon get his revenge.

Then, suddenly, his insides quivered. An infamous pain stabbed his abdomen. He did not understand what was happening.

"I'm sick of lies," the king whispered in his ear.

He lowered his head to find the king's sword stuck in his gut up to the hilt. It was inconceivable. Dwarven smiths boasted that their steel was impenetrable.

"The kingdoms will be mine. Selena will die today under my steel, just as you have. My son will return to me, whoever has him."

Triar pulled Nobulka back and hurled him over the balustrade into the fiery maw of the wall pit with a mighty kick to the chest.

# 9

Lady Cilux kept the pressure on the wretch's throat. In her left fist, she accumulated her remaining energy. She tasted the pulsing of the earth to create a punishment to match the crime committed. Not only had she been stripped of her apprentice, her legacy, but Égredor was like a son to her. This shoddy mage would pay dearly for his audacity.

Out of nowhere, a flash of light to her left made her blink. Without knowing why the mage fell at her feet. Her hand still held him by the neck. Something or someone severed her arm below the elbow.

Without even looking, she launched the dark-energy discharge looking for her assailant. Instantly, she bent down with alacrity to pick up her severed limb. That's when she saw her. A mage who seemed to be barely a young girl; a youth that contrasted with the deep wisdom that her countenance gave off.

"I know you. You were Shao's lover. I met you years ago when my master and I visited yours. Since then, I knew you were not to be trusted."

"I also know you and remember you. I hear you dwell in the Great Salt Lake. I guess the fish didn't teach you anything?"

Cilux gritted her teeth. Her eyes flashed with rage.

"You attacked me treacherously, without honor, just like this outcast who killed my apprentice from behind."

"We are at war, didn't you hear? War is not fair; it is not honorable. It is war. I won't let you leave this world thinking the fight was unfair; I want you to leave knowing that you tried with all your might. Come on, put that arm back together. Take a breath. Focus. Take as much time as you need. You will die knowing that you are nothing compared to me, and your corpse, and that of your beloved apprentice, will be devoured by the vermin of the forest. There will be no rest for you; you will mourn your failure for all eternity."

The Mistress of the Lake did not flinch at the threatening words. With gentle, firm gestures, she joined her forearm to the stump. Concentrating, she cauterized the wound and restored the flow of blood, the connections of her nerves, and the interweaving of her muscles. There was no scar left when she was done, no mark to reveal where she was wounded.

"I appreciate the gesture, but you shouldn't have done it. I am no longer the girl who visited you centuries ago. I am a member of the Council. I will finish you off!"

Lady Cilux analyzed her closely. This woman orchestrated this tragedy. If she destroyed her, the threat would cease. She would kill her without mercy.

A bolt of crimson energy snapped her out of her reflection. The damn woman was attacking. With a quick gesture, she repelled the discharge.

"Are you making fun of me? A child would do better."

In response, another attack. Diversion. Attack. Deflection. What was her intention? The blows were light, ridiculous. A distraction!

"What are you up to?"

"Remember, this is war. There are no rules, no limitations. There is only the desire to win at any cost. You are not my target; you are an obstacle."

A faint smell of decay reached her nose. She looked around. Nothing had changed. The Resandians' corpses, her apprentice's body, and the other mage as an inert lump; everything was still the same. She felt a bead of sweat running down her right temple.

If she wanted to treat her like a second-rate mage, she would prove to her that she was not. She threw fireballs with both hands. They flew swift and deadly.

At the last second, Nadia stopped them with a slight gesture. She did not deflect them; she stopped them. The spheres remained suspended a couple of inches from her face, inert, harmless. She took each one of them.

"Nice try. You lack imagination. You spent too many years in the comfort of the Council, propped up in a chair discussing trifles. On the other hand, I spent many years understanding the true power of Panameria, making it mine, bending it to my will."

Nadia indifferently released the two orbs she held. As they fell to earth, two columns of yellow light rose.

Lady Cilux stepped back, waiting for the counterattack. Again, the smell hammered her nostrils. Now it was not faint but intense, as if she had been dipped in putrid offal.

The pillars increased their brightness so much that she had to cover her eyes. When brightness ended, it gave way to absolute darkness, dense, sticky darkness, which seeped into the skin, numbing the inside.

"Show yourself!" ordered Lady Cilux.

The silence was the only answer.

She lit her hands to get some vision. The glow barely penetrated a few feet of darkness.

"Mistress, help me."

Égredor's staggering voice reached her ears. Égredor! She saw him die. Could he still be alive, or was this just a trick to get her to lower her defenses?

"Mother Ci," said the mage before starting to cry.

A huge sorrow settled in the sorceress' heart. Égredor was an orphan she had rescued from a sinking ship on her precious lake. When she took him under her tutelage, the boy was only about five years old. She always introduced him as her apprentice, and he kept his composure by calling her 'mistress'. At home, it was different. Mother and son.

"My son, I'm coming to get you."

She concentrated her energy on widening the circle of light. Beads of sweat trickled down her forehead. Why was it so hard for her? What kind of magic was this? She moved forward, feeling her way with her feet. Something soft. She crouched down.

Her hands illuminated Égredor's body. Blood was pouring from his chest and mouth. Badly wounded, alive! And, if he was alive, she could heal him, she could bring him back. She would take him away from here, to their home.

"Mother, it hurts."

"Calm down, Égredor. We're going home. Everything will be all right."

She hugged him warmly. He was cold. She didn't feel his heart, not a breath of life. Nothing. She reluctantly let go and stood up.

"Stop it, get out of my head!" demanded Lady Cilux.

Fury and rage ignited her spirit, breaking the bond that trapped her. Clarity came back to her world.

She met Nadia's eyes above her own. She could feel the warmth of her breath.

"Here you are, damn you, now I'll get rid of you," threatened the Mistress of the Lake.

"You freed yourself, I'll give you that, but it's too late."

A hellish pain shot through Lady Cilux. She felt as if her soul was splitting in two, and her chest was bursting into flames. She looked down, searching for the cause. Her adversary's right arm was inside her body. Then she understood the pain. Nadia's fist closed over her heart, digging her nails in and tearing the tissue. She held the woman's wrist, trying to repel the aggression. It was useless; pressure increased, compressing her vital organ to the limit.

Deceived. Defeated. Lady Cilux, Mistress of the Great Salt Lake, perished with one last breath.

Nadia withdrew her hand and shook it to remove the traces of blood. She looked for Béldar's lying body and advanced towards him.

## *10*

Selena followed Cedric's fall until she saw him sink into the burning waters that licked the walls of the fortress. Triar deprived her of facing that traitor. She would have loved to have killed him herself; now, she could only focus on the attack.

A couple of hundred of her soldiers were dying or dead, victims of the king's archers. Her troops stopped and watched as the wall of the left keep fell, leaving a clear path for the invasion.

"What are you waiting for? An invitation? The way is clear, and victory awaits us," Selena shouted loudly to her men.

In response, the queen's troops resumed their march toward the city.

Selena sensed someone at her side. The wet nurse was approaching her with a mournful gesture.

"Your Majesty, riders from the east," she announced, pointing with her hand to the group of horses coming down from the hills.

The warrior saw them. Their number must be close to four hundred, so they would make a strong dent in her infantry. They were approaching at a gallop, rapidly closing the distance.

Her captains marched on the front with more than half of her army. She reared her horse, which reared up on its hindquarters.

"Soldiers! Follow me," she shouted to the group that lagged. "Pamela, come with me. These bastards intend to crush us like a clamp. We'll stop them."

That said, the mage spurred her mare to meet her rivals. She was closing the distance. The small militia accompanied her, and the girl rode to her left. Beyond Pamela, she could see her men about to penetrate the city. If all went well, in a few minutes, she would accompany them.

Selena unsheathed her sword. She still felt fatigated from her attacks on the walls. She had to try. She connected with the earth, with the very essence of life. A discharge of energy flooded her, so strong that the animal, the unfortunate driver, perished on the spot. The warrior took advantage of this power surge to rise into the air and fall in the middle of the cavalry. She channeled all her magic towards the steel. Holding the weapon with both hands, she unloaded a blow on the nearest rider. She could clearly see the terrified face of her target, who tried to dodge her with little success. The blade of the sword not only opened the skull as if it were a grape but also caused an explosion that threw half the army to the ground. Mounts and riders flew stunned around her.

Although exhausted by the effort, Selena stood up with authority.

"Finish them off!" she howled and threw herself into the fray.

# *11*

Their beautiful home was now in complete chaos. The ancient pine and fir trees were broken by magic. The melting snow created puddles of water that mingled with the blood of her brothers and those damn murderers. His wolves, his precious pets, were devastated by the vile Resandians. The sky was covered by black and greenish clouds, a mixture of death and ancient magic. His nose screamed in pain from the pestilent effluvia of corpses.

In the distance, his former love had just knocked down Lady Cilux in a most bizarre feat. Now she was bending over the traitor, perhaps tending to his wounds.

Shao cursed the woman with all his might. As centuries passed, not only did her hatred germinate resoundingly, but also her power, which rivaled his own. For the first time, he hesitated about victory. He recognized, with terrible bitterness, that he had erred in his judgment by underestimating the determination and capability of his enemies. Nadia, besides being extraordinary, also wielded an iron will.

He tried to mentally connect with the remaining members of the Council. They were scattered in the vicinity, battling, defending, and annihilating. After Cilux fell, there weren't many left. There would have to be enough of them. The Council would endure.

"Brothers, sisters, come to me," he mentally commanded.

He observed sparks in several places as the mages returned to the original formation. Perlion materialized to his right, still holding the limp body of a Resandian.

"Casualties?" he questioned the head of the Council.

There was a sepulchral silence broken only by the howling of the wind.

"Lady Cilux and Égredor fell before Nadia and Béldar," answered Perlion. "I have not seen Landros nor Martio."

"My master fell protecting me and taking about ten of those demons with him," added Calia, Landros' disciple, sadly.

Shao bowed his head at her with sorrow reflected in his eyes.

"Who else?"

"My faithful Tricio didn't stand a chance; he was still young. We were ambushed by more than a dozen," Fergissa pointed out.

"I lost my son, Dolego," Birzo sobbed.

The mage's forlorn image contrasted with his size.. Birzo was over six feet tall with equally broad shoulders. The stories about him said that his master picked him up after he was thrown out of a circus caravan where he performed feats of strength. His pointed ears hinted at a mixture of human and elven blood.

"I understand, brother," Shao consoled him. "We will avenge them all."

"You don't understand, Shao; he was my son, my real son. I dragged him into this madness following you. I don't regret being here, but he wasn't ready. I should have known. How will I explain it to his mother?"

The big man slumped down and sat on the ground. Abundant tears rolled down his cheeks, wiping away the traces of soot and blood that smeared his face.

"I will not fight anymore. I resign from the Council. I'm leaving," he announced as he stood up.

"You can't do that. We need you," Shao replied.

He could understand the fear, the frustration. He had doubts, too. They would only come out of this together. The Council would prevail; he would make it prevail. Together they would.

"Look," he announced as he pointed towards where Lady Cilux fell, "they are also regrouping. There are no more than twenty Resandians left. Nadia must be exhausted, and Béldar wounded. We can only stop them if we attack together. The future of the Council, the future of Panameria, everything is at stake."

"I'm sorry, Shao, I'm leaving," said the half-elf.

Shao's eyes radiated anger and despair. This could not end like this. Triumph was near. It would be difficult and full of sacrifices. But they would win, he was sure; well, quite sure. Centuries of leadership would not end that way. This insubordination could not, must not be allowed.

Then, he held the giant's maroon robe with both hands.

"I COMMAND YOU TO FIGHT!"

Birzo easily shook off the old man's grip and turned his back on him, walking away.

"Bloody coward."

The anger turned to rage, the rage to fury, and the fury to energy that permeated the hands of the mage, who channeled it towards the deserter. A discharge with enough power to finish the man off.

Lady Fergissa and Perlion intervened quickly. With mutual effort, they barely managed to stop the petty attack.

"What are you doing, Shao?" the northern mage confronted him.

What had he done? He was breathing heavily. A feeling of iciness ran inside him. Fear. He remembered the last time he had felt such an unpleasant sensation. His master had cornered him in his quarters. He was looking for an answer about his affair with Nadia. He wanted to know the truth from his disciple's own mouth. "I don't love her," Shao had lied at the time, "there is nothing between us." He didn't believe him. With no escape plane and cornered against the stone walls, his master plunged his finger slowly into his chest. Cold seized him, torturing him as he had never experienced in his life. Terrified, he confessed every detail, even the new life on its way. And then, when he mutilated her, he did nothing, nothing, because terror gripped his heart.

Now he felt the same way. He broke the rules. In front of the dwindling Council, he attacked one of his brothers. There was no apology. There would be no peace. Not for him.

"You are on your own. You are no longer one of us," Perlion said bitterly.

Without waiting any longer, they disappeared from sight. As they proclaimed, they abandoned him.

In the distance, a burst of female laughter burst out, laughter that reverberated in his ears as if telling him, "I will have my revenge."

## *12*

She was beautiful, graceful, and deadly. From the hillside, King Ivanivok did not lose any combat detail. Accompanied by little more than a hundred men, Selena was destroying his ambush plans by deftly undermining his cavalry.

The horsemen from Glastia were legendary for their bravery and expertise in using pikes and spears. That was not enough to stop the magical attacks that the warrior lavished in both directions. Once the equine defense was broken, the queen's soldiers polished off the northern subjects.

Triar had the mages' support, so he had to agree to accompany him in this feat. He put his warriors at his disposal and now was watching them perish. He thought of the mothers, fathers, brothers, sisters, wives, daughters, and sons to whom he would soon have to give the news. His people trusted him to lead them, to protect them. He failed. If his father were still alive, he would rebuke him for his naivete. "Dead kings are good for nothing, only fertilizer for the plants. Intelligent actions shape the future of a kingdom, and sometimes those actions begin with recognizing mistakes," he would tell him repeatedly so that he would understand that the most powerful weapon was not the sword but intelligence.

His escort awaited an order. The horses neighed, and the stench of sweat and rage overwhelmed him. He clenched his hands. Twenty more men would not make a difference. Twenty fewer faces to apologize to, twenty fewer families dressed in mourning. His soul would not forgive him if he gave the order; his soul would not forgive him if he did not.

Swordsmanship had never been his forte. He was comfortable with long distances. He gripped his bow. He carved it himself from a yew log he cut in the Honey Mountains. He spent a whole summer shaping it. His father congratulated him when he showed it to him.

I had a chance to end this. The queen was distracted. He took an arrow from the quiver he carried at the side of his mount. He tensed the shaft. He paced his breathing to the same rhythm as his steed. He removed from his mind any distracting thoughts. The process took only a few seconds. He was ready. He sought out the red-maned figure and aimed. Let Salmur guide his projectile.

As he was about to release the arrow, she looked at him. She felt those green eyes boring into her brain. She was still, steel in hand, and surrounded by corpses lying on a grass carpet. He sensed a crimson glow on her body, some kind of aura enveloping her. Magic!

He saw her stow the sword in its sheath, then open her arms. "Try, come on, try." It was as if her voice crept into his head, challenging him.

Ivanivok sighed and lowered the weapon

"Retreat!" he ordered his escort as he led his horse northward.

His horsemen followed him.

## *13*

One by one, the mages vanished. Nadia's laughter haunted his ears. The smell of burning flesh reached so deep inside him that he thought it would never leave him. He felt his side. There was no trace of the wound. He closed his eyes, concentrating the Earth's energy, making it rise and permeate his every cell. He felt good.

Nadia conversed quietly with the Resandians. There were just sixteen of them. The battle had been devastating on both sides. Fortune and mastery favored them. Shao was alone. But she sensed that he would not surrender.

"I want him alive," said Nadia in a quiet voice.

"Steel and fire on our enemies," he heard the warriors mutter.

"Steel, fire, and honor!"

The combatants dyed their attire black. They rummaged through the cloth; now Béldar knew there were no hidden pockets, only cryol tattoos, and then whips appeared. They raised their hands as if to strike and vanished.

Instantly, Béldar turned to the head of the Council. The black figures appeared around the old man and completed the gesture they started before teleporting. Their whips flew with expertise. They immobilized his limbs, trunk, and neck expertly. Blue sparks shot from the straps and licked the distance to the mage.

Then, it happened. Emerald flames swept through the attacking Resandians. Half of them managed to drop their whips in time, the others were consumed, and their ashes fell to the muddy ground.

The remnants of the scourges began to dance in search of their victims. Wrapped in flames, they became a powerful threat.

The Resandians jumped, dodging the attacks, which raised greenish smoke after burning grass and mud upon impact with the earth. They wielded the magical blades with their hands, trying to stop the symphony of blows.

Béldar did not lose any detail of the combat. Shao didn't even move, but he controlled the tentacles with great skill. He could see energy rising through his feet and feeding those appendages.

The Resandians were being overcome. Six of them laid inert. The remaining two ran towards Shao, executing several feints while holding their scimitars. They cut off the mage's new 'arms' with accurate slashes. They were no more than five yards away from their adversary. Four. Three. Two. They swung their weapons, one horizontally and the other vertically, anticipating any possible escape of their adversary.

And Shao vanished.

The two assassins positioned themselves back-to-back and began to turn slowly.

"UP!" shouted the mage in desperation.

When they looked up, they were impaled by the mage's improvised weapons.

The demoted head of the Council of Mages of Panameria rubbed his hands together as if he were wiping them and began to walk, staring at Nadia.

## 14

Shouts of pain, clashing of steel, and the crackling of burning wood greeted Selena when she crossed the threshold of the collapsed wall of Perennia. Everywhere, her men were slaughtering adversaries, who resembled armed farmers more than soldiers.

Soon, this too would be her kingdom. She liked its location by the lake. The walls could be repaired. Perhaps moving her residence here would be timely. To maintain control, she would have to control the kings or, perhaps, replace them with men *loyal* to her. Yes, it was a good idea. From here, she and Béldar would reign.

How was the combat against the mages turning out? She was uneasy about the power of the Council. She had to trust her *mother* and the Resandians. The root of all their ills was the Council, and it had to be destroyed. The fighting here would soon be over, and she could go to their aid. She had to focus on finding and eradicating Triar.

She looked around her. She enjoyed her pilgrimage to Lebassi to face the king for the first time! She still enjoyed it; however, she had to think as the future monarch of the human kingdoms. Each decease would represent one less pair of hands to build the future. It would also mean deep hatred and resentment, more than already existed. She could manage hatred and resentment, but why turn her reign into a continuous struggle when she could stand as a righteous queen. Enough blood ran through the streets.

Suddenly, an enemy henchman ran towards her, weapon in hand. With a simple gesture, she threw him to a bead stand. The soldiers approached her to protect their queen.

She raised her hand, stopping them.

"Drop your sword, and I will spare your life!" shouted Selena to the fallen man.

Staggering, the man stood up. His knuckles turned white from how tightly he gripped the hilt.

"Fucking foreign bitch. My wife and children are dead. My tent is burning in flames. I will drop my sword after I pierce your black heart."

Instantly, an arrow pierced his throat, and the merchant fell again. A pool of blood began to spread as he lay down, dying.

"Thank you, Pamela."

"My pleasure, Your Majesty."

Just because one individual did not agree to surrender did not mean that the rest would make the same decision. She approached a half-ruined staircase and climbed up to a part of the wall that resisted. She raised her sword and launched a lightning-like discharge into the sky.

"Soldiers of Perennia!" he shouted, magnifying his voice. "Whoever lays down their weapons will be spared. Surrender, and you will live. Face me, and you will die. The decision is yours."

Silence reigned for a few seconds. The fighting stopped.

"Tell me, bitch, will you spare me too?" Triar shouted from the middle of the square.

Another arrow flew swiftly towards the royal flesh. The former King of Lebassi caught it in flight with his left hand. Then, demonstrating his dominance, he tossed it aside.

"Now you let little girls fight for you? Face me!"

From on high, Selena watched her fate. Although she was created for this, she was no longer driven by the same impulse. She was now a different person. Now she was a person, not a magical entity without reasoning, without freedom. And, with that free will, she made her decisions, not moved by other force, neither magical nor mortal; only her. She drew her sword.

"Stand back!" she ordered her soldiers. "He is mine."

## *15*

The mage walked parsimoniously towards them. There was no fatigue in his countenance, only weariness. His robe fluttered in an icy breeze that reminded him that they were in the middle of the mountains. The cold left no mark on the mages, but Béldar felt his soul freeze. His skin crawled, and he had to restrain the clinking of his teeth. The icy sensation contrasted with the radiant sunshine.

"You are the only one left. It is useless for you to fight," said Nadia.

"Yes, we are only two elders with a lot of history behind them," Shao added.

"History? Now you call it that."

The breeze turned into the wind, carrying small snowflakes with it, even though the sky was still clear.

"It's all we have left."

"After today, you will have nothing left."

"Give it a go, Nadia. The same master, remember."

"No! You are wrong. He is no longer my master. He expelled me. I learned from other teachers."

"Magic is magic, darling."

"Don't you dare call me that!"

The wind became a gale. Small branches accompanied the snow. Béldar braced his feet so as not to be swept away. Voices came to him distorted.

A violet glow enveloped Nadia, who launched a beam of energy toward her former lover. The young mage was sure the attack had the strength to bring down an entire castle. It never hit its target. A colossal wall of ice had risen, separating them. The blizzard ceased.

"Béldar, help me take it down."

In response, the mage launched several fireballs. Nadia remained focused. The obstacle began to melt away.

What was Shao's intention? To delay them? He might have escaped. A mage of his level could hide forever in any corner of Panameria. They would never find him!

To his surprise, he was still there. He took advantage of the distraction to back away and lean next to the bodies of his wolves.

The barrier exploded, spewing chunks of ice in all directions.

He and Nadia advanced with determination. If what the mage said was true, they would have a very good chance of defeating him.

A translucent golden-colored dome rose above Shao and the wolves. Small flashes of lightning formed inside, and the bodies began to tremble, driven by the concentrated magic.

"What is he doing?" asked Béldar.

"I suspect that despair has driven him to an aberration. At some point, he must have toured the Liamen Archipelago."

"The land of the dark elves?"

"The elves are famous for creating chimeras. Have you heard about that?"

"Fantasies, only legends."

"Your legend is waiting in front of us. Get ready!"

A huge lightning bolt shot out of the dome, cracking it completely. An amber smoke spread, carrying with it a caramel, fruity smell. Then a roar slapped them in the face.

The creature stood up on its hindquarters, a mixture of human legs and wolf's paws. It was completely covered with silver hair. The creature's size was so portentous that its head reached higher than the roof of any house. Its chest, with a patch of green fur in the middle, resembled two barrels of beer. The long, muscular arms were topped by claws as long as daggers. Although his hairless face featured a snout with sharp fangs, the mage's features still prevailed.

"You're crazy, Shao! Look at you. You're nothing but an animal," mocked Nadia.

Thick strands of saliva hung from the being's mouth.

"More than an animal. A god!" Shao spat.

"Soon, you will be a carpet, I promise."

The mage launched a swap with such speed that it tore the mage's robe.

"Damn." Instantly, Nadia materialized a shield and a sword. "Chimeras are pure magic, boy. Arm yourself!"

Since when were mages warriors? He had never trained with swords; that was what soldiers were for. He looked down at his hands, closed his eyes, and summoned them: in his right hand, a double-bladed ax; in his left hand, a mace with sharp points. Slashing and smashing. If he had to fight like a warrior, he would. He held the mace in a protective gesture in front of him and raised the sword, ready to strike.

A bite from the creature was dodged by Nadia, who counterattacked with her sword, hitting the creature in the right thigh. The wound exposed muscles, and, as the blood started to gush out, it also bubbled. The cut healed in seconds.

Shao's throaty laugh echoed.

"I am a god!"

The chimera clenched its fists, and an aura of crimson light enveloped it.

A powerful force pulled Béldar's weapons towards the creature. He held them tightly. Tension was increasing. Laughter hammered in his ears. Nadia was also struggling to hold on to her weaponry.

"It's mine. Give it all to me," added the mage mockingly.

Béldar's sword and mace vanished in threads of magic flying towards the wolf. Beside him, the sorceress kept up the fight and still maintained control.

"Mine!"

To his surprise, his weapons were recreated between Shao's claws, magnifying their size.

Nadia charged. Quick and accurate slashes painted a maroon cross on the belly of her adversary. The shield rattled as it parried a blow from the mace, and the sword's blade passed inches away from the lady. The wounds closed.

The young mage backed away unarmed. Shao looked invincible. His companion could barely keep him at bay with rapiers and swords. Unlike him, her training must have trained her in the art of armed combat. She was a true master; there was no doubt about it. How long could she hold him off?

A roar brought him out of his reverie. Nadia's shield exploded into pieces, which the wolf absorbed.

"Mine!" Shao repeated.

Béldar scanned his surroundings. He had to find something useful. He found only destruction and death. The thick trunks of the collapsed hut were scattered. The trees were destroyed. Lifeless bodies of mages and Resandians. Nothing.

The sorceress screamed as the canid's jaws closed on her left forearm. Seizing the opportunity, she struck it in the shoulder. The sword greedily penetrated the flesh and embedded itself in the bone.

"Mine!"

Shaking his head, Shao tore muscles and tendons, tearing the woman's forearm. He stood up to his full height.

Nadia had to drop the sword, which the wolf assimilated.

The abomination began to chew; blood mixed with saliva soaking its jaw and mottling it with scarlet hues. Flesh and bone were gobbled up, leaving only a smile on the mage's *face*.

"You were mine. You will be mine. All mine."

The words were followed by a thunderous roar that caused his ears to ring.

For the first time, Béldar saw fear reflected on Nadia's face. He had to help her. How? Next to these colossal creatures, he was nothing more than a helpless child. Both had the same master to then take different paths. Shao became head of the Council. Nadia, expelled, drank from the ancestral knowledge of the Resandians, who proved to be wonderful warriors. The Resandians! Maybe, just maybe. She might have a chance.

"Nadia! Hold it a little longer."

The woman wrapped her stump with her right hand; faint wisps of steam rose from the wound.

"He hasn't beaten me yet. I got this puppy right where I want it," replied Nadia, catching her breath.

Selena's lover visualized the last fallen Resandians' bodies. *The fresher, the better,* he thought. A distraction, he needed a distraction. He focused his mind. A thick, dark fog rose, separating them from the monstrosity.

Nadia thanked him with a slight nod. He took the opportunity to materialize near the assassins' corpses.

He hoped it worked. Squatting down next to one of them, he opened his clothes, exposing his chest. He placed his hand on the skin. He felt it! The tattooed lines came to life and began to bubble. Slowly, the cryol began to flow into his fingers. Yes, an opportunity.

## *16*

The main square of Perennia was a wide place with a circular structure where six streets converged. In its center, a beautiful fountain of the whitest marble from the quarries of the west with the sculpture of a maiden with soft features and long hair raising her hands in a welcoming gesture; at her feet, four goldfish spat jets of water towards the cardinal points. The waters of the pond were tinged red with spilled blood. The square was the nerve center of the city's commerce, with stores, stalls, and hucksters.

After coming down from the tower, Selena paid no attention to any of it. Finally, Triar! Inside her, something drew her to him and made her think of destroying him at all costs. She supposed it was difficult to erase the reason for her creation.

"Will we fight today, or will you continue to admire me?" Triar questioned with a smile sculpted on his face.

The king proved his worth to her once, but he also proved he was no match for her. Why did he feel so confident about winning? Revenge? That she could understand. She killed his wife. His son was dead or lost. The kingdom he treasured so much now belonged to her. She could understand he wanted to get back at her for all that, but openly confronting her was unwise.

She carefully analyzed her surroundings. She could not hear any fighting. A crowd was milling around the circumference of the square; Perennia's soldiers behind Triar, his own behind her. They kept their weapons ready and their attention on the deed that was soon to begin. On the heights, roofs and rooftops were clear; no archers, no visible threat.

The clashing of swords against shields startled her. The Perennial defenders cheered Triar on. The invaders, her troops, responded briskly, adding their own chords to the existing cacophony.

"Will you also ask me not to use magic this time?"

Drawing his steel, Triar replied:

"You can use whatever you please. It is your fate to die today."

"Fate? There is no fate; there is will. The same will that took away your kingdom, your queen, and your son. My will!"

The former ruler of Lebassi carried two swords. He kept one with a golden hilt and without ornamentation in his belt. The one he wielded had a long, thin blade, which she sensed was very sharp. The blade had a dark hue with reddish flashes; almost matching it, the hilt was a deep black, like the soul of an assassin.

She walked towards him with her guard up.

"Finally, let's get started."

Triar ran towards her. On the run, the king's left hand drew his second weapon. He stopped only a few feet away from her. He crossed the two blades in front of him in a defensive stance.

She threw her first punch, feeling him out. He dodged it.

*Who are you?* A voice in her head distracted her. She repelled Triar's counterattack with a simple gesture. She recognized that the king had a good technique. She had much quicker reflexes and found it easy to anticipate his moves. *Who are you?* Again, the voice.

"Who's talking to me?" shouted Selena.

"What? I didn't say anything," said Triar.

The blades fought against each other, raising sparks.

"Shut up! I'm not talking to you."

Another blow. The dark blade tore into her abdomen this time, making her move back. She silenced the moan that wanted to come out of her throat. She stepped back. She was stronger and faster; how did he hurt her?

*I like your taste!* Again, the voice echoed inside her. Whoever it was, it wasn't Triar; she was sure.

"Ha, ha, ha. The first blood is mine."

She had to focus. The defeat was not an option; it could not be. Suddenly, she understood. Some mage had to be hidden and coaxing her mind to give the sovereign the upper hand. Of course, that was it.

Triar's slashes were more frequent. She stopped the edge of the crimson steel that sought her neck. The king pressed with his corpulence, forcing her to take a step back to contain the onslaught. At that moment, the thrust slowed, and her attacker turned to the right, making an arc on her side with the other blade. Damn! She brought her left hand down and parried the blow with her fingers. Before she could react, Gregor's grandson viciously pulled the blade, cutting her. Drops of blood fell on the cobblestones of the square.

*NO! What a waste. That blood must have been mine.* What was the mage playing at? What was he trying to do? Scare her with that 'ghostly' game? Make her think she was crazy? This didn't make sense.

The armor felt heavy. Three blows in a row from her adversary. She dodged the first two. The third required her full effort to block it. The reddish-red blade was only a few inches from her face. There was a flash as if the sword was looking at her and winking at her.

She stepped back. They both stepped back.

Triar's left arm began to tremble. After what seemed like a spasm in his hand, he released the golden-handled sword. The king's countenance looked bewildered.

*Now it's just you and me.*

The revelation hit her like a bucket of cold water in the middle of winter. No mage was trying to distract her. She didn't understand. It couldn't be. Whether she believed it or not, that sword spoke to her. Triar's certainty made sense. He wielded a magical weapon. Those damned mages, what other surprise did they have in store?

"Tell me, Triar, did your friends, the mages, give you that sword?"

The king smiled.

"Do you like it?" he asked as he lifted it and spun it gently. "Its name is Nobulka, and, with it, I will slice your throat."

"Did it make you drop the other one?"

The smile disappeared, giving way to a violent attack. This time, Selena contained it with ease.

"I know your secret. You won't distract me anymore."

"You're crazy, bitch."

Another hit, another, another. Although the expertise was still there, it was not enough. She knew his wiles. He was no match for her. It was time to strike.

"My turn," announced the queen.

She lashed out at him. She alternated thrusts with lateral slashes looking for a hole in his defense. The attempts were unsuccessful.

*Now it's my turn. I want to taste you again.*

A blow from Triar slipped through her defense, wounding her below the shoulder, barely a scratch, and the sword flared with a faint red aura.

*Uhm, delicious!*

The king held the weapon with both hands and returned to the vanguard. Blow after blow, she felt her resistance undermining. It was the sword; it gave him strength, it helped him. She felt weaker and weaker. She did not know how long she had been fighting, but her steel weighed her down.

Her adversary raised the weapon above his head. The dark blade came down swiftly, leaving a maroon trail. She reined in the attack by crossing her blade horizontally. The power of the blow shook her muscles and shattered her rapier as if it were made of glass. The blade hungrily tore through the breastplate of her armor, throwing it to the ground from the forceful impact at the same time.

With her knees and hands on the ground, she was helpless. A kick in the abdomen threw her violently to the cobblestone. It was inconceivable that she was losing. Her campaign could not end like this. She felt the blood in her mouth.

The king's boot mercilessly trampled the fingers that still held the remains of her sword.

"Finally, at my feet. You didn't stand a chance."

Selena felt the pressure on her hand increase. She heard some bones break. She screamed.

"You cannot imagine how much I am enjoying this moment. Finally, my dream is coming true."

The tip of the sword approached her face. It began to tear her left cheek. The blood that spurted out was immediately absorbed.

*Your blood reminds me of Rumlas'. Those were great times.*

The weapon continued down, seeking her neck, tracing a long wound, feeding on her.

She would die today; if it were meant to be, it would be. She would face death with honor. No pleading, no begging. Her only consolation was the thought that the Council would be destroyed. She trusted Béldar; he would do it.

"Just get on with it!" cried the queen.

There was no reply from his executioner nor voices in her head. The market itself fell silent, waiting for the outcome. The king's arm raised, preparing for the final blow.

## *17*

For what seemed like hours, Béldar extracted as much cryol as he could from the inert bodies of the Resandians. A small sphere of liquid metal levitated above his hand. It had to be enough; he couldn't wait any longer. Near him, Nadia was fighting, trying to keep the creature at bay, thus giving him valuable time. He would not let her down. The Council seemed to have turned its back on Shao; his defeat would pave their way to triumph.

He felt the power of the mineral pulsing. He placed his other hand on it to contain and mold it. As if it were a mental forge, he began to stretch it, trying to create a blade that would serve to destroy the abomination. Small sparks jumped from the surface as it elongated, and a pungent smell hit his nose. The material resisted, and sometimes small tendrils would rise as if trying to escape. Delaying it any longer was dangerous. He focused on finishing by applying more and more magic. Good, at last!

As long as his arm, the resulting blade was dark crimson with a slight sheen on the edge. It vibrated, and tiny strands of energy danced on it like miniature lightning bolts during a summer thunderstorm. The rapier lacked a hilt, so when the mage held it, he sensed the mysticism of his creation directly. He felt energy, strength, and power.

He turned his attention to his enemy. He was biting and clawing at the woman. He saw a gesture of rage and pleading on Nadia's face, showing him he was her last chance.

He sighed. If he failed, it would be the end. This was their last chance. His ally's resistance would soon end. This malignancy was too vigorous; even if Selena defeated Triar, she would be helpless against something like this. His mind flew to her for an instant. He prayed that she was well. He prayed to see her again. What began as an assignment from the Council, as an act of conquest, ended with an act of surrender on both sides. Thinking of her reinvigorated him, and memories infused him with energy and passion. She was there, far away, but also very close. For him, she was no longer the queen or the murderer, never again the devastator of Lebassi; for him, she was only *his love.*

With determination, the mage grabbed the cryol weapon with both hands. With the tip straight towards the front, he rushed towards the creature. Last chance! Shao's back was his target; he would thrust the blade at an upward angle so that the metal would damage the internal organs as much as possible. The distance became infinite. He was breathing with agitation. His lungs burned; whether from exertion or anticipation, he did not know. The stench of the monster was worse than that of a slaughterhouse. A little more, just a little more.

Nadia fell. Blood gushed profusely from three ugly scratches on her face. The claws shattered her right eye.

"Mine, mine, mine!" the beast exclaimed.

At that moment, Béldar thrust his sword in briskly and plunged it in until his fingers were covered by the wolf's fur. On its way, the blade cut nerves, muscles, and organs until it exited through the creature's chest.

Shao howled. He turned quickly; there was more anger than pain in his eyes.

Béldar tried to place a barrier between him and the monster. He thought he would succeed, but the beast threw itself on top of him, pinning him to the ground. He had no escape. He turned his gaze to Nadia, who did not move. He was alone.

"You bastard!" Shao spat. "You will suffer, you will die, and you will be mine."

Béldar shrieked as the being's claws dug into his abdomen, churning his insides. Tears escaped from his eyes, showing his suffering.

The wolf's jaws approached his face. The stench was revolting.

"It will be slow," he whispered in his ear and then bit his shoulder.

Every blow was torture. Shao was making sure to prolong the agony. The little hope of victory he previously harbored was dissipated. He would not escape alive, and the head of the Council would endure. Selena, his Selena, would succumb to this abomination.

Shao's nails caressed his thorax, tearing his robe. Then, they dug in and tore apart his bones, making their way to his heart. He watched him lick the blood that splattered on his muzzle. Shao smiled viciously.

The torture was such that his nerves became numb to pain. His consolation came in the thought that the end was near. His martyrdom persisted as he realized he would lose Selena. He was losing what he longed for so long, marked his life as a human and a mage with regret, and finally obtained: love. His heart did not belong to him. That muscle that still throbbed inside his chest was just that: one more muscle. The perfect idea of love was not there because he gave it without qualms to the woman who now inhabited his dreams, whom he decided to love, and from whom he expected to be loved.

Shao paused for a moment. He stood upright, observing the hole he had dug.

"Mine."

Béldar saw the tip of the sword emerging from the wolf's chest. The attack did not turn out as expected; deep inside, he had harbored the hope that the magical metal would easily destroy the chimera and lead them to victory. It did not, and the exposed edge was a reminder of his failure.

What if... Maybe... It could be... The last chance. The world was sometimes full of multiple last chances.

He saw the monster's puzzled look as he raised his hand to grasp the sword.

"Spread out, destroy!" ordered Béldar.

A crimson glow erupted from the weapon. The metal began to gurgle and melt. A few drops remained in his fingers; the rest went inside the body of the leader of the Council.

"All yours!" said Béldar.

The beast writhed as it felt the liquid mineral spreading through its body, destroying it from the inside. More than that, the cryol broke its connection with Panameria, destroying the illusion of the chimera. Desperate, he threw a punch toward Béldar's heart, tearing it mercilessly.

The young mage's mouth filled with blood after that last blow. The end! There was no doubt about it.

Thick pieces of skin fell from the creature's body. It staggered away and soon stumbled until it fell flat on its face into the mud. Small intense-maroon flames devoured the flesh. The destruction brought a fetid effluvium of blood and sewage.

Béldar, mustering what strength he had left, brought his hands to his chest to cover his exposed and sullied heart. He closed his eyes, seeking connection in a last-ditch attempt to heal his wounds. Nothing! He felt nothing.

A hand rested on his. Somehow, the sorceress crawled up to him and gave off some energy to heal him. The current running through him was so slight he barely noticed it. He could see the effort on Nadia's face. In addition to the wounds on her face, thick gashes on her body attested to much more deadly damage.

"Take care of her! She is not my daughter, but she is the future of Panameria. I lied to you. I never looked for the child torn from my body," Nadia confessed while coughing. "I deceived you into fulfilling my revenge."

"I will take care of her," promised Béldar.

Nadia exhaled her last breath, leaving him. The strength yielded to him was fading. The pain was disappearing, while fatigue was taking its toll on him. He would only close his eyes for a moment, just a moment to rest.

# 18

"Nooooooo!" Selena shouted.

Claws tore at his stomach. Teeth like daggers tore his shoulder apart. His chest opened up, exposing his heart. He heard the wailing. He felt the salty taste of tears. It was killing him; Shao was killing Béldar. For some reason, he connected with him at this moment of maximum suffering. Another shriek, charged with rage and helplessness, came from her throat. The queen's body began to burn. Reddish-orange flames engulfed her.

The arm descending towards her hesitated, then maintained its trajectory. That moment of hesitation was enough for the flames to create a cocoon around her body.

"You witch, you damn witch! I had you," Triar insulted her.

*Hide if you want; I'll still feed on you.* The voice of the sword flowed again like a snake through her head.

Again and again, useless blows fell on the armor.

The iridescent flares were growing. Triar turned away from one that licked his boots. The soldiers in the square backed away.

Inside the magical wrapping, Selena was reborn. She remembered the moments when Panameria endowed her with life. Magic flowed into her as if for the first time. She stretched out her fractured hand and watched with delight as her fingers rebuilt themselves intact. The pain disappeared. What was happening? She sensed communion with the earth, with all of nature, as if the torture her love experienced had awakened her, making her reborn. Her love! Yes, she loved him, she loved him!

If she wanted to rescue him, she had to hurry. There was not much time left. Her enemy was waiting for her.

Little by little, the flames faded away, revealing Selena. Her armor looked restored, of impeccable copper color, with no dents, no signs of blows, spotless as if it had just come out of the forge. Her uncovered face showed no wounds.

A sigh of relief burst from the throats of her followers, who began to acclaim her. From the other end of the square, the cries "Witch", "Murderer", and "Damn you" were not long in coming.

"Captains, get the troops out of here. They won't want to be around," Selena commanded.

The young wet nurse took a few steps forward.

The queen confronted her. "Go, Pamela, that's an order."

"Your Majesty, let me..."

"Go!"

"Yes, Your Majesty."

The troops retreated. In response, the defenders of Perennia cheered King Triar, urging him to end the duel.

"Rise, Panameria!" ordered Selena.

A sepulchral silence loomed over the square. Thick clouds covered the morning sun, darkening the city. A tremor, a crunch. Deep cracks ran across the cobblestone floor. Steam with a pungent smell of sulfur rose from the depths.

"Order your troops to evacuate Perennia," Selena suggested.

"Never! You will not defeat me," replied the king.

"It is your decision, but you will die knowing that you condemned an entire city." Selena did not wait for Triar's answer and added: "Soldiers of Perennia, I recognize your courage, but this is not your fight! Leave the city, save yourselves and your families."

A bubbling reddish-orange liquid followed the strong odor. Lava was rising along with heat from the underworld itself. There were murmurs and then shouts from the defenders' side. What the warrior's words failed to accomplish, the liquid fate did. Triar's hosts fled.

Selena extended her right arm towards the seething fluid and began to draw it into her hand. A sorrel tentacle wrapped around her limb, swiftly forming a single-bladed ax topped by a long tip. Meanwhile, her other forearm wielded a shield of black basalt. The queen struck sword against shield, creating a thunderous sound that resembled an earthquake.

"Face me and die!" said Selena.

A black halo enveloped Nobulka. The hilt lengthened. The blade stretched out several palms, and its width stretched proportionally. The aura extended into Triar's body.

"I wield Salmur's sword, the same sword that defeated his brother, Rumlas. You are only a nightmare that today comes to an end."

Triar lunged forward, forming a vertical arc aimed at the mage's head.

*What this jester says is true. I defeated the twin of darkness. Your blood will be mine, and, when I pierce you, I will banish your soul to the realm of the fallen god.* Again, the sword's words crept into her brain, seeking to distract or frighten her.

She deftly dodged the attack with her shield. The impact was much greater than expected. Undoubtedly, this Nobulka had to be supporting Triar not only with its blade.

"I don't care how many gods you've defeated; you've never faced me," Selena pointed out.

*Foolish words from a mere woman.*

"Didn't you hear? Triar said that I am a bad dream; I am your nightmare."

The queen counterattacked by first shoving Triar with her shield, knocking him off balance, followed by a short, firm slash that tore the former Lebassi king's lower abdomen.

She was still surprised by how she was reborn; she could not define it in a better way. Her strength and her powers were restored. It had been a long time since she had felt this way. She had to take advantage of this good moment to strike the final blow. The sword wielded by the sovereign was powerful; she could not be careless. Attack, strike, give him no time to think. She had to finish him off.

Nobulka intercepted her second blow. A few feet away, Selena felt that not only Triar was looking at her; she also felt the sword's 'eyes' fixed on her.

The weapons creaked under strain. The blades threw sparks. Sweat was running down Selena's armor from the effort, as well as from the heat of the lava. The lava level was rising. Several stands succumbed to the flames, and both adversaries moved to a higher position.

The queen used her shield to throw magma splash at her adversary. The liquid adhered to the armor causing black burns. The feint did not harm the king, but it did distract him. She seized the opportunity to slash the king's left calf.

Triar avoided falling to the ground by violently jabbing Nobulka, like a cane, into the stones.

Now he was at her mercy. She would have no mercy. She fixed her gaze on the warrior's right wrist. Her ax tore the air violently and separated his hand from his arm in a second. The sword fell free a very short distance from the red-hot fluid.

*Take me. I will serve you faithfully.*

She ignored the voice. She fiercely kicked Triar's face, throwing him into the lava. The king scrambled, screaming, looking for a way to get up. Reflexively, he rested his stump on the liquid. The scream that rose surpassed the walls of the city.

Selena walked slowly towards him. She let go of the shield, which shattered when it touched the surface. She placed her foot on the king's chest, forcing him to fall back into the magma.

Triar screamed again. Part of his scalp caught fire, and a smell of burning flesh wafted into the air.

"I defeated you when we first met. I still don't know how you survived, but today your dream ends. Only I am left."

"My son," Triar pleaded.

"Your son does not interest me, nor you or your people. Your legacy will die with you."

His flesh crackled. The armor was beginning to melt with the man inside. The screams turned to howls.

"I have learned to be compassionate," Selena said as she decapitated Triar with her sword.

Within seconds, armor and body were consumed.

*I'll be your slave; just keep me away from the fire.*

The queen lifted Nobulka holding it by the handle, and smiled at it.

"For a god's sword, you beg a lot."

*Thank you, my Queen. I will keep my word.*

"I'm sure of that," Selena emphasized. She put the sword in the sheath hanging from her waist.

She gazed at the scene. Parts of the city were burning. Lava was spreading greedily around the corners. She stretched out both arms as she walked toward the collapsed wall. Lava receded, returning to the bowels of Panameria, leaving trails of desolation in its path. Selena contemplated her handiwork. She liked the city.

The clouds dropped their load. A light rain soaked the buildings suffocating the remaining fires and leaving a delightful effluvium reminiscent of spring rains.

She walked towards the outer plain where her troops were waiting for her. There they were. Of two thousand soldiers who participated in the siege of Perennia, she saw no more than five hundred, and many of them looked wounded. They trusted her with their lives, and she managed to lead them to glory. As one being, her hosts brought their fists to their breasts and bowed with one knee on the ground.

Pride flooded Selena, seeing how her fate was forged and how her existence had meaning, leaving behind being the capricious desire of a dastardly king. At last, she had complete control over her life, and the occasion was propitious to bring a new order to the kingdoms of men.

She took a few more steps forward. A light breeze ruffled her red hair. She grabbed Nobulka with her right hand and pulled it briskly out of the sheath. Lifting it and pointing to the sky, she sent out a bolt of thick vermilion lightning that tore the celestial dome, clearing the clouds completely. The roar shook the walls of Perennia.

"Victory is ours!" proclaimed Selena, the new ruler of the human kingdoms.

# 19

Gregor was walking along the castle's breakwater with Agatha. After their initial encounter, they became good friends. She would be fourteen in a few months and had been under the protection of King Sabilo since she was three years old. No, she was not his granddaughter; there was no kinship between them. As everyone knew, the king never married and never had offspring. The girl was an orphan, just one more, one of many, until she crossed paths with the kindly king. He took her into the palace, and, from then on, he began to call her granddaughter, and she called him grandfather. They had told each other about their entire lives during the last week.

The day was splendid. The breeze was raising light waves on the surface of the lake. The sun was shining gloriously, and dozens of fishermen and sailors were crossing in both directions.

"Will you stay?"

"I don't know, Agatha. I don't know what to do. That murderer owns Lebassi. I am not strong enough."

"Then you must stay. Become strong here. My grandfather will help you. Wars are not won without preparation. I will fight with you."

"Don't talk nonsense. You're just a girl."

"I am a woman."

"Women..."

What was he going to say? He sounded like his father. Was he going to say that women couldn't fight? Cruel fate proved them wrong. A woman was now the ruler of their kingdom. If King Sabilo were not a man of honor and unquestionable loyalty, he might have killed or handed him over to that harpy.

"What were you going to say?" Agatha interrupted his thoughts.

"I was going to say that it would be an honor to fight alongside you. We will surely win if your sword is as sharp as your tongue."

The girl burst out laughing and punched Gregor's arm affectionately, making him blush.

"Come. The blue boat at the end always brings the biggest crabs you've ever seen."

And she pulled him by the hand, making him run after her.

Suddenly, a reddish glow rose over the eastern sky, beyond the Great Salt Lake. It could be in Perennia. A shiver ran down his spine, and his blood ran cold. A vision of his father's death haunted him.

"What is that?" Agatha asked.

"I don't know."

"Your hand is cold! Are you all right?"

The King of Lebassi was motionless. He saw it all too clearly. That witch killed his father again. Again. He did not understand how. No, it did not make sense. He thought of his brother, whom he had never met. A thirst for revenge flooded him inside.

"I will stay. I will get ready. We will get ready," Gregor announced.

# 20

Selena walked sadly through the mountain landscape where, until this morning, Shao's hut was located. Although the combat in Perennia was atrocious, it did not surpass in cruelty the battle against the members of the Council. The scene in front of her was desolate. Nature destroyed, melted snow mixed with the blood of mages and Resandians. Trees consumed in their entirety bore witness to the bloody struggle. The smell of ash mingled with the stench of death and torn viscera.

Behind her, she heard the retching of the former wet nurse. She looked over her shoulder at her. She had made a mistake bringing her here. Even she wasn't prepared for this spectacle. She kept moving forward.

She kept track of the bodies in mage robes, or remnants of robes, in her mind. She could say that a little more than half a dozen had fallen. On the other hand, the remains of Resandians were so many that she had little hope that any of them had survived.

A stench of caged beast hit her all at once; to her left, a pile of what appeared to be animal remains mixed with human parts, half wrapped in a green robe with gold trim that she recognized instantly. Shao? What happened here? The stench was unbearable.

Before she saw him, she heard it. A faint heartbeat. A soft breath. Her *mother,* motionless, with one hand on Béldar's open chest in what seemed to be a protective gesture.

She ran to him and threw herself beside him. She moved Nadia's limp body. She hugged Béldar tightly, who let out a murmur of pain. Selena laid him gently on the ground.

"You're alive!" sobbed the queen. "You're alive!"

She tenderly caressed the face of the mage, whose eyes were glazed; thick tears streamed down his cheeks.

"We won, Béldar, we won," Selena announced as tears also began to flow from her eyes. "I will get you out of here. You will be fine."

Selena noticed that Béldar's hand was closing over hers. It was a gentle squeeze, very faint. His fingers were icy. The mage tried to speak, but a sudden cough stopped him.

"Calm down, my love!" she murmured, trying to calm him down. "Let me heal you."

Béldar's hand stopped her.

"It's fine; it's too late," whispered Béldar. "I love you!"

"And I love you, so I can't let you go."

She leaned over him, seeking his lips. She kissed him. They both closed their eyes. Selena enjoyed the warmth of the kiss. A multitude of moments flew into her mind. She remembered arguing with Béldar, fighting with him. She remembered how he made her feel like a little girl, insecure and helpless. Again and again, he provoked her. But he was always there, by her side. When something went wrong, he took care of her. When she insulted him or yelled at him, he was still there. He loved her. And she loved him too. The victory was nothing without him. Victory… Life was nothing without him!

She heard nothing. Nothing. No heartbeat. No breathing. The hand that held hers did not squeeze. The fingers were cold, like a river in winter.

She slowly separated from him. His eyes were closed. If it weren't for the numerous wounds, she could say he was sleeping. On his lips, there was a smile.

Selena burst into tears. She hit the mud hard, again and again, helpless. This wasn't fair. It couldn't be; not him, not him, please!

A hand rested on her shoulder.

"Your Majesty, Béldar is gone. Let him rest."

Yes, he was gone; he had left her. Knowing that didn't erase the pain; it made it worse because she would never see him again. Never again. With all her power, there had to be another way; there had to be an option. She did not understand gods; she did not understand the path souls took. It didn't matter; where there is a will, there is a way, and if she had anything, it was will.

She stood up. She kept her gaze fixed on him. She wiped away her tears. A cold breeze caressed her face. She was the absolute ruler of the kingdoms of men. King Triar had fallen at her feet. She was undoubtedly the most powerful ruler of Panameria, and, moreover, she was not only the fruit of magic but she had been rescued from the realms of darkness. She was proof that a return was possible.

Her eyes filled with hope. If she came back, Béldar could come back too. Looking up at the sky, she smiled. She would not stop trying to have him by her side again. She had the power, the magic, the resources, but, above all, she had the will. She needed nothing else.

Lightning flashed over the mountains announcing that a storm was approaching.

# EPILOGUE

A shiver ran through the body of Jana Ank, daughter of the Great Siasse Ank, when Nadia let out her last breath. A little over two hundred years ago, their father, the patriarch of the Resandian tribe, had bound them together with the strongest bond their race allowed: 'Sand Sisters'.

She was sharing the day's meal with his beloved father. It was never a good time for death.

"Father, I must leave," Jana announced.

Her father looked at her strangely.

"I'm sorry, father, my sister Nadia is dead," she added.

Her dad's hand, covered with a red glove matching all his clothes, squeezed hers. A comforting warmth came over her.

"Go, my daughter. Take care of pending matters."

Jana stood up, leaving the delicacies on the table. With a slight nod, she said goodbye before leaving the tent.

Half a hundred tents surrounded her father's in concentric circles, in perfect harmony. Hers was in the first circle. She walked towards it with firm and determined steps. She felt pain in her eyes. No longer blue, they glowed yellow, filled with grief. Her companions from the camp moved out of her way.

Her awning, matching her gray attire, was small, just for her. Just enough and necessary. The Resandians were famous for their itinerancy. Anyone who didn't know them would think they wandered the desert. That was not what they did. They lived; they communed with it. They were part of the desert. Brothers, protectors, sometimes executioners.

She rummaged in a corner. There it was: a small box made of Galadian willow wood, no bigger than a wolf cub. It was bluish-green with no lock or lid. She placed the palm of her hand on the wood. A tingle caressed her fingers as the material faded. Beneath the veils that covered her face, Jana smiled.

Two daggers emitted twin indigo flashes. One looked untouched as if it had never been used. The other had a much smaller blade, just as sharp but smaller.

She took the complete one and encircled the hilt with both hands.

She sighed, trying to calm down. The color of her eyes mutated, back to the bluish hue usual for her race. She disappeared.

Jana materialized in front of the entrance to her sister's abode. The black darkness that served as a door was gone. Another twinge assaulted her. She entered.

Everything was as it was last time, but nothing was the same anymore. She walked through the corridors carved into the rock until she reached the pond. The golden glow was waning. The green basket still floated in the water. Her friend's world was beginning to fade.

She stretched her arms towards the basket. Slowly, the basket woven from vines approached her. Inside, asleep, was Magnus, Triar's son.

The Resandian removed her gloves. Her hands were completely gray and covered with medium-sized scales, almost as if she were wearing a coat of mail. She stretched out her fingers, displaying long, sharp nails. She removed the cloth covering her face. The scales on her face were much smaller and of a darker shade. It had no lips; her mouth was cut out, resembling the arc of a crescent moon. For a nose, she had only two diamond-shaped orifices. The smile was riddled with triangular teeth.

She picked up her claws and held the child.

The cocoon had done its job. The baby was no longer a baby, not anymore. Magnus, born barely a month ago, looked like a child of about two years old.

Jana stroked the infant's forehead gently and lovingly. The little boy opened his eyes. They were the same color as the sky.

"Mom?" Magnus stammered.

The patriarch's daughter's two hearts shrank. She could not cry. Her irises darkened to resemble ashes.

"Yes, I'm mom."

"Mom!"

Gently, she placed him on the grass of the cavern. She removed the blanket that barely covered him. From among her clothes, she took out the small dagger.

"It won't hurt, I promise."

Delicately, she drove the blade's tip into Magnus' left forearm. A faint purplish glow emerged as Jana tattooed a dagger on the skin. As the cryol blinked, the boy smiled, fascinated by the colors.

Printed in Great Britain
by Amazon

14517865R00214